Reluctant Consent

Margaret Barnes

Published by Scribbling Advocate in 2018

First Edition

ISBN 978-1-9164471-3-4

The cover design is by Berni Stevens @bernistevensdesign.com.
The photograph is of Middle Temple Lane London.

Acknowledgements

This second Cassie Hardman novel has taken considerable time to come to fruition partly because of the delicacy of the subject matter – a trial for rape. The case described in these pages is entirely fictitious but it draws on a number of similar trials in which I defended the accused.

I would like to thank a number of people who read the first and subsequent drafts. They include Diane Riddell, Michael McCormick, Maggie Harkness and her writing group. I would particularly thank Marila Hargreaves who read, commented and edited the early drafts. Kate McCormick again acted as my writing buddy and contributed her usual pithy comments.

I found a lawyer Lesley Jones of 'perfecttheword' who did the final edit on my novel and I am grateful for her work in making this as good as it is. All the mistakes are mine.

Again I want to thank my husband Alan Taylor for his forbearance and support.

Margaret Barnes

Chapter 1

9th May R v Sadler

The Old Bailey. Court 12. Light wood panelling, green leather under the harsh glare of lights flickering subliminally. The faint smell of yesterday's aftershave. On the wall behind the judge's elevated bench was a stylised version of the royal coat of arms: the lion and unicorn overseeing the proceedings with sardonic eyes. For the lawyers in the room, including Cassie Hardman, all this was familiar, their place of work. For witnesses and jurors it must have been intimidating.

The trial of Paul Sadler for the offence of rape had started with the jury being sworn in and prosecuting counsel opening the case to the seven women and five men. Their ages ranged from early twenties to late sixties. The eldest was a woman; she was casually dressed in a cardigan and round-necked T-shirt, nothing very expensive. The youngest was a slender male, a stud in one ear and a permanent grin. Cassie wondered what he would make of the case, whose side would he be on. There were a couple of women in their late twenties, possibly early thirties. They were likely to believe a woman wouldn't allege she had been raped unless it was true.

Once the screens were in place and the court had reassembled, Emma Gilbrook took her place in the witness box. Gone was the gleaming girl of the selfies taken with Cassie's client; the young woman before the court looked much younger. Her tawny blonde hair was scraped back into a ponytail. She wore no make-up and her eyes were red rimmed. Cassie felt a finger of ice stroke her as she looked at the witness, knowing, as she did, she would have to call into question the woman's credibility.

Hugh was good with vulnerable witnesses. Cassie assumed it was that ability to treat them gently that accounted for him being instructed in cases where victims made allegations of sexual assault. He was the same outside the courtroom, although he had been terse with her when she requested some further enquiries should be made.

'Miss Gilbrook, can you tell the court your full name, please?' he said.

'Emma Gilbrook.'

'And do you live in North Kensington with your mother, Rose?'

'Yes. I do.'

'Can you look at this please. Exhibit one, My Lord. It's a copy of the *Metro* newspaper dated twenty-third of February. At the bottom of that page there is a section called "Rush Hour Crush".'

Emma Gilbrook turned the newspaper over and stared at the page. She pointed a well-manicured finger painted with dark purple nail polish towards it.

'Do you recognise one of the messages?'

'I do. The one from the man in the grey suede jacket. I'd been at Holland Park station with a garment bag the day before. Taking a gown to a client.'

'Quite. You recognised the description of yourself?'

'And the man. The station wasn't very busy and I realised somebody was looking at me. I looked up and saw this man watching me. I smiled at him.'

'Why did you do that?'

'I … I think I was flattered by his attention. He was handsome … well dressed. A well-cut jacket. I notice that kind of thing.'

'Did he respond?'

'I think he took a step forward, but the train came. He wasn't in the same carriage as me. I went to my appointment and didn't think anything of it.'

'When you saw the message in the newspaper, what did you decide to do?'

'I thought it was quite funny at first. I told my friend Anita …'

'That's Anita Connor?'

'Anita. Yes. I told her the man was very attractive and it might be fun to contact him. She wasn't sure but said to keep him to coffee and cake.'

'As the message suggests. Did you do that?'

'I contacted him through the newspaper and think he responded by text. I'd said I'd meet him for coffee and he suggested that Saturday at the café in Holland Park. I was happy with that. It's very public, lots of mums with their kids, dog walkers, lots of people around.'

'So, you met there. How did the meeting go?'

'Good. We had coffee. Talked a lot.' She nodded. 'I thought he was good company. He made me laugh.'

'Did he talk about himself?'

'He told me he lived with a relative, an aunt, I think, in Ealing. His parents were separated and his mother had remarried. He didn't get on with his stepdad. And I think he said his father lived abroad.'

'Did he say where he worked?'

'He told me he was on the ground staff at Heathrow.'

'And his age?''

'He said twenty-nine.'

'Did you tell him how old you were?'

Emma looked down. 'I told him I was twenty-four.'

'That wasn't true was it?'

'No, I'm twenty, but I wanted him to think I was older.' She paused. 'I don't know why.'

Hugh Palmer alternated between reading the papers in front of him and glancing at the witness, looking over his glasses which were perched on the end of his nose. Cassie took another mint from the packet on the bench in front of her and observed the jury. There seemed to be very little reaction to the admission by Emma that she had lied. Probably too early in the trial.

'Was there any physical contact between you?'

'Not really. A peck on the cheek when we parted. Actually I'm not sure about that.'

'Did you meet Sadler again?' Hugh asked.

'I think about five, possibly six days later. Must have been Thursday. I was working the next day.'

'Where did you meet?'

'We went to a pizza place on the Gate.'

'How did the evening go?'

'I enjoyed it. As I said he made me laugh. Telling stories about work and things like that. Travellers making strange requests, that kind of thing.'

'Did you have any alcohol with the meal?'

'I didn't but I think Paul had a beer.'

'Who paid for the meal?'

'We shared the bill. He paid a bit more because of the beer.'

'Was there any physical contact between you this time?'

'He walked me to the bus stop and we held hands. He stayed with me until the bus came. Gave me a hug and a kiss on the cheek as we parted.'

'Did you arrange to meet again?'

'No, we didn't. Not then. He said he'd text me.'

'Did he?'

'At the weekend. He suggested we went out for dinner at Kensington Place. I told him I couldn't afford it. That's when he said it was his treat.'

'You went to the restaurant and had a meal there. Did you have anything to drink, any alcohol?'

'We had a glass of wine each. It's expensive.'

'Sadler was paying?'

'I did offer to pay my share, but he insisted he'd invited me and he was going to pay.'

'Was there any physical contact in the restaurant?'

Emma Gilbrook put a hand across her mouth and her voice dropped. 'We held hands across the table while we waited for the bill.'

'Do you know what time it was when you got the bill?'

'Quite late. After eleven, I think.'

'Were you working the next day?'

'I should have been. I should have gone home.' She took out a handkerchief and blew her nose. Hugh waited and then asked her why she had not.

'I wanted to take Paul to meet my friend Anita, so I suggested we went to her flat.'

'Had you told her you might go and see her?'

'I had mentioned it. It wasn't definite … I didn't know if he would.' She was pulling at the corner of the handkerchief she was still holding in her left hand.

'Was Anita there?'

'No. I have a key so I let us in. I thought she'd be back soon.'

'What did you do when you were in the flat?'

'I hung up my coat and went to make us some coffee. While I did that Paul had taken his jacket off and hung it over the back of a chair. I said I didn't think it would be long before Anita got back. We sat down on the sofa and …' Emma looked around the courtroom and then asked if she could have a drink of water. The usher handed her a glass and she took a sip.

'Do you want a break? It's nearly time for the luncheon adjournment. Mr Palmer, I assume Miss Gilbrook's evidence will take a little while yet,' said Judge Tyte.

'I don't think we will complete her evidence before lunch, My Lord.'

'I thought not. I think we'll break now. Miss Gilbrook, it's better that we hear the rest of your evidence in one session. Do you understand?'

Emma Gilbrook nodded and stepped out of the witness box.

'Right, members of the jury, can we start at one forty-five? Does that inconvenience anyone?' The judge didn't wait for a reply.

Cassie had spent the short adjournment trying to dismiss from her mind the witness's obvious distress. Sometimes she hated her job. She would not have liked the most intimate part of her own life being examined in the way this young woman's was, and it was going to get worse.

Hugh recommenced his examination in chief by reminding Emma Gilbrook how far she had got with her evidence. 'You were sitting side by side on the sofa, and what happened then?'

'We drank our coffee and then Paul put his arm round me and kissed me on the lips.'

'Did you respond?'

Emma bent her head. 'Yes.' Her voice was a whisper. 'We kissed and cuddled each other and then …'

'And then? Tell us in your own words what happened.'

'He put his hands between my legs. I pushed his hand away and said no.'

'What were you wearing?'

'Jeans and a silk blouse I'd borrowed from work.'

'Did he touch you over or under your clothes?'

'At first over my clothes. He touched my breasts.'

'Did you object to that?'

'No. I should have. Then he undid one of the buttons on my blouse and pushed his hand onto my breast and played with the nipple. I think I said not to. I can't remember really.'

'Did you stay in the living room?'

'After a little while he stood up and took hold of my hand and pulled me towards Anita's bedroom. There's only one.'

'Did you want to go into the bedroom?'

'I kind of hung back. I didn't pull away from him. Went more slowly.' Emma dropped her voice and began to search in the pocket of the jacket she was wearing. Cassie could see she was on the verge of tears. The usher rushed forward with a box of tissues and handed one to the witness. Hugh turned towards the jury and waited, allowing them to absorb how upset Emma was.

'What happened in the bedroom?'

'We lay on the bed. Then …' Emma's fists were gripping the side of the witness box. 'He got on top of me, took my jeans off. He …' She began to cry.

'Take your time. If you want a break just say so,' Judge Tyte said.

Emma blew her nose with the remains of the tissue. Cassie tapped her fingers on her thigh; the memory of her own experiences nudged at her thoughts. She pushed them away to concentrate on the witness.

'He put his hand between my legs and his fingers into my vagina. I told him to stop.'

'Did he remove his hand?'

'Yes, he did.'

'And then?'

'He unbuttoned my blouse. I took it off – I had borrowed it from work and I didn't want it spoilt. He undid my bra and I took that off too. He kissed my breasts and then he put his hand between my thighs and his fingers in my vagina. He asked me if that was alright. He asked if I was enjoying it.'

'Did you reply?'

'I couldn't say anything. I realised his penis was hard. He unzipped his trousers. I knew he was going to penetrate me.'

'Is that what happened?'

'Yes … not immediately. He removed his trousers and underpants. Then he told me to stay there and he went into the sitting room. When he came back he had a condom packet with him. He opened it and … he couldn't get it on.'

'Where was he while he was doing that?'

'By the bed.'

'Was he holding you in any way?'

'He was struggling with the condom. I helped him put it on.'

'You helped him put it on. Why?'

'I knew we were going to have sex. Taking precautions …' Emma mumbled the next few words until Cassie heard '… was sensible.'

'Did you agree to have sexual intercourse with him?'

'I didn't want to.'

'Did you have intercourse with him?'

Emma nodded, her eyes fixed on some point on the other side of the room, somewhere above the heads of the jurors.

'What happened afterwards?'

'We lay side by side. He went into the bathroom, came back and lay down next to me. He put his arms round me and pulled me on top of him. I realised he had put another condom on. I had one leg either side of his body. He put his penis inside me. We had sex again.'

'Did you agree to having sex with him on this second occasion?'

'I didn't agree … I didn't want to have sex with him.'

'What was the next thing that happened?'

'I got dressed. I told him I expected Anita would be back soon and he should get dressed as well.'

'Did he?'

'He put his clothes on while I straightened the duvet and plumped up the pillows. We went into the sitting room and almost straight away Anita arrived. I introduced them and we chatted for a few minutes. He said he'd better go. I said I wanted to stay for a few minutes with Anita.'

'How long did you stay at Anita's?'

'About half an hour.'

'Did you say anything to her about what had just happened?'

'I felt too embarrassed. We'd been in her bed.'

'You went home. Tell the court what happened the next morning.'

'I overslept. My boss rang and told my mum about the blouse. She came in and asked me where I'd been and I told her I'd been raped. She called the police.'

Judge Tyte said, 'You've been giving evidence for quite some time now and I think we'll start cross examination tomorrow morning.'

Chapter 2

Cassie had spent a restless night, her thoughts hopscotching between the questions she needed to ask Emma Gilbrook the next day and the events fifteen years before that had caused the final rift between her and her husband. But, once in the courthouse, she dismissed all thoughts of her ex-husband and concentrated on preparing for the day ahead. In the Bar Mess she saw Marcus Pike, who had led her in the Barker case. 'You look a little down, Cassie.'

'I've got a rape case. I really hate doing them. What's more, the evidence against this guy is slim. He should be acquitted but …'

'Prejudice – does he look like a rapist? I read somewhere about "fair labelling" – that's what makes the difference. Will he come across as a bully in the witness box? Or very arrogant. Whatever the jury thinks makes a rapist. Do you remember a case where the man said something to the effect that he'd paid for the tickets to a dinner and because of that he thought she would consent to having sex with him?'

'I'm not sure …'

'It's a silly comment like that from a defendant that can get them convicted. I was the junior in that case. Until he said that in the witness box, I thought he'd be acquitted. One of the advantages of Silk, one doesn't get instructed in rape trials anymore. Anyway, you girls are so much better at them.'

'We get instructed in them too much,' Cassie retorted.

'Who's your judge?'

'Tyte.'

'Ralph Tyte. Typical public school. Women either angels or whores. Nice girls don't and all that.'

'You went to one of those schools!'

'Mine was co-ed.' Marcus smirked and then looked up at the clock over the servery. 'I'd better go.'

Cassie left too. As she went down the spiral staircase towards the wide corridor outside the courts, she put on her wig. Often she didn't wear it until just before she went into court, but today she wanted to hide in her professional persona. She was an advocate putting a client's case; her own feelings were of no importance.

She began her cross examination of Emma Gilbrook by asking her questions about her friendship with Anita Connor.

'You met Miss Connor when you were still at school, didn't you?'

'I wanted a Saturday job in a fashion shop. She was the manager for a small independent in Westbourne Grove. I went to work there. We became friends.'

'She's some years older than you?'

'Ten years older. She was more interesting than my school friends.'

'Would it be right that you sought her advice about your career?'

'She helped me get my current job.'

‘A job you enjoy?’

‘Very much.’

‘You sought Miss Connor’s advice about meeting Paul Sadler, did you not?’

‘I showed her the message in the newspaper column.’

‘Did you say you were thinking of contacting the man in the grey suede jacket?’

‘We discussed it. I described him and she said it might be a good laugh, but I should stick to coffee and cake as the message said.’

‘There was no suggestion that it might be dangerous?’

Emma Gilbrook shook her head. ‘I didn’t think so.’

‘You met Paul Sadler twice before the evening of the ninth of March and throughout those two meetings he did nothing to make you frightened or worried about his behaviour?’

‘I wouldn’t have agreed to see him again if there had been. I’ve said he made me laugh a lot. We got on well.’

‘Can you remember what you talked about?’

‘Work. Clothes and music.’

‘Nothing about previous relationships?’

‘I think he mentioned a long-term girlfriend but she had gone to live abroad.’

‘Did he tell you how old he was?’

‘We played a guessing game.’

‘You knew he was twenty-nine?’

‘Yes, I guessed correctly.’

'He asked you if you were twenty-one and you said no, and he then said twenty-four and you agreed?'

'Yes, I did.'

'Why was that?'

'I don't know.'

'Did you want him to think you were more grown up than you were?'

'I don't know why I said it.'

'Anita Connor is about ten years older than you. Do you like having friends older than yourself?'

'They're more interesting. They've done more.'

'You wanted to be more interesting to Paul Sadler?'

'I suppose so.' Emma dragged out the words. Cassie took the opportunity to glance at the jury. She saw a woman with dark curly hair and glasses with bright green rims in the front row; she was leaning forward, her elbows on the bench and her head propped on her hands. There was no time to make any assessment of the woman's attitude to the evidence she was hearing.

'Were you looking forward to the night out with Paul at Kensington Place?' Cassie asked.

'I thought it would be a nice evening.'

'You had told Anita Connor you were meeting him and you suggested taking him to her flat. She told you she was going out that night and she wasn't sure when she would be back.'

'I don't …' Emma looked around the room and sucked her lips. 'I don't remember that.'

‘Didn’t you say that didn’t matter? You’d take Paul Sadler to her flat and if she turned up before you left she could meet him?’

‘Possibly.’

‘You knew she was unlikely to be there but it would give you time alone with Paul. You couldn’t take him home, could you?’

Emma looked behind her as if she was checking who could hear her. DC Pomfrey was sitting under the public gallery, her face impassive. Was Emma looking for help from the policewoman? Cassie couldn’t tell.

‘No, I couldn’t.’

‘Is that because your mother is disapproving of you having a boyfriend?’

‘She thinks I’m too young.’

‘Do you think you are too young?’

‘Of course not.’

The reply was firm and brisk. That was good. Emma Gilbrook was showing she had some fight in her. She wasn’t and wouldn’t have been submissive.

‘When you went to Miss Connor’s flat that night you anticipated having some time alone with Paul Sadler before she came home. You would not have done that if there had been any reason to be afraid of him, would you?’

‘I wasn’t afraid of him.’

‘Before this evening the only physical contact between you was him kissing you at the bus stop?’

‘That’s right.’

‘There was some chemistry between you?’

Cassie liked the word chemistry; it suggested people behaved like atoms obeying immutable laws of attraction. That was what her question implied.

'I guess so … there was a feeling … we were alike or something.'

'You found him a very attractive man?'

Emma paused, clearly struggling to find an answer, then said, 'I … most women would.'

'During the evening in the restaurant, you held hands across the table? Paul Sadler was attentive?'

'He was very nice to me.'

'I want to show you a photograph.' Cassie picked up a bundle of pictures from behind her and handed them to the usher, who gave one to Judge Tyte, one to Hugh Palmer, and the rest she distributed round the jury. 'That's a selfie taken in the restaurant?'

'I'm not sure if it's a selfie. One of the waiters may have taken it. I don't remember.'

'But it was taken in the restaurant?'

Emma Gilbrook looked at the photo and a thin smile passed across her lips. Cassie looked at the jury. This time the curly haired woman was looking at the photograph and then at the witness, clearly comparing the two. Emma Gilbrook put the photograph down. 'It was taken in the restaurant that evening.'

'After you had eaten, he suggested going on to a club, but you said you didn't want to be late but if he would like you could go to your friend's flat?'

'Yes. He agreed. I told him Anita would probably be there.'

'Paul Sadler wasn't unhappy about that?'

'He didn't appear to be.'

'You let yourself in with a key. You didn't ring the doorbell or knock on the door?'

'I had a key. Why would I ring the bell?'

'You didn't ring the bell because you knew Anita Connor would not be there, isn't that right?'

'I … don't remember if I rang the bell or not. It didn't matter if Anita was there or not.'

'You knew she wouldn't be there because she told you she was going out.'

'I've said I don't remember her saying that. I know she says she told me, but I don't …'

'You don't remember because you were taking this man back to her flat so that you could be alone with him, not to introduce him to your friend, isn't that so?'

Emma shook her head and repeated that she couldn't remember.

'You wanted to pursue your relationship with Paul Sadler in private, didn't you?'

Emma shook her head. 'I don't think … I don't know.'

'You made some coffee?'

'Yes. I did.'

'Despite Anita not being there?'

'I knew where the coffee was.'

'After you'd had your coffee, Paul put his arm round you and you began kissing? That was entirely mutual?'

‘I told him to stop when he put his hand between my legs.’

‘You responded when he was kissing you?’

‘Yes, but that was as far as I wanted it to go.’

‘You didn’t stop him from touching your breast over your blouse and then under it?’

‘I can’t remember what I said to him. I didn’t want him to touch me there so I must have said something like *stop*.’

‘You said nothing at this stage. That’s right isn’t it?’

Emma put her head down and mumbled.

Judge Tyte said, ‘Can you please speak up, we need to hear you.’ And then, ‘Members of the jury, the microphone doesn’t amplify – it is simply to record what’s said.’

Emma apologised and said she didn’t recall what she had told Sadler, if anything.

‘He continued caressing your breasts for a little while and then you both stood up, he took your hand and you went with him into the bedroom?’

‘The door of the bedroom was open. He could see the bed.’

‘He didn’t use any force to get you to go into the bedroom?’

‘No. I dragged my feet a bit.’

‘But not enough that he had to use any force to make you go with him, did he?’

‘I guess not.’

‘You both lay on the bed. He didn’t push you down or threaten you to get you to lie on the bed?’

Emma wiped her eyes and then put her hands on the edge of the witness box. She had a tissue in her right hand and she was picking at it, tearing small pieces from it that floated down to the carpet. ‘No, nothing like that.’

‘You didn’t have to lie on the bed, did you?’

‘I didn’t know what to do.’

‘Your jeans – how did he get them off?’

‘He unzipped them and pulled them down.’

‘Can we have exhibit two please,’ Cassie said. DC Leanne Pomfrey got up and went to the exhibit table, picked up a brown exhibit bag and handed it to Hugh Palmer. He tore the bag open and pulled out a pair of dark denim jeans. He passed them to the usher who went to stand by the witness box.

‘Are those the jeans?’ Cassie said.

‘They are,’ Emma replied.

‘How would you describe them?’

‘They’re slim fitting. They have a zip at the ankle.’

‘Is that because they are very tight?’

‘They are tight, yes.’

‘I’ve got another photograph here. Is that you wearing those jeans?’

Copies of the photograph were handed round the court. It showed Emma Gilbrook wearing a pair of jeans that fitted as if they had been painted onto her. Emma said it was.

'Did Paul Sadler use one hand or two to pull them down?'

'Two hands.'

'He wasn't holding your arms down.'

'Just the weight of his body.'

'Your hands were free – you could have pushed him away from you or at least tried to, but you didn't, did you?'

'I don't know why I didn't push him away.'

'Let me help you. You didn't push him away because you helped him take your jeans off. You rolled them round your bottom and then undid one of the zips on the ankle while he undid the other.'

Emma made no attempt to reply to the statement. She looked round the courtroom, up at the judge, and then put her head down and began to shake. Judge Tyte lowered his voice. 'Do you want a break?' Emma shook her head. The judge looked at Cassie and indicated she was to continue.

'Paul Sadler put his hands between your thighs and his fingers into your vagina?'

'I told him to stop.'

'Your blouse, you took that off and your bra. When you removed them where did you put them?'

'I … let them fall to the floor. I was on the bed.'

'But you didn't want the blouse damaged, did you?'

'No, I didn't.'

'Yet you dropped it on the floor?'

'I'm not sure, I …'

'Didn't you get off the bed and put them on a chair by the dressing table?'

'I don't remember. I might have done.'

'You knew he wanted to have sex with you, didn't you?'

'By this time, yes, I did.'

'But knowing he did you got up, removed your blouse and placed it on a chair.'

'I've explained I didn't want it to get spoilt. Damaged.'

'You went back to the bed?'

Emma Gilbrook looked down, took a handkerchief from a pocket and wiped her eyes.

'Miss Hardman, I think it would be better if we took a short break now, before you continue,' the judge said.

'As you please, My Lord,' she replied, although she knew it would give the witness time to compose herself a little and she wanted to get this part over with.

As Emma Gilbrook walked towards the door, the judge said, 'Don't talk to anybody about your evidence, please.'

Chapter 3

Cassie walked over to the windows that looked over the street. The clouds were a dark grey and the pavements wet. Cross examining a young woman like Emma Gilbrook was distasteful. She found herself examining her own sexual experiences, as she had so often when she defended in a rape trial. As her understanding of her own needs and desires had broadened so she had become more aware of how much physical contact she could or would tolerate. She enjoyed the physicality of a sexual relationship. Was that how Emma Gilbrook felt, or was she unsure of her reaction to Paul Sadler's touch? These were intensely personal and private matters. Cassie would not have wanted them investigated under the bright lights of the courtroom. The usher distracted her train of thought, calling her back into court.

Cassie continued her cross examination. 'You were naked on the bed with Paul Sadler on top of you, and he again put his fingers into your vagina. He asked you if you were enjoying it?'

'I didn't want him to do that.'

'What did you say in answer to his question?'

'I said … nothing.' Emma put her head down but she wasn't crying as far as Cassie could see.

'Sadler got up and took off his jeans and underpants.'

'Yes, his penis was erect.' Emma paused and then turned towards Cassie. 'I know what you're going to say. Why didn't you get up? I don't know. He told me to stay where I was.'

'He didn't use any force or threaten you, did he?'

'He told me to stay on the bed.'

'And you do everything you're told to do, do you?' Cassie could hear the sarcasm in her own voice. She didn't like doing this but she had a duty to her client. There was no reply from the witness. Cassie repeated the question a little more gently.

'No, I don't do everything I'm told to do.'

'You could have got up and put your clothes back on.'

'I could, but …'

'You didn't. Could you see Sadler from where you were on the bed?'

'He went to his jacket and took the condom from his pocket.'

'You saw that, so it was obvious he was intending to have intercourse with you, yet you stayed on the bed?'

'I had been told to stay there.'

'You weren't forced to stay there?'

'No, no I wasn't.'

'After he opened the packet containing the condom he was standing by the bed struggling to get it on his penis and you helped him do that?'

Emma Gilbrook didn't reply. 'You helped him put the condom on?'

'Yes. I knew what was going to happen … I though it better. I was protected.'

Cassie paused and looked towards the jury. The eldest of the female jurors was shaking her head. Two of the other women were looking puzzled as well. She hoped they were finding this part of the evidence unbelievable.

'Afterwards you lay with Sadler on the bed. He went to the bathroom. Was he in there for a few minutes?'

'He was.' Emma Gilbrook shrugged her shoulders and stared at Cassie before dropping her head.

'You had the time to get up and put your clothes on?'

'I suppose so, but I didn't.'

'He got on the bed and put his arm round you and pulled you on top of his body without any protest from you?'

'I didn't resist.'

'You were straddling his body and you had sexual intercourse with him in that position, didn't you?'

'He had sexual intercourse with me.'

'You were totally cooperating with him and consenting to having intercourse, weren't you?'

'I did not want to have intercourse with Paul Sadler.'

'You both got dressed and went into the sitting room and Sadler said he was working over the weekend but he would contact you during the next week. You said that was fine?'

'He did say something like that. I didn't want to see him again.'

'You were still in the living room when Anita came back, and soon after Paul Sadler left?'

'I went home. I went to bed and the next morning I told my mother what had happened.'

'Was that the first thing you said to your mother – that you'd been raped?'

'I … don't know.'

'Let me help you. The next morning you overslept and your mother came into your bedroom to wake you up. You told her to go away, but she dragged the bedclothes off you and you began to argue with her.'

'I wanted to be left alone.'

'The two of you argued about the time you came in and where and who you'd been with?'

'She was going on at me.'

'So you told her you'd been raped?'

'It was true.'

'Was it? Isn't the truth you were very attracted to Paul Sadler? You were aroused by him and responded to his lovemaking?'

'I didn't want to have sex with him.'

'You agreed to have sexual intercourse with him.'

'I didn't want to …'

Cassie sat down. The worst part of the trial was over. Emma Gilbrook would leave the courtroom and Cassie wouldn't have to think about her again.

Chapter 4

Six weeks later

As soon as Cassie reached the robing room at Snaresbrook Crown Court, she turned on her mobile phone and looked at the long list of emails that had accumulated in the inbox while she had been in court. Amongst those from fashion houses, stores and restaurants she saw a message from someone called Malcolm Delaney. The name was unfamiliar and her first inclination was to delete it as being a scam of some sort, but the subject matter was Paul Sadler. The first line read:

'*Miss Hardman, I want to congratulate you.*'

Her curiosity was aroused; she was a little flattered that someone wanted to show their appreciation of her advocacy skills. She opened the email and read the contents:

'*… on your representation of Mr Sadler. You are a very talented advocate. I would like to invite you to have lunch or dinner with me. We can arrange a time or place later. I look forward to hearing from you. Malcolm.*'

She wondered who Delaney was and how he had found her email address. She had no intention of accepting his invitation or indeed of replying, but she didn't delete the message; an unknown admirer would make an amusing tale for her colleagues.

When her train arrived at Chancery Lane Tube station, she made her way through Stable Inn Court where the rain had enhanced the scent of the roses; she inhaled the perfume – better than the sweaty smell of the Underground. She turned left from the Inn into Chancery Lane, by the Document Exchange. Coming towards her with a sack truck piled high with brown envelopes and boxes was the office junior, Roger Hales. He smiled at her but didn't stop.

'Alright, Roger? Bit of a pull uphill with all that.'

He started at her words as if he hadn't seen her approaching. 'Yes, Miss.' He didn't stop but pushed his way into the office building where the DX was housed.

Cassie continued along Chancery Lane, a route she took frequently. To her right was the solid wall of Lincoln's Inn and on the east of the street was a row of shops. They were forever changing – fewer offices and more coffee shops and takeaway sandwich bars. But at the junction with Carey Street, where it had been as long as she could remember, was the firm of Ede and Ravenscroft, purveyors of robes and wigs to her profession. She could remember buying her wig and gown from them over seventeen years ago. The wig, made of horsehair, had been carefully fitted to her head by one of the female assistants. It had been very white then, betraying her status as a newly fledged barrister.

She crossed Fleet Street, busy with vehicles, and turned under a stone arch into the calm of Middle Temple Lane. She loved this place, with its history, its sense of continuity. Her step instinctively slowed as if the pace of life inside the

Temple was that of an earlier time, and she wandered into her chambers at 3 Burke Court. The clerks' room was anything but peaceful, the tranquillity disturbed by the clatter of fingers hitting keyboards, and the shrill voices of the junior clerks chattering into the mouthpieces of their phones. Jack, the senior clerk and the man who held the reins of her practice, was in his room overlooking the open-plan office occupied by the rest of the staff.

Cassie went to the row of pigeonholes and pulled out her mail together with a couple of briefs tied with pink tape. She glanced at the two sets of papers and was separating her letters into those for the rubbish bin and those she needed to read, when Jack beckoned her to join him. On his desk were four lever-arch files that showed the signs of being well handled. On an A4 sheet tucked under the pink tape holding them together was the title 'R v David Winston Montgomery'. Jack's shirtsleeves were rolled up and his butterfly print tie tucked between the buttons of his white shirt; he tried to look busy even if he was just checking the racing results. He sat down, looked up at her and beamed. Cassie waited for him to speak, although she knew exactly what he was about to say.

'I've managed to get you a leading brief in a murder at the Bailey. I assume you'll want to apply for Silk in a couple of years. This is quite a good case. You're ready for it, even though it's a murder. None of the Silks want it. Scared they'll get tarred with a racist brush, I dare say. A woman won't, of course. Judge Crabtree is in a bit of a panic thinking the defendant might want to represent himself. I said to Colin in the list office, my Miss Hardman can handle it. Spoke to Tim. Didn't take long to persuade him you could do it. So, there you are, a leading brief in a murder.' He leant back in his chair with his hands behind his head and smiled at her. Cassie thanked him and picked up the files. Jack was a confident East Ender, a combination of butler and used car salesman. He often claimed that a good clerk needed to be able to lie and have no sense of geography.

She knew he was lying now; he had not got the brief for her. Tim Durrant, the solicitor for Montgomery, had spoken to her the previous evening and told her his initial choice was Eleanor Hesketh. She was the only female Silk in chambers, but she was in the middle of another case. Unable to defend Montgomery, Eleanor had suggested Cassie. Tim had instructed Cassie before and, even though it was usual to instruct a QC in a murder case, he didn't have much time to find someone who was available and who he trusted. Facing that dilemma he had decided to send the brief to her. He had made it clear she was senior enough and, he thought, competent enough to take on a murder case. 'He's got some very racist views. It makes dealing with him difficult, but I'm sure you can handle him,' and then after a pause, 'he's sacked a couple of barristers already.' She hadn't liked to ask why.

Cassie hadn't been over-keen on representing a racist but the opportunity to have a leading brief in a murder trial was unlikely to happen again at this stage in her career. Even if the client was convicted, if she had done her best it would help her application for Silk. In addition, Tim instructed her regularly and she didn't want to let him down.

'Are you going home now? I'll get you a taxi, shall I?' Jack said.

'Thanks, if you would. That would be very helpful. I don't think I can manage this on the Tube.'

Cassie knew better than to argue with Jack, or to confront him with his obvious lies; he must know Tim would tell her why he'd chosen to instruct her. But, she knew he wanted the brownie points for getting her the case. He was thinking she might apply for Silk, and she would need his help for that, so she said nothing.

Cassie's flat was on the top floor of a white stuccoed terraced house in Notting Hill. The small front garden was looked after by the woman in the basement flat and in early summer it was still a little bare. The front door was boot polish black and the brass doorknob gleamed ferociously. Carrying heavy bags up the three flights of stairs made her wonder if she had been sensible to buy it, but once inside she knew why she had. She loved the light and the views over the gardens at the rear of the terrace. She put the files down on her desk, one of her most treasured possessions. She undid the pink tape and opened up the files. Under the cover of the uppermost file was a DVD labelled 'Christopher

Young'. She assumed it was the recording of the video interview with him; he was an eyewitness to at least some of the events that had resulted in the death of his fifteen-year-old brother Albie. Under the DVD was the single sheet of A4 paper bearing Tim Durrant's instructions. They were, as she expected, extremely terse, leaving her to read the papers but making it clear that the client was trying to dictate tactics. He added that the defendant's attitude could only lead to disaster.

Chapter 5

DC Alexis Seymour picked up the forensic report. As she anticipated the wrap of white powder was cocaine. The small quantity, only enough for personal use, had been found in the trouser pocket of a seventeen-year-old male who had been stopped leaving a nightclub in North Kensington. She was about to put it to one side for the uniformed officer who had conducted the original search, but the final paragraph in the report caused her to think again. The forensic scientist had analysed the drug to ascertain its purity and had identified the dilutant as Phenacetin. He advised steps be taken to identify the source as the filler was a known carcinogenic.

She turned on her computer and found the details of the arrest. The youth was named as Roger Hales; he was described as mixed race and his address was a flat on the Lancaster Estate, North Kensington. As she reached for her mobile, Chris Dundy walked through the door.

'Look at this,' Alex said, handing him the report. 'We need to see this kid and try and get him to tell us who his supplier is.'

'Is he on bail?'

'He's due back today. I'll tell uniform we need to see him before they charge or caution.'

'Has he any previous?'

'No. No cautions either.'

The two of them began to shift the files of paperwork from the night duty. They were still reading when the custody sergeant told them Hales had arrived.

Chris brought the young man into the interview room, along with the smell of frying fat wafting in from the direction of the canteen. He was well built, with dark, tightly curled hair and ears that stuck out. His shirt was open at the neck but his light grey suit was distinctly formal. Alex pointed to a chair on the other side of the coffee-stained table she was sitting at and switched on the recording device. She introduced herself and asked Chris to do the same.

'We're in the interview room at Ladbroke Grove Police Station and with us is – can you give us your full name, please?'

'Roger Hales.'

'And you're how old?'

'Seventeen.'

Alex cautioned him. 'You don't have to say anything but it may harm your defence if you do not mention when questioned something you later rely on in court. Anything you do say may be given in evidence. Do you understand?'

He nodded.

'Do you know why you are here?'

He nodded again.

'Can you say yes or no. The recorder doesn't pick up a nod.'

'I was stopped and searched and a wrap of some white powder found.'

'That powder has been analysed and it's cocaine. A Class A drug. Illegal. Now I should ask you if you want a solicitor present while we interview you.'

'I don't want anyone to know. I didn't know what it was.'

Chris shifted in his seat. 'What did you think it was?'

'I knew it was some kind of drug. I wasn't sure what it was.'

'Haven't you used drugs before?' Alex said.

'Smoked a bit of weed, but not now.'

'So, where did you buy this wrap?'

'I don't want to say.'

'Any reason for that?'

'I'm not answering your questions anymore.'

'Nice suit you're wearing. On your way to work?' Chris asked.

'Um, yes.'

'Where do you work?'

'Not saying.'

'We're not going to go and tell your boss if that's what you're worried about,' Alex said.

Roger Hales looked first at Alex and then at Chris, before turning back to Alex. 'I work for some lawyers in the Temple.'

'Which set of chambers?'

Hales took a deep breath. 'Three Burke Court.'

This time it was Alex who took a sharp intake of breath. The address was familiar to her. One of the tenants there was Cassie Hardman, a woman whose skills as an advocate she had come to admire when she was the exhibits officer in a drugs case some years ago.

'Well then, you know the importance of telling the truth, don't you?'

Hales put his head down. When he looked up, he said, 'I'm not answering any more of your questions.'

'This wrap contains not just cocaine but a substance called Phenacetin, which is dangerous, and we want to find the supplier quickly before large quantities are on the streets. We want you to help us. Do you understand?'

Hales shook his head and repeated he was not going to answer any further questions.

Alex turned the recorder off. 'Roger, I'm going to release you on bail for a further week until we decide what action to take.' She saw Chris screw up his face as she picked up her papers.

The two detectives walked with Hales to the front door of the police station and watched him walk south towards Holland Park Road.

'Why didn't you charge him?' Chris said.

'I'm going to speak to Cassie Hardman and see if she can get the information from him. I'm sure she'll be keen to prevent one of her clerks getting a conviction.'

Chapter 6

Cassie toyed with watching the video immediately but decided she was hungry and wanted her supper. Cooking was the one thing she still fitted into her busy life. She had to eat and she found preparing a meal, even if it was just for herself, relaxing. Her kitchen was tidy – red units with black granite tops – only affordable because of its very small size. She put spaghetti on to cook, sautéed some raisins and pine nuts, and then added some tender spinach. While she waited for the meal to cook she opened a bottle of red and poured some into a glass. She sipped slowly as she stirred the sauce into the pasta; in the familiar process her resentment of Jack's dishonesty finally dissipated.

Once she'd eaten, Cassie inserted the DVD into her computer and, while the disc was being read, she found the transcript amongst the files. The screen leapt into life showing one of the cameras panning the interview room, so that anyone viewing the recording would know there was no one hidden who might influence the child's evidence. The room was impersonal, the walls an institutional cream and the furniture dark brown; the only indication of any association it might have with children was a box of toys, brightly coloured like Smarties, placed on a low table.

After about thirty seconds the door opened and a woman wearing a dark straight skirt, it could have been navy or black, and a yellow shirt, came into view. She raised her arm with her hand outstretched, clearly inviting someone to enter the room. A young boy of about nine slid through the door. He was well dressed in what appeared to be a school uniform, grey trousers and a dark green sweatshirt with a shield on it in gold. His curly hair was brushed back from his face. The pupils of his dark eyes were dilated and they darted around the room as if he thought something or someone might be concealed waiting to pounce on him. Following him was a man carrying a writing pad; he was wearing jeans and his dark beige polo shirt was open at the neck. Trying a little too hard to look less intimidating to the schoolboy, Cassie thought. The male officer took a seat to the right of the screen and waited while the woman motioned to the boy to sit on the sofa next to her.

'Come and sit here, Christopher, or shall I call you Chris?'

The boy moved towards her and sat perched on the edge of his seat, facing the woman but looking at the man. He didn't reply to the woman's question. She asked again if she should call him Christopher or Chris.

He turned to look at her and said, 'Chris.' The woman then introduced herself as Detective Sergeant Angela Kotzeva and the man as Detective Constable Craig Hadley. She asked the boy to give his full name.

'Christopher James Young,' he replied. Kotzeva then pointed towards one of the cameras and then to others positioned round the room. At the same time, she explained they were recording the interview. Chris looked up at the cameras as she talked. At one point it seemed to Cassie that he looked straight at her, and she could see a hollow look in his eyes. She turned away. What would it be like to lose a sibling, the hole created by the loss of someone who she had known all her life? She would have felt like she had been torn in two if her younger sister, Amanda, had died, particularly in such a tragic incident.

She pushed those thoughts to one side; she had to think about the defendant and how best to fight his case. Chris Young was not going to be easy to cross examine, no juvenile was. The jury would be sympathetic towards him and she'd have to be careful not to antagonise them. But that was in the future, now she was looking for flaws in his account of the events leading to his brother's death and checking to see if the interviewing officer had asked any leading questions, or tried to guide him in any way.

Cassie switched her attention back to the screen; Kotzeva began to tease his story from the boy, letting him tell her in his own words what he had seen and heard. He described seeing his brother go into Montgomery's shop with his two friends who he called Loveday and Jas. Kotzeva asked him if he meant Leon Campbell and Jonathan Wilding. He agreed that was who he was talking about. His brother, who he called Albie, didn't like him hanging around with them, so he'd waited outside.

Kotzeva asked him if he could see what was happening inside the shop. Cassie noted the boy looked down, away from the officer, and plucked at his sweatshirt, before saying, 'Not really. I could see them moving around, reaching up but nothing else.'

'Could you see the shopkeeper?'

Chris Young shook his head. 'I take it that's a no?' Kotzeva said.

'No.' He nodded.

Kotzeva asked him what had happened next, and he told her he had seen Jas coming towards the door, followed by his brother and then Loveday. All three of them came rushing outside followed by the shopkeeper.

'The man was nasty – like, angry, very angry. He was shouting at Albie, calling them niggers, black bastards,' Chris said. He sat upright and swung his right arm across in front of himself, and added, 'He was swinging this club thing, a golf club.'

'What did he do with the golf club?' asked Kotzeva.

'He, the man, hit Albie with the club, and he just fell, fell to the floor.' Chris started to sob and the male officer handed him a tissue. 'I ran to him, and called his name, but he didn't move and I threw myself at the man and screamed at him, "You've killed my brother".'

Now tears were streaming down his face. The two police officers waited for the weeping boy to cease crying. Chris used the tissue he had been given to wipe his face and then he blew his nose. Once he had calmed down Kotzeva asked him to go on. He described how the man had pushed him off and gone to Albie and then turned and dashed inside. Chris had stayed with his brother stroking his face and calling his name. 'I wanted to wake him up,' he said, sobbing.

'Was he still breathing?' Kotzeva asked.

'I don't know, no, I don't think so.'

He started weeping again, wiping his face with the crumpled tissue. Kotzeva asked him what had happened next, and he told her a policeman turned up, followed by an ambulance and they took Albie away.

Cassie pushed the pause button and looked carefully at the tear-stained face of Christopher Young. She believed him: he was telling the truth, but not the whole truth. He hadn't seen all the events of that afternoon. Was he confused or was he hiding something? That was what her cross examination should reveal.

She opened the files and found the first witness statement. It was that of a boy called Jas Wilding. Cassie ignored the declaration that the contents were true and read the first paragraph. His full name was Jonathan Darius Wilding. He admitted he had been in the sweet shop with his two friends Loveday Campbell and the dead youth Albie Young and they had damaged what he described as girlie magazines.

She continued reading. 'Then Monty asked us if we had come to pester him or wanted to buy something. I said I wanted some sweets, but Loveday and Albie both wanted cigarettes.' She thought the interviewing officer had intervened, not only because the next words were, 'I didn't know they wanted cigarettes,' but also she was sure Wilding would have said fags, not cigarettes. The statement continued: 'Albie said they were for his mum, cause he's sold them to us before when we've said that. This time he told us to piss off, he wasn't selling us any cigarettes. "You're too young," he said. Albie began to argue with him and called him names. We all joined in. Someone called him a wanker and I think Loveday said he was a perv, a paedophile. I think I was the one calling him a wanker.'

She tried to picture the three boys and Montgomery in the narrow aisle, squashed between the shelves of sweets and the racks of magazines, but without having seen the shop she found it impossible to create the scene in her mind.

'When Loveday said he was a paedo, Monty went mad and told us to get out. We just laughed at him. Then he picked up a golf club from behind the counter and charged out towards us. I ran out of the shop. I can't remember if I was the first out. Just as I got outside I saw Chris, Albie's brother, next to the shop window. He's a nuisance, hangs around, you know. I stopped and turned to see where Monty was, he was still swearing and cursing us, calling us black bastards and stupid niggers.'

One of the officers must have asked him if he was scared, because the statement continued, 'I wasn't scared. I thought I'd be able to keep out of his way.'

Cassie pushed her hand through her short brown hair, and sighed. How could Montgomery use that kind of language, no matter how offensive they had been? For a second she had visions of refusing to do the case, but that was against the cab rank rule; she had to take it. Then again, it was a leading brief in a murder case and that was a significant step in her career.

'Albie was just outside the door and Loveday was a step or two nearer to me. Monty was in the shop entrance swinging this golf club. He must have caught Loveday on the arm because I heard him yell and then Chris … he started screaming. Both Albie and me ran towards Chris – he's only nine. I was nearest and as I got closer to Monty he hit out with the club, catching me in the chest. I wasn't really hurt, but winded like. I moved back a bit. Albie came between me and Monty and I saw the club hit him across his head and he fell to the ground.' Cassie underlined the words 'in the shop entrance'.

She sat back pondering why the police had not video recorded the statements of Jas Wilding and Loveday Campbell. The two boys were under sixteen and could have been treated as vulnerable witnesses, in the same way as Christopher Young. Perhaps the boys were too unruly to put in front of a camera and the police were relying on them being more subdued in the courtroom, or they had simply forgotten to check the age of the witnesses and couldn't be bothered to start again. Further, they had not been interviewed until the next day. There was nothing to indicate why that was. Had there been the opportunity for them to talk about the incident and agree what to say? Was it just a cock-up or some unfathomable conspiracy?

She was about to turn over the page to the statement of Loveday Campbell, when the telephone rang. Stephen Burnett, who shared a room with her in chambers, said, 'Cassie, I hear Jack's got you a leading brief in a murder. Need a junior?'

'I think it's a bit of a poisoned chalice – no one else wants to do it. You don't want to be led by me, do you?' Before he could reply, she added, 'You're far too senior.' Although she liked Stephen he was the last person she would want as a junior. He would be a distraction, with his practical jokes and silly pranks. She had co-defended with him once when he had brought a glove puppet into the courtroom and played with it on the edge of the work bench, hiding it from the judge and jury behind the rows of files and trying to make her laugh. She didn't want a repeat of that.

'As usual, Cassie, you're right. Do you know who Tim is thinking of? It might be good tactics to go for Ayesha. May help with the racist slur to have a coffee-coloured face on counsels' benches. And she is quite seductive – impress the male jurors even if the defendant isn't too keen.'

'Stephen, really – and do you have anything other than sex on your mind? Anyway, I gather he won't accept anyone who isn't white, Anglo Saxon and probably protestant as well.'

'That rules out quite a lot of the Bar then.'

Cassie laughed; Stephen was good at making her see the funny side of her problems. 'Look, the choice of a junior is vital. He'll not have anyone from any ethnic group. I think it's one of the reasons he sacked previous counsel. It's only two weeks to trial and my instructions are to not be sacked before the end, never mind get an acquittal.'

'Actually, that wasn't why I rang. I heard Eleanor having a real go at Richard, something to do with fees and Jack. Do you know anything about it?'

'I've not been told anything. Eleanor doesn't confide in me. You'd better ask someone else.'

'I've done just that and, reading between the lines, Eleanor's very upset because she has some rather substantial fees outstanding and Jack says he hasn't time to chase them. When she went to Richard to complain he brushed her off. The consensus is she believes chambers ran much better when Richard was in Hong Kong, and she was acting as head in his absence.'

'Really,' said Cassie as she tried to work out where the conversation was going; sometimes talking to Stephen was a bit like a game of chess. 'Well, I don't want to get involved. I have an awful lot of work to do for this trial. See you soon.' She put the phone down, pondering over the row between Eleanor and Richard Jago. Was Eleanor hoping to be the next Head of Chambers? And where would Jack stand in all this? If Richard stood down, would Jack go as well? What of her own ambitions for Silk, would she be better with Jack still the senior clerk or not?

She shuffled the documents in front of her and the bundle of photographs fell against the computer mouse, causing the screen to come to life.

She noticed there were a few unopened emails, amongst them one from Malcolm Delaney. She opened it.

'*You haven't replied to my earlier email. I was so looking forward to meeting you in person, but never mind, if you change your mind do contact me – or if not I shall be watching you.*'

Cassie paused; this email didn't have the same courtesy of the earlier one. Who was Malcolm Delaney anyway? She reassured herself that his pronouncement that he would be watching her was not a threat, just confirmation that he was one of the regulars at the Old Bailey who came to watch the trials or simply to get out of the cold. The staff at the court called them the Bailey groupies and said they each had barristers they preferred to watch. She hoped that was the answer.

Chapter 7

Alex was eating breakfast, looking forward to her day off, when the phone rang. Her shoulders dropped, anticipating it was her boss asking her to come to the station.

'You're at home.'

'Dad. I do get some time off.'

'Good. Are you working this evening, because if …'

'I'm not on duty again until Thursday.'

'How would you like to go to Covent Garden tonight?'

'What about Mum?'

'She's got one of her charity functions. So get yourself dressed up and meet me at the theatre at six.'

'How dressed up?'

He laughed, a deep throaty sound, a sound she'd always loved. It signalled he was in a good mood. She hadn't seen much of him lately and the last time had been for lunch with both her parents. He had been taciturn. Her mother had chattered the whole time. Things were not right between them. She knew her father had kept a mistress at the flat she now lived in, but her mother had not, to her knowledge, sought a separation or divorce. Financial matters bound her parents together now.

'Definitely not your leathers. How about a cocktail dress? We'll have dinner at the theatre and you can tell me what you've been up to recently.'

'Do people still dress for cocktails? Six at the theatre. See you.'

She walked into her bedroom with its walk-in wardrobe. It was ages since she'd worn an evening dress. She'd been to a ball in one of the Inns of Court, Gray's Inn, with her older brother Peter and some of his friends from Cambridge who were reading for the Bar. She sighed; Peter had been killed five years ago in an avalanche. He'd been twenty-seven and it was his death that had made the rift between her parents unbridgeable. She hadn't helped by deciding to join the police force.

She foraged through her clothes, the racks of jeans, smart skirts and white shirts she wore for work, until she found the pale blue taffeta dress wrapped in a white linen cover. She tried it on, hoping she hadn't put on weight from eating in the station canteen. It fitted. She looked at herself in the mirror and held her blonde hair up, emphasising the low-cut neck of blue silk. She hoped her father would approve.

She got to the theatre early and stood waiting in the foyer for her father to arrive. She must have missed him coming through the doors, because suddenly he was standing next to her. He bent over and kissed her on her cheek.

'You're looking lovely.'

'Thanks, Dad.' She beamed back at him. Even at sixty he was a good-looking man. He still had all his hair, although it was no longer dark brown.

'Shall we go to the restaurant? There's time for the first course.'

Later, after the music, they were sitting in the dimly lit restaurant having dessert and a final glass of Champagne, when her father took hold of her hand. 'Alex. I don't suppose it will come as a shock to you, but we've decided to separate, your mother and me. We'll wait until we can divorce by consent, two years apart.'

Alex felt tears come into her eyes. She looked away towards the bright lights in the bar that now appeared to be surrounded by rainbows. She blinked. 'Is there somebody else? Are you leaving Mum for somebody else?'

'As it happens I'm not. But your mother has been seeing another man. That's not the reason. It's not been the same since, Peter … well, you know.'

She squeezed his hand. 'I know. I just didn't think we'd all get so …' She struggled for the right word. 'So apart. We were a family before …'

'I guess so, but your mum and I, well, we'd not been getting on before and when Peter … that was the final straw. Your mother will stay in Richmond and I've bought a flat overlooking the river in Battersea.'

Alex nodded. She was their child. She didn't want this to happen. She wanted to be able to go to their home. For them all to be together. She told herself she was nearly thirty, old enough to know these things happened and she had her own life. She stood up. 'I'd like to go now.' Her voice sounded, even to her own ears, faint and far away.

'Of course, I'll get you a taxi.'

Back home, Alex ripped off her evening dress and poured herself a large glass of whisky. *Damn them*, she thought. Despite the Champagne she had drunk earlier, the whisky had no effect. She was still sober. She checked her watch. It was too late to phone her mother and she wasn't sure she wanted to speak to her anyway. But she turned on her mobile and found a message from Mel Haskins, telling her there was a briefing in the CID office at nine in the morning. She was to be there. That was her day off gone. At least she would have something else to think about rather than the announcement her father had made.

The office was buzzing when Alex arrived. Chris Dundy, her oppo, was already there. She had worked with him for the last four years. He was a tall man and bulky with it, but she found his size reassuring. Mel Haskins, his ginger hair cropped closely, was leaning against the wall. He was the local Intelligence Officer. Part of his job was to man the computers for the drug squad, collating the relevant information gathered on the patch. Alex didn't know the five other men. The presence of Mel Haskins suggested this was a drugs investigation. She hoped it would be a little more exciting than the routine street robberies that were an almost daily occurrence in the area, and that it represented a return to favour for her after her unconventional involvement some time previously in a murder investigation. Amongst the group, she was the only woman. Mel Haskins leant over her. 'I didn't know you'd been moved to the drug squad.'

'I think it's just for this operation. I was told this job needed more feet on the ground.'

'Nice to have a pretty face amongst …' Mel looked round at the other officers.

Alex ignored the comment. 'Do you know what it's about?'

'Not really. Something to do with contaminated drugs.'

Alex looked around the room; it was quite small and smelt of cigarettes even though there were large signs proclaiming that Ladbroke Grove was a no-smoking station. She was sitting with her feet under the table, her navy jacket over the back of her chair and the sleeves of her pale blue shirt rolled up. Chris Dundy was next to her and the rest were lounging around a dilapidated table on which a collection of pens had been slung along with a number of notebooks.

She didn't have time to observe all the other officers before a man in his mid-thirties walked into the room with the air of authority that made it clear he was the boss. He unzipped his brown leather bomber jacket and his light blue eyes swept round the group of officers. He perched on the edge of the table at the front of the room, pulled a mobile from his pocket and put it down together with the sheaf of papers he was carrying. There was a shuffling of chairs as the seven men in the room rearranged themselves so that they could all see him. Alex too turned her attention towards the senior officer.

He introduced himself as DCI Saltburn and then said, ‘I think you all know that a couple of weeks ago, a man called Roger Hales was arrested in possession of a wrap of cocaine. It was cut with a carcinogen. The cutting agent mimics the effects of the cocaine and increases its potency. In addition it makes it dangerous, and the traffickers a lot of money. Until a couple of days ago, it looked like it was one-off, but we’ve now had about twenty arrests, all in the West London area, cut the same way. The aim of this investigation is to find the source. Identify who’s cutting the cocaine, who’s distributing it and who’s importing it. I want all the persons found in possession to be re-interviewed and pressed about their supplier.’

He handed round lists of those who had been arrested. ‘Can we split them up and interview them again. Only three of them have previous convictions for drug offences. The rest can be told they will be cautioned if they cooperate. Tell those with previous we’ll put letters in saying they’ve helped us find the supplier.’

Alex looked at the list, which included Roger Hales. ‘Sir, we’ve spoken to Hales. He works for a set of chambers in the Temple and he’s learnt enough law to refuse to answer questions. But …’

DCI Saltburn screwed up his face. ‘I suppose we can expect some to do that.’

‘I was about to say …’ Alex said.

'She has some really classy friends,' Dundy added.

Chapter 8

Cassie's room in chambers was on the top floor overlooking a rather dingy courtyard where a London plane tree's spindly branches struggled to find the light. Three others shared the room with her; the desks were all arranged higgledy-piggledy and each one, even her own, was covered with papers in untidy piles and half-filled coffee cups. Along one wall were more stacks of paper hoarded from long-finished cases. The room smelt of dusty paper and stale bread left over from half-eaten sandwiches. She didn't want to have the conference with David Montgomery there. It was unlikely to impress any client, particularly one who had been persuaded that his barrister should be a leading junior, as she was, rather than Queen's Counsel. Rather reluctantly, she had asked Eleanor if she could have the conference in her room.

'But of course,' Eleanor had said. 'Just don't move any of my papers.'

The conference was due to start at six o'clock, but Cassie went to Eleanor's room some ten minutes before. A pupil, Spencer Watson, was working at the desk; he looked at her through thick-lensed glasses as she asked him to leave.

'I was told the room was free,' he said, trying to explain his presence there, as he moved his bulk out from behind the desk.

'I hope you haven't moved anything. Eleanor is very fussy about her papers.'

'No, no. I haven't, I haven't moved a thing.' He kept repeating the words as he manoeuvred round the open door.

Cassie smiled; pupils were very easily unsettled. She knew she shouldn't tease, but sometimes she couldn't resist. She put the Montgomery brief on the oak desk. The room faced west and caught the evening sun, flooding it with light that bounced off the highly polished surface. The chair was made of black mesh and rather throne-like; Cassie's feet didn't quite touch the floor. She adjusted it to her own height and, once it was at a level that allowed her to write at the desk, she opened her papers.

While she waited for her client to arrive she took the opportunity to look around Eleanor Hesketh's room. Unlike the office occupied by Richard Jago, which, to Cassie, fitted the description of a library in a gentlemen's club, this was tastefully decorated, the walls a fashionable shade of dark cream, the chairs upholstered in beige and red-check wool. The library shelves had the same books as Richard's, the black bindings of the All England Law Reports neatly arranged against the red of the Criminal Law. There were three etchings on the walls, all by Eric Gill, the simple monochrome shapes emphasised by heavy black and silver frames. Cassie admired the Gills, although she wondered why Eleanor had chosen drawings by a man who had committed incest. Her sister, Amanda had emailed her about going to Manchester to see an exhibition of Lowry's paintings. Perhaps some day, if she got Silk and if she ever had a room of her own, she would have a print by Lowry on the wall. She loved the matchstick figures and it was one way of reminding her of her roots in the north.

Cassie's mobile rang. She checked the screen. 'Alex, nice to hear from you. How are you?'

'I'm fine. Cassie, this is a bit difficult. I'm making enquiries about a Roger Hales. He says he's one of your clerks?'

'The gofer. He's very junior.'

'How well do you know him?'

'He's been with us for about six months. Our senior clerk thought we looked a bit too white and he knew Roger's family. His dad probably played cricket with Jack. He seems willing enough.'

'He was arrested about four weeks ago in possession of a small quantity of cocaine. When we received the analyst's report it says it was cut with Phenacetin. It's used because it mimics some of the effects of cocaine. The punter thinks he's getting the real thing but the dealer makes a lot more money because it's cheap. The downside is it has some dangerous side effects. It's carcinogenic for one.'

'Are you saying he's dealing in drugs?'

'No. When we interviewed him …'

'Did he have a solicitor there?'

'I asked him but he declined. He said he didn't know what the powder was but more importantly from my point of view he wouldn't say where he bought it. I'm fairly sure if he provided the information about his supplier we would caution him for this offence.'

'So you want me to talk to him and see if he'll tell me?'

'Something like that.'

'And if he won't?'

'I can't say. He may be charged with possession. It's only a small quantity. Personal use only.'

'I'll try.'

They both knew Cassie felt under some obligation to assist Alex and she wanted to help. She knew how dangerous drugs could be and it was worse if they were contaminated. She put her mobile on the desk and sighed. She didn't really want to speak to Roger, but …

As Cassie considered how to approach the clerk, there was a gentle tap on the door and Hamish, another of the junior clerks, poked his head round the frame and then ushered Tim Durrant and Montgomery into the room. Cassie's first impression of her client was of a short, elderly man, older than his age, which she knew from the papers was fifty-eight. He was neatly dressed in grey flannels and a jacket of blue tweed, with a dark blue shirt unbuttoned at the neck and a glasses case stuck out of the breast pocket. There was an air of the military about him, but the most striking thing was how little expression there was in his face; his dark eyes and thin lips gave nothing away.

Tim Durrant, his solicitor was, as usual, scruffy. His shirt looked like it had not been pressed, his tie hung loose around his neck, and his navy suit didn't quite fit. His appearance was deceptive, hiding a sharp intellect and sound judgement, which he always used to the advantage of his clients. Cassie liked him even though she could find him irritating, particularly when he gave every appearance of not doing any work on the cases he sent to counsel. She believed he kept his instructions short not because he didn't have ideas or hadn't read the documents, but because he found the process of preparing a brief time consuming and he had better things to do. His domestic problems impinged on his time too.

Tim took a Winnie the Pooh spectacle case from his briefcase and placed a pair of dark-rimmed glasses on the end of his nose, before introducing Cassie to her client. She smiled at Montgomery to try and instil some confidence in him, and then asked him to tell her about the shop on Barlby Road.

'It was my father's shop, Miss Hardman. He'd bought it just after the war. We lived in the flat upstairs when I was a kid. Dad stayed there after Mum died. I'd joined the navy by then. Eighteen I was. I helped him out when I was on leave. Then when he retired, this Indian guy, something Singh, I can't remember his first name, took over the shop. He paid rent and that was my father's pension, like. He got a lump sum for the goodwill and he bought a little flat out at Hayes. He died about four years ago. I'd left the navy a couple of years before and got a job in a builders' merchants at Park Royal, stock control, same thing as I'd done in the navy, only bricks and plumbing fittings instead of munitions.'

'How long have you been running the shop?' Cassie asked.

'We've only been there about eighteen months. Mr Singh left, gone back home I assume. Never had much to do with him – he gave me a month's notice and was gone. I'd been made redundant a couple of months before that and at my age, well, it's hard to get another job, too many foreigners taking them.' He paused and waited. He was trying to provoke her, she thought, but she didn't respond and he carried on. 'I, well, me and Val …'

'Val's your wife?' Cassie said.

'Yes, Miss. There's just the two of us.' Cassie nodded at him to continue. 'Well, we thought it would be a good idea to take over the shop and run it ourselves. A bit of income to add to my pension and there was the flat over it. No rent to pay either. I used my redundancy money to restock it, and to sort out the upstairs rooms, new kitchen, new bathroom. That kind of thing.'

'Does the shop make much money?'

'No way.' There was a bitter edge to his voice. 'I soon realised why old Singh had left, crafty he was – got out while the going was good. Been there about seven years I guess. Things had changed in that time, were changing before that. A lot of the old houses had been knocked down, and council flats built, social housing. Then the site by the canal became a supermarket selling newspapers and sweets. We couldn't compete on price. I tried to be a bit different – trade on being old fashioned, sweets in jars instead of packets. Tried to start delivering newspapers, but couldn't get the lads to do it for the money I could afford. These black kids would rather sell drugs.'

'But you got the schoolkids coming in?'

'Yes, cigarettes, that was what it was about. If they bought some sweets or something, I'd sell them cigarettes. I knew I shouldn't, but if they said they were for their mums or dads, usually it was mum, I'd let them have the fags.'

'Was this the first incident with boys from St Colomb's?'

'No. It started almost straightaway. At first it was little things, like dropping a drinks bottle on the floor so that it spilt and then refusing to pay for breaking it. Looking at magazines and pulling them apart was another favourite. Then they started stealing, picking up an extra bar of chocolate as they left, that kind of silly petty theft. I'd yell at them asking them to bring it back, but they'd just ignore me.'

'Was it always the same boys?'

'I don't think so. They'd come in in groups. I'd be watching one and then the others would start. It was impossible to tell them apart. All big lads. Black lads. I knew what to expect when they started coming in.'

'Did you call the police, go to the school?'

'Police, they were bloody useless. Tell them someone's stolen a fifty pence bar of chocolate and they don't want to know. Bigger fish to fry, I suppose.'

'Did you do anything, a CCTV camera or something like that?'

Montgomery looked puzzled. 'I thought you would have seen the recordings. The police took them.'

'No,' said Cassie. Then to Tim, 'Do we have DVD recordings taken at the shop?'

Tim said he hadn't seen any, but he would check the schedule of unused material and ask the CPS for them.

Cassie turned back to Mr Montgomery. 'When did you put the CCTV in?'

'About six weeks before. It's quite expensive and I've only one camera at the back. It moves all the time, catches people in different parts. You never get a complete picture. The kids soon cottoned on to it and would duck down behind the central gondola, or wait until it moved round to another part of the shop.' He shrugged his shoulders. 'But you can see their faces clearly on the screen.'

'We'll get hold of the discs. I hope I can identify the right boys.'

'I think it's probably the last few minutes. I stopped it just after I rang for an ambulance. Didn't want it to delete the recording. It does that if it's left running. They were the only ones in the shop.'

'Right. I just want you to tell me in your own words what happened that day. What time was it?'

'I think just after three thirty, after school had finished. These three black lads came into the shop. They'd been in before. They started playing up, throwing magazines about, stealing sweets and then demanding cigarettes. I'd had enough of their behaviour and told them to get out.'

Cassie stopped him. 'Did you swear at them. Can you remember what you said?'

'I told them to get out. I probably told them to bugger off, called them black bastards or something like that. They were calling me names and one of them said I was a paedophile. That was it. I'd had enough of them. Told them to get out. They were sneering at me. I got a golf club from behind the counter. Swung it around at them. They ran out. I followed. They'd stopped just outside the shop. I was in the doorway. They were still shouting at me. One pulled a knife. I saw it – something metallic in his hand. It was a knife. He began swinging it around in front of him. I told him to drop it, but then he lunged towards me with it and I thought he was going to stab me so I swung the club down towards his arm. Suddenly there was this other lad there. I must have caught him on the head. He went down. I was shocked – he'd come from nowhere. And then a much younger lad ran over to him, knelt down, and then ran towards me shouting I'd killed his brother. The little 'un began to hit me. I had to push him off. I ran inside and dialled 999 for the ambulance and police.'

'You're sure there was a knife?'

'Yes, absolutely. I saw a knife in one of the buggers' hands and he was threatening me with it. They may be schoolkids but they're all over six foot, and I knew they were going for me. You're a goner, I thought. Three onto one and this knife as well.'

'Were you still in the door?'

Montgomery paused. 'I may have stepped forward. A step. They were pushing at me.'

'The golf club was in the shop?' Cassie asked.

'Yes, I found it, by the canal. It had been thrown away with a load of other bits and pieces, part of a washing machine and a toddler's cycle, I think.'

'These boys had left the shop, but you followed them outside, didn't you?'

'A step, at the most, I wanted them far enough away from me that I could shut the door. I wasn't going to turn my back on them.'

'Are you sure there was just the one blow?' Cassie said.

Montgomery looked down as if searching through his memory. 'I'm not sure. I may have caught the lad with the knife on the arm. But he still had it in his hand, so I'm not sure.'

'Ok, that's all I want to ask you at the moment. There is just the question of a junior. Has Mr Durrant discussed that with you?' She saw he looked puzzled, so she added, 'It's usual to have two barristers rather than one in a case like this, and we need get someone instructed fairly quickly.'

'I'll have anyone you and Mr Durrant choose, Miss, but I'd rather not have some darkie. Don't like 'em.'

'It would help your case if we did. I can't emphasise enough how much better it would be if we choose someone of Afro-Caribbean descent like these boys. Not only would it show you weren't prejudiced, it would give us more insight into their behaviour in court.'

'No. Not having anyone who's black. I'm not having it. The shop was a nice little earner, now it's nothing, worth nothing. Surrounded by wogs I don't like them over here. I'm not having it. That's final.'

She wanted to scream at him about his prejudice but her instructions were to keep him sweet, prevent him sacking her as he had his previous counsel, so she said nothing and instead sucked in her lower lip. Tim intervened. 'Ok, David, we'll find someone suitable and let you know in a day or two. I want to have a word with Miss Hardman about a couple of technical matters so if you want to get on your way, I'll be in touch.'

Tim got to his feet and opened the door for Montgomery who left without a word to either of them. As soon as Cassie heard his footsteps moving away she said, 'I had to tell him what I thought was best for his case, but if he doesn't want a black barrister, we'll have to accept it. Have you any ideas about a junior? I thought about James Callan, at least he's Irish.'

'And a redhead.' Tim laughed. 'But it's not a bad idea. I'll ring Jack tomorrow and get that fixed.'

After Tim had left, Cassie picked up her papers and looked carefully at Eleanor's desk, hoping everything was where it was meant to be. Down in the clerks' rooms she checked her pigeonhole; she was hoping that any fees paid to her over the last couple of weeks had been processed. She knew she was owed quite a considerable sum for a trial she had completed about five months ago. There was a thin white envelope waiting for her, the type in which the cheques were usually placed. She opened it, but instead of cheques or the notice of a transfer to her account, there was a postcard with a Lowry print on the front. A typed note was stuck to the back of the card. 'I'm still waiting to hear from you. Delaney.' A tremor went down Cassie's spine. How did this man, whoever he was, know she had been thinking about owning a Lowry print?

Chapter 9

The postcard from Delaney was not only menacing, but she was puzzled as to who he was. She didn't remember anyone with that name involved in the Sadler case. The trial had only finished some six weeks ago and she was sure she would still have the file relating to the case on her computer. It didn't take long to open it. The list of witnesses was short.

Cassie scanned the statement of the forensic scientist. He had examined the swabs taken from Emma and the semen in the condoms found in the flat, and compared the DNA with samples taken from Sadler. There was no dispute her client was the man Emma Gilbrook had named as her assailant. The scientist's evidence had been agreed. The medical examiner's statement made her smile. They always had a sentence that said the witness had found the use of the speculum to examine the complainant's vagina uncomfortable. Some prosecutors would say that was a sign that intercourse had been forceful. Hugh prosecuted often and was fully aware the same instrument was used when a cervical smear was taken in tests for cancer and most women found it uncomfortable. He knew she would ask questions along those lines and what the response would be so he had agreed to leave out that part of the doctor's evidence.

Her aversion to defending in rape trials came back to her. She hadn't wanted to do this case, but she had warmed to the defendant and she really liked Lee Shaw. She hoped they would continue to work together. Lee described Sadler as a very attractive man, charming too. He didn't fit the 'fair labelling' description Marcus Pike had talked about.

Cassie found the transcripts of interview. The first one on the day of his arrest was short. He had said he didn't want a solicitor to begin with but had changed his mind and the interview had stopped. In her instructions Lee noted Sadler felt he was being bullied by the male officer, DI Nigel Crawford. Cassie had listened to the original recordings of the interview. She had wanted to hear the tone the officer had used. But even from the transcript it was clear the interviewing officer did not believe Sadler's account.

DI Crawford. Tell me how you came to meet Emma?

Sadler. I'd seen her at Holland Park Tube station so I sent an email to the Rush Hour Crush column in the Standard, *or is it the* Metro.

DI Crawford. And?

Sadler. Look, I don't know what she's said, but we had sex at her friend's flat. She took me there ...

Sadler must have been angry as the DI had said, '*Ok, Ok calm down.*'

Sadler. She was quite happy about it. Consented.

DI Crawford. Really. That's not what she says.

Sadler had been quite emphatic that he and Emma had consensual sex. The officer, DI

Crawford, had noted the age difference and his questions continued to probe Sadler about it.

DI Crawford. She was quite young, wasn't she?

Sadler. She didn't look that young.

DI Crawfod. Quite a bit younger than you?

Sadler. She wasn't under sixteen. Was she? I'm sure she wasn't. She told me she was twenty-four. She couldn't have been under sixteen. She was working – left school must have been sixteen. She seemed to know what she was doing. She helped me put a condom on. We both wanted it.

DI Crawford. Are you sure?

Sadler. Yes. I am.

After that Sadler refused to answer any more questions. The female officer, DC Leanne Pomfrey, asked him if he wanted to see a solicitor. Sadler said he did, so the interview was terminated.

The DI wanted to make further enquiries and had released Sadler on bail. Cassie thought there was sufficient evidence to charge her client at that point. He didn't, hoping, no doubt, further enquires would provide more evidence on which Sadler could be questioned. Preferring charges may have prevented that.

She would object to the first interview being given in evidence because of the officer's line of questions. The officer had tried to mislead Sadler about Emma Gilbrook's age and he should not have done so. Judge Tyte had refused that application so the interview had been before the jury.

The second interview was longer and this time Lee Shaw had been present. In her instructions Lee referred to what she thought was a deliberate attempt by the officer to mislead her. Before the interview began, DI Crawford had provided Lee with a brief outline of the evidence against Sadler but he had failed to mention they had discovered Paul Sadler had placed more than one notice in the Rush Hour Crush column.

DI Crawford had asked Sadler again about how he had met Emma Gilbrook and their subsequent meetings. Sadler had given a very full account of the three occasions he and Emma had met. Then DI Crawford had produced copies of the notices in the *Metro* without saying anything to Lee about them.

Miss Shaw. What are these? I've not been shown these. I don't think...

Sadler. I didn't place those notices.'

Miss Shaw. I need some time with my client if you are going to persist in asking him questions about these notices.

DI Crawford. Do you want to speak to your solicitor?

Sadler. They're not mine.

DI Sadler. I have here a statement from an employee of the newspaper confirming the contact number is the same as your mobile?

Sadler. No comment.

In her instructions Lee had described how they had left the interview room and immediately Paul Sadler had admitted he had placed the other notices.

‘Why didn’t you say so? It’s not a crime wanting to meet young women,’ she had said.

‘I felt embarrassed in front of the officer. I was…well, like a dating agency,’ Sadler had said

Lee had advised her client that they should go back into the interview and he should admit the lie and explain to the officers why he had denied the notices.

The transcript continued with Sadler giving his explanation, then DI Crawford started to ask questions about the notices. Over a three-year period, Sadler had placed six different requests in the newspaper.

DI Crawford. Let’s start at the beginning, shall we? First one, the girl in the Burberry raincoat at Hammersmith. Do you remember that one?

Sadler. Not sure. I think so.

Miss Shaw. Is there anything else? Burberry raincoats are fairly generic. No other description?

DI Crawford. Miss Shaw, I’ll ask the questions the way I want.

Lee had scribbled a note in the margin of the transcript. ‘Oops in trouble again!!’

DI Crawford. Dark haired, got off at Chiswick Park.

Sadler. Right. Yes. I don’t think she responded.

DI Crawford. Why did you pick on her?

Sadler. She looked nice. Well dressed. I like women who go for good clothes.

DI Crawford. Next one. Again Hammersmith.

Sadler. Piccadilly line. The one I use to get to work.

DI Crawford. Ok. Description refers to reading a Kindle with a bright pink cover?

Sadler. I remember her. I think she was called Karen something. Can't remember the surname.

DI Crawford. Chambers, Karen Chambers. Did you meet her?

Sadler. Yes. We went for a coffee on King Street. She was good looking but no sense of humour.

DI Crawford. Do I take it from that you didn't see her again?

Sadler. That's right.

DI Crawford. A woman with a cherry red briefcase?

Sadler. Yes. She phoned me and we had quite a long conversation. She said she'd been flattered that someone wanted to meet her, but she told me she was living with someone. I think we chatted on the phone a couple of times, but it never went any further.

DS Pomfrey. Why did you keep doing this Rush Hour Crush? You weren't getting anywhere with it?

Sadler. Element of surprise. Would there be any response and what would they be like.

DI Crawford. Would they be vulnerable enough so that you could rape them, that's why you kept on. Looking for women to sexually assault?

Sadler. No. No. Nothing like that.

DI Crawford. Next one. Dark trouser suit with a floral scarf.

Sadler. Angie Williams. I did meet her a couple of times. Met for coffee once and then at The Dove on the river. She worked for an employment business in Hammersmith. We got on well but there was no chemistry and so I didn't answer her calls after that. Rather rude of me, but I just wasn't keen enough.

DI Crawford. The one before Emma was at Earl's Court. Green eyes and red hair.

Sadler. I don't think she responded.

DS Pomfrey. Why Earl's Court?

Sadler. Not sure. I might have been on my way to Gatwick.

DI Crawford. We've looked at the text messages on your mobile and in addition to the texts arranging to meet Emma, there's one call to her home address on the morning after you raped her.

Sadler. I didn't rape her.

DI Crawford. But you did ring her the next morning?

Sadler. I rang her mobile and her mother answered.

DI Crawford. You wanted to persuade her not to complain about the rape, didn't you?

Sadler. No. I wanted to tell her I wouldn't be in touch for about a week because I was working a late shift.

DI Crawford. That's not what her mother says.

Miss Shaw. Is that a question?

Sadler. Mrs Gilbrook was going on at me. How dare I phone her daughter? Who did I think I was? I didn't know what to say.

Cassie shook her head and poured another glass of wine for herself. The trial had been straightforward. The facts were largely agreed. The only issue was whether Emma Gilbrook had consented to having sexual intercourse with Sadler. If she had, why was she alleging he had raped her? She couldn't imagine what the emails were about or who might want to contact her other than one of the Old Bailey groupies, but the man, she assumed it was a man, was getting persistent.

Chapter 10

Despite the imminence of the Montgomery case, Cassie continued working on other cases, going to court every day. The opportunity to speak to Roger Hales came a few days later, when she finished a trial in the early afternoon. She dashed back to 3 Burke Court hoping she would get back first. To her relief her shared room was empty. She took a deep breath and using the internal telephone asked if Roger could run an errand for her. She was a terrible liar and felt herself blushing as she made her request. She had hardly put the phone down when she heard Roger's heavy footsteps pounding up the stairs and along the hall to the door.

'Come in,' she said. Roger walked to the front of her desk. 'Roger, can you sit down please.' He towered over her and she felt uncomfortable enough as it was. 'I understand you were arrested a few weeks ago and some cocaine was found in your pocket. Is that right?'

His eyes widened. 'How did …Yes, Miss Hardman. Will I get the sack?'

'I haven't told anybody yet. Where did you get the drugs?'

Roger hung his head, 'I'm not sure I want to say. I don't think you'll believe me.'

'Let's take it one step at a time. You were stopped and searched?'

'I don't know why they stopped me. There were hundreds of us queuing to get in the nightclub.

They were pulling over all the black males. It's always happening.'

'Did you have the drugs on you?' Cassie wondered if the drugs had been planted on him by the police. It wouldn't be the first time that had happened. Too many officers applied the three Bs: big, black and bad.

'They were in the pocket of my jeans.'

'Had you bought them?'

Roger didn't reply but shook his head.

'Roger, I understand the cocaine was cut with another drug. A drug that is dangerous and can cause cancer. So it's important for the police to find the dealer who's doing this. If you help them they'll just give you a caution. I can guarantee that.' Alex's promise was a clear inducement and could be used if any officer tried to pursue a charge of possession.

'Can you tell me who your supplier was?'

'I found the wrap.'

'Where?'

Roger Hales pursed his lips and looked down. 'Here.'

'Here. What do you mean here?'

'Here. In the toilet on the first floor.'

'In the toilet here – in chambers.' Cassie was well aware cocaine was the drug of choice for many high fliers. It kept them going, working long hours and enabled them to party just as hard. But one of her colleagues? And bringing them into chambers. Usually it was alcohol. Sometimes, she thought, she was too ready to go for a drink after work or to open a bottle of wine with her evening meal. But never drugs.

'It was nearly time for going home. I went to the toilet and saw this white paper on the floor. I picked it up. Opened it and saw … I didn't know what it was.'

'Didn't you realise it was cocaine, some drug at least?'

'I did think so. I was tempted to try it … I didn't – too scared. I put it into my pocket and forgot about it until the police stopped me. I should have got rid of it.'

'Yes, you should.'

Roger's face crumpled and his eyes filled. Cassie could feel his distress. She believed him, but she wasn't sure Alex Seymour would.

'Will I get the sack?' Roger swallowed and looked up at the ceiling.

'Roger, I am not going to do anything at once. I think you are telling me the truth, but the police may not. Now go back downstairs and try to get on with your work.'

When he had left, Cassie picked up her mobile with the intention of contacting Alex and telling her what she had learnt. She scrolled through the contact list and then put the phone down. Would Alex believe Roger's account of finding the wrap? If it was true, then someone else in chambers had bought the drugs. Cassie had no idea who that might be. Was it one of the clerks? One of her colleagues? A conviction for possession of a Class A drug would result in that person being disbarred. She found it hard to believe anyone would be so foolish as to bring drugs into chambers. Of course it might have been a client. That must be the answer – it was a client.

She hesitated. Whoever it was, if Alex wanted to continue her enquiries, she or other police officers would want to question members of chambers, the clerks and the clients who had come for conferences. She couldn't let that happen. She would have to tell someone, the Head of Chambers, Richard Jago, the senior clerk, Jack, or someone else. Not now though; it was Friday night and Ben was coming for supper.

She picked up her bag and ran down the stairs, but as she got level with the door to the clerk's room, Eleanor came out onto the landing. Eleanor. Of course – Eleanor was the best person to tell about Roger. Eleanor didn't have the responsibilities of being Head of Chambers, nor was she in charge of the clerks' office. She looked at Eleanor's face. Would now be a good time? She wanted some input quickly, before Roger was due back at the police station, or Alex started to want answers. She had already decided she would accompany him when he answered to his bail and see if she could persuade Alex to caution him. She hoped Eleanor would approve of that course.

Eleanor wasn't in the best of moods, but Cassie decided it was possible this would be the only opportunity to ask for advice.

'Eleanor, can I ask you about something?'

'Sure, some difficulty with your case?'

'No, it's something else. Can we discuss it in your room?'

‘Sure, but …’

Eleanor led the way up the stairs. Cassie closed the door behind her as Eleanor sat behind her desk. ‘It’s Roger. He was arrested in possession of a small quantity of cocaine. A police officer I know rang me and told me the drug was cut with a dangerous chemical. They are anxious to know who supplied him. He’d refused to answer questions in interview …’

‘At least he’s learnt something while he was here.’

‘But if he helps them, she’s promised he’ll get a caution rather than be charged.’

‘So, what’s the problem?’

‘He told me he found the wrap in one of the toilets here.’

‘Difficult …’ Eleanor sucked at her teeth, clasped her hands and then put a thumb to her mouth. ‘Is he telling the truth?’

‘I think he is. He thought he might experiment with it but wasn’t sure what it was so he just stuck it in a pocket.’

‘He should have thrown it away.’

‘That’s what I told him. He’s due back at the police station next week and I thought I’d go with him. Make sure my friend keeps to her promise. But what if she wants to start interviewing us? No one’s going to admit they take drugs.’

‘You’ll just have to persuade her she won’t get anywhere. I’m sure you can do that. Now, I have other things to do.’

‘What about Roger?’

'He's got us over a barrel, hasn't he? If we sack him he'll blow the whistle and there will be an investigation by the Bar Standards Board. No – we need to keep this in chambers. Let me know how the interview goes. We might have a better idea about what's going on.'

Cassie arrived back at her flat minutes before Ben. She heard him tear up the three flights of stairs without getting out of breath. Cassie was surprised – she had never known him do any exercise. Not that she did very much, but a lifetime of walking in the hills around her home town of Lancaster, and using stairs rather than the lifts, even at the Bailey, kept her relatively fit.

'Have you got a bottle open yet?'

'In the fridge.' Cassie smiled up at him. She liked his face. He wasn't traditionally handsome but his eyes were warm and intelligent and his mouth was usually curved into a smile. She reached up and traced the outline of his lips with her little finger. He put his arm round her as they went inside her flat.

It was a warm evening and she had put a bottle of Chablis to chill. Once their glasses were filled they exchanged their news. Ben was in a good mood; his research was going well, and he was excited by an invitation to attend a scientific conference in Washington. Cassie was less pleased with the week despite the leading brief. Montgomery's racism had upset her. She was struggling with managing a man whose views she found unacceptable but who she was bound to represent. The arrest of Roger Hales and the emails from the unknown Delaney had added to her stress. Ben frowned when she told him she had received a third communication about the Sadler case. 'Shouldn't you report it to the police?'

'I've thought about it, but …'

'You still don't think it's serious, and you haven't got the time.'

'There aren't any threats. Just he'll be watching me. Could just be a guy in the public gallery. And you're right – I haven't got the time. Anyway, I gather the police aren't very good with stalking cases.'

He pursed his lips; the smile had gone.

'Let's forget about it. It's Friday night. I'll order a pizza, make a salad and then there's strawberries and home-made ice cream. We can watch a film or whatever,' she said.

Ben pulled her to him.

Chapter 11

Cassie met Roger outside Holland Park Tube station. His eyes betrayed his anxiety and although he tried to smile at her, he couldn't. It was a short walk to Ladbroke Grove.

'Now let me talk to the officer. I know DC Seymour and I trust her. But they'll want you to tell them where you found the wrap, and you must tell them the truth. I do believe you and I hope the police will as well.'

'It is the truth, Miss Hardman.'

Inside the police station Cassie asked for DC Alex Seymour and explained who they were. While they waited she looked round at the posters, warning of pickpockets, car thieves and burglars, peeling from the wall. After a few minutes they were escorted into the custody area, where Roger surrendered to his bail. The custody sergeant was completing the forms when Alex came into the room and on seeing Cassie raised her eyebrows.

'Miss Hardman, you've come with Mr Hales. Are you acting as his legal representative?

Cassie said she was.

'Perhaps you'd like to come this way and I'll tell you the details of the offence,' Alex said to Cassie. 'Perhaps Mr Hales would wait here.'

Cassie wasn't surprised by her friend's reaction. It wasn't normal for a barrister to turn up at the police station with a client. She assumed Alex was expecting a solicitor to attend the interview and she knew her presence would raise questions.

Once inside one of the interview rooms, Alex said, 'You know the details of the offence. He was stopped and searched outside Peaches nightclub …'

'Probably illegally.'

'No comment, but the wrap was discovered and when it was analysed it was found to be twenty-five per cent pure. As I told you, the cocaine was cut with a drug called Phenacetin. It enhances the effects of cocaine but can have serious consequences with long-term use.'

'I understand, and I know you want Roger to tell you where he got the drugs. If he does he'll be cautioned rather than charged. Is that right?'

Alex nodded.

'Right. I'll tell you what he told me, but I don't think it will help you very much. He says he found it in one of the toilets at Three Burke Court.'

'How convenient. I guess he doesn't know who left it there. I'm not sure I can swallow that.'

'Alex, I think he's telling the truth. He could have played the race card, an illegal stop and search, a wrap planted. It's been known. He hasn't done that. Have you got the notes the officer made at the time? The record of the stop? The grounds for it?' Alex didn't reply. 'The whole thing would be concocted after he was charged. Let me guess – *I saw Hales turn away from me as if trying to conceal something. I went up to him and asked him to show me what was in his pockets and he refused.*

I took hold of him and he struggled etcetera, etcetera. Sound familiar?'

'Ok. I could start an investigation into the tenants in your chambers.'

'I know, and that's the other reason I'm here. First, I don't think it will help you. No one is going to admit it. There are fifty-three tenants, six pupils, seven staff, as well as any clients, both professional and lay, who come to chambers. What's more, they are on an open staircase that leads from Middle Temple Lane into Burke Court. So any number of passers-by would have access to them.'

'I'd like to interview your boy …'

'Don't call him a boy. It's patronising.'

'Ok, Ok. I'd like to interview him under caution.'

Cassie nodded. 'Sorry I was a bit sharp, but the trial I'm doing at the moment has a strong racial dimension. The defendant is a racist and I'm having to keep quiet so that he doesn't sack me.'

'Right. Do you want to be present when he's interviewed?'

'He's entitled to a lawyer. I haven't advised him to refuse to answer questions, but I don't think he'll say anything different.'

Cassie waited in the interview room while Alex went and got Roger Hales from the custody suite. She pulled the file towards her and began to read the document on the top of the bundle. It was a copy of a police officer's notebook and, as she had guessed, referred to Hales turning away from him as if concealing something. When he was searched the packet was in the right-hand back pocket of his jeans. How had the wrap got from his suit to a pair of jeans?

Roger repeated his account of finding the wrap, and although Alex pressed him he didn't change it. Cassie thought Alex had missed the inconsistency regarding Roger's clothing, but then Alex asked, 'Do you normally wear a suit to work, Roger?'

'Yes, miss.'

'When you were arrested you were wearing jeans.'

'I can't remember.'

'You must have taken the wrap from your suit and put it into your jeans?'

'If I was wearing jeans that night. I can't remember. I know I found the packet in the toilets in chambers and put it in my pocket, that's all I can tell you. I don't know where it came from.'

Alex looked at Cassie and pulled her lips into a wry smile, before saying the interview was over and the case would be referred to the Crown Prosecution Service for their consideration.

Chapter 12

The next day as soon as Cassie got home, she changed out of her dark suit into jeans and a bright yellow jersey. She wanted to look at the scene of the alleged murder. It had started to rain quite heavily and she reluctantly decided to drive. Moving her coffee-coloured Mini out of the parking slot she had secured four days ago meant when she came back she would have to drive around until she found a different space. She checked the status of the traffic along Ladbroke Grove on her mobile. The app advised her it would be slow. The evening traffic was building up, and it took her nearly fifteen minutes to cover the mile or so to the row of shops at the junction of Barlby Road and Ladbroke Grove. She turned into a side street close by and found a resident's parking space; fortunately, her permit allowed her to park there.

The brick-built terrace looked worse than it did in the photographs. Sandwiched as it was between the car park of the supermarket, the railway line, the canal and the Harrow Road, not even a bright summer sun could have made the scene attractive, never mind under the grey clouds of a rainy day. One of the houses could have been occupied but it was difficult to judge; instead of curtains, a sky-blue sheet had been hung across the windows on the first floor. The remainder were protected from prying eyes by dirt. The property to its right was boarded up, covered in graffiti by an untalented artist. Cassie couldn't tell if it had been a shop or another house. Next to that was the building she had identified as a hardware shop in the photographs. She had gone with her grandfather to a similar shop in Lancaster when she was a child. She recalled wandering around while he chose a tool he needed for his work as a cabinet maker. She was curious about all the tins and tubes she could see, and trying to read the labels she had accidently moved one that was propping up a small pyramid. There was a clatter as they fell to the floor. Her grandfather had apologised to the salesman and ushered her out of the shop. Montgomery's newsagents too gave the impression of being from a previous era. Her client's despair at the loss of business was tangible to her as she surveyed the row of properties. This small corner of London had missed the jaunty progress of the nineties and the continuing austerity would in a short time, she guessed, sound its death knell.

The sweet shop was still open and, without really thinking about what she would do, she pushed open the door. There was a smell of decay, aniseed balls, methylated spirits and stale tobacco, a smell she had not anticipated from the pictures she had examined. A bell sounded at the back, a snatch of 'Hearts of Oak' which she recognised from her schooldays. A woman in her late fifties, not much younger than her own mother, came into the shop and stood behind the counter. She was clutching at the sleeves of a dark grey cardigan and wrapping it round her body. She didn't smile in welcome, but asked Cassie if she could help her.

‘I was looking for Mr Montgomery, or rather I wanted to look at the shop.’

‘Why would you want to do that? Who are you snooping around here? Another reporter? My husband’s not seeing anyone.’

Of course, Cassie thought, dressed like this no one would think she was a lawyer. ‘Sorry, I should have explained. I’m Cassie Hardman, the barrister representing your husband. I wanted to get a feel for the place. To know what the shop is really like. You must be Valerie.’ She hadn’t expected her client’s wife to be there, he had said she hated the place, and wouldn’t work in the shop because of the abuse they both got from their young customers.

Cassie held her hand out in anticipation of shaking hands with the woman; Mrs Montgomery did not respond but let her arms fall by her side, and then put one hand on the counter and said, ‘He’s not here.’ Her voice trailed off. ‘Have a look round. I’m sure there’s not much to see. We’re trying to keep going. We don’t get much from it, but apart from his pension from the navy, and these days it’s not enough, it’s all we have.’

Cassie walked up one side of the central gondola and looked at the racks of magazines, the shelves of sweets and cigarettes, the three-dimensional view that the photographs had recorded in two. She reached up and took down one of the magazines from the top shelf; she had to stretch to pick it up. The boys captured on the CCTV had not.

When Cassie turned towards the counter she became aware of Mrs Montgomery watching her every move. 'It must be very difficult for you …'

'It's awful, just awful. We've had dog dirt through the letter box and abuse scrawled on the windows. He's not really evil. For years he was away at sea for weeks, months and then home for a few weeks. When he finally left the navy … well, the world had changed. Changed too much.'

Cassie didn't know what to say to the woman. Seeing the newsagent's shop in context had made her feel a little more sympathetic to her client. He was trying to keep his father's business going against the pressure from supermarkets and with vandalism rife in the area. He didn't have enough money from his time in the armed forces to give up the business, and he was too old to start something new. The best he could hope for was that the whole terrace would be sold for redevelopment, but this was not the time.

Cassie thanked Mrs Montgomery and made her way to the shop door. She opened it, took a step forward to the threshold and stood for a few seconds as she thought her client must have done. The pavement in front of her was quite wide, plenty of space for the three boys to stand in a circle around the entrance. She looked to her right to where Chris Young had been standing at the moment his brother received the fatal blow. The distance between them would not have been more than twelve feet. As she turned to walk back to her car she glanced back into the shop and saw Mrs Montgomery still standing behind the counter hugging her cardigan to her.

On the way back to her flat, she thought about the difference between her life and that of her client. She lived in a more prosperous part of Kensington, in a home she could afford from her earnings in the profession she enjoyed. It wasn't the first time she had compared her own life with that of her client and been thankful for her good fortune.

Once inside, she went over to the desk. It was the last piece her grandfather had made. He had lost his job with Gillow's, the furniture manufacturers, when he was fifty-five, almost the same age as Mr Montgomery. Even with his skills, her grandfather had found it difficult to get another job and had scratched a living making the odd piece of furniture. He had known what it was like to struggle late in life, but she could not imagine him expressing the sort of views her client did. Then again, Lancaster in the nineties probably didn't have the same sort of racial mix as London in the early part of the twenty-first century.

In addition to the Montgomery brief another one was open on her desk; she had promised to do an advice on evidence for her instructing solicitors, but the visit to the sweet shop had taken longer than she anticipated and she was hungry. She checked the contents of her fridge and decided to have some prawns with feta cheese, parsley and lemon on some pasta. Pasta again, but it was quick and tasty. While she prepared her meal, she sipped at a glass of Chianti.

David Montgomery's reaction to immigrants had been expressed very forcefully to her in conference and she had wanted to argue with him, to protest that whatever anyone's skin colour, we were all part of the same species, that the difference in our DNA was negligible. She hadn't, because she didn't want to be sacked by him, and she knew it would be a waste of time. He wasn't for changing. She wished she hadn't accepted it, but getting a leading brief was too good an opportunity to turn down.

Once she had eaten she turned on her computer to start work on the advice she had promised to have ready by the end of the week, but first she checked her emails. Her sister had sent some photographs of her two nephews and the sandcastle they had built on the beach. The two boys were standing either side of the turreted cone of sand, holding their spades aloft, waving them in triumph, and in the background was Blackpool Tower, apparently growing out of six-year-old Jeremy's head. The next email was from Delaney. Cassie shuddered. Her unknown admirer was becoming a nuisance. At first she decided against opening it, and went on to the next email on the screen, but her curiosity prompted her to see what he had to say – perhaps it would help her to identify him. It was still headed Paul Sadler but the contents appeared to be unrelated to that trial.

'*As thorough as ever, I see. Did you enjoy your visit to Montgomery's this afternoon? I hope you found what you were looking for. I'll be seeing you. Yours, Delaney.*'

Cassie swore to herself. How could he have known she had been to the shop? She hadn't told anyone, not even her clerk. *He must be following me*. All thoughts of work vanished. She went over to the windows from which she could see the street. She looked down; there was no one loitering outside. Then she studied the cars; she had managed to find a parking space only a few bays away from the one she had left earlier. In front of her car was the blue Peugeot belonging to one of her neighbours and behind, the Volkswagen Golf driven by the lady who lived opposite. On the other side of the road was a white van; for a moment Cassie thought it had been there earlier, but one white van looked like another and they were ubiquitous in London. She saw a man leaving the front door of one of the houses opposite and get into it. Once it had vacated the space, a black-and-cream Smart car belonging to a local firm of estate agents dashed forward from where it had been hovering. Mr Delaney couldn't possibly be one of the not over-bright but terribly well-connected young men employed by them. What was his interest in the Sadler case?

As she finished work on the advice, a pop-up told her Ben was online, and seconds later she heard the ringing tone telling her he wanted to speak to her. She ignored it; she didn't want to tell him she had been sent another email by Delaney. He would want her to go to the police and she didn't want to do that. It would be too distracting. Then she felt guilty but by that time he was offline. She would contact him later. She opened up her inbox, looked at the message from Malcolm Delaney, shuddered and hit the delete button.

Chapter 13

Standing in the doorway of 3 Burke Court, Alex ran her eyes down the board with the names of barristers painted in black on a white background. About a third of the way down was Miss Cassie Hardman. Alex pushed open the swing door and walked into a dark hall. Facing her was another door that led out into a dismal-looking square and to her left was a wooden stairway. Painted on the wall was a hand pointing up and next to it the words 'The Chambers of Mr Richard Jago QC.'

At the top of the stairs there were four doors. Three of them were unmarked but the fourth had a brass plate with the word 'Reception' on it. Alex looked for a bell or knocker but couldn't find one. She hesitated and then pushed the door open. She found herself in a small hallway with a glass screen on her right and a large open office behind it. She could smell toast and coffee as well as a heady perfume. Sitting round a group of desks were five men and one young woman, each wearing head phones and each studying a computer screen. One of the men was Roger Hales. He blanched. She shook her head to indicate she wasn't there to see him.

'Can I help you?' said a woman sitting at a desk to the right of the doorway to the office area. Alex hadn't noticed her until she spoke.

'I'd like to see Miss Hardman, please.'

'I'm not sure …' The receptionist picked up a phone and punched in a short number. 'I'm not sure she's back from court.' While she waited, Alex took the opportunity to observe the activities in the clerks' room. She had never been in a barrister's chambers before and wasn't sure what to expect. There weren't any signs of affluence; the desk and chairs a little smarter than the ones in the station, the computers a little more up to date. There was a pause while the phone rang. 'Is Miss Hardman there?' Whoever it was who'd answered must have said yes. 'There's a lady here to see her.'

The person at the other end relayed the message, and then said something Alex couldn't hear.

'Your name?' said the receptionist.

'Alexis Seymour.'

The receptionist repeated her name and then put the phone down. Seconds later Cassie was at the door of the hallway. 'Alex, come on, this way.' Cassie held the door open and ushered Alex out. She led the way across the landing towards the door on the opposite side of the stairway. As she did so she pointed towards the other two doors. 'Those are the toilets. I think Roger found the wrap in the one on the right. Do you want to see?'

'Not at the moment.'

Coming down the stairs towards them was a tall man dressed in a dark grey suit. Alex thought he was probably about the same age as she was, and although she would not describe him as good looking he was striking, with dark hair and lively hazel eyes. He held her gaze, smiled and lifted one eyebrow, then he nodded at Cassie and pushed open the door to the reception.

Cassie took Alex into a large room, the walls of which were lined with bookcases. 'We don't really need these now. Virtually everything is online, but sometimes … sometimes it feels right to use a real book. Now, what's brought you here?'

'I was hoping you might help me. More of the contaminated cocaine has turned up and we need to find the supplier quickly. We're trying to interview the buyers, but I'm doubtful we'll get anywhere with that. Even offering them a caution won't mean much.'

'What are you getting at? Someone here is more vulnerable?'

'Barristers can't afford a conviction for possession of a Class A drug. Wouldn't they be disbarred? Is that the right word?'

'Probably. But nobody will admit having any drugs. They know their rights.'

'I'm sure they do. But they might tell you.'

'Are you asking me to question my friends?'

'Yes. Look, I know it is rather, well, underhand, but …'

'I'm not going to grass on any of the other tenants. I'm not an informant.'

'It looks like there's a large quantity of this contaminated drug. Serious addicts are at real risk, and that might include some of your colleagues. I'm not asking for names, just where they get it from. I'm assuming none of them is the supplier.'

Cassie put her hand up to her face and looked down. 'I don't know of anyone who takes drugs regularly. Alcohol, yes, but not hard drugs.'

'How much time do you spend with them when you're not working?'

'Not that much. Mainly I'm with Ben.'

'You're still seeing him?'

'We spend most weekends together and …'

'And?'

'I'm not their type. Brought up in a different world.'

Cassie noticed the screen on her mobile showed she had received an email from Delaney. She shook her head.

'So you wouldn't know who might use cocaine at the weekends or when they're burning the candle at both ends?' Alex said.

Cassie only vaguely heard her. 'Sorry, what did you say?'

Alex repeated her question.

'I don't spend much time with the other tenants apart from after work when we might go to one of the pubs or wine bars round here. The Cheshire Cheese, El Vino's, the Devereux. The weekends … most tenants are with their families. Like I spend time with Ben.'

'Look. It's up to you.'

'Fine. That's it then.' Cassie looked at her mobile again and tightened her lips into a thin line.

'I know it's rather a lot to ask of you but I didn't expect it to upset you …'

'It's not that.' Could she tell Alex without it going any further? 'I've been getting emails and notes and things from some guy called Delaney. I don't know who he is, but he heads the emails "Paul Sadler". That's the name of a defendant in a rape trial I did about six weeks ago.'

'And?'

'I can't see any connection between this man and the case.'

'Have you reported it?'

'No. There haven't been any threats. It's just that he seems to know such a lot about me. Not just details from our website. It's a bit unnerving. Actually, it's getting to me.'

'You should make a complaint.'

'I've thought about it but I've a really difficult trial about to start.' Cassie stood up and then sat down again. 'I don't want to waste time making a statement when it might be nothing …'

Alex nodded. 'Will you think about the drugs … if any one of your colleagues knows anything or says anything. It may be our best chance of catching this dealer.'

After Alex had left, Cassie remained in the library, her mind jumping between the Montgomery case, Delaney, and now Alex's plea for help. Perhaps Stephen – he was such a gossip; he might know who was taking drugs.

It wasn't difficult to contrive having a drink with Stephen. He was always ready for a night in a wine bar. They headed for Daly's on the corner of Essex Street and the Strand. It didn't take long for the conversation to turn to the problems of fee collection.

'What's going wrong? Any idea?' Cassie said.

'Not really. I've asked Zoe and she shrugs her shoulders and blames others for not submitting their fee notes.'

'I've asked her to chase some fees, but she says she hasn't time. It could be there's too much work for one person. Chambers is nearly double the size it was.'

'Jack could get someone else if that was the problem.'

'Someone else to pay. And with the cuts in Legal Aid …'

'Would be difficult. I can see that. Changing the subject – Roger …'

'What about Roger?'

He leant forward and lowered his voice. 'I've heard he was arrested with some drugs. Personal use only, but still.'

'And we're still employing him?'

'Apparently he says he found the wrap in the toilet.'

Cassie opened her eyes wide. 'Really?'

'And Jack decided it was better to keep him on. Didn't want him saying one of the tenants took drugs. Actually I'm surprised Jack is so naïve.'

'Who uses drugs? I can't think of anyone who does. Are you saying you believe his story?'

Stephen nodded. 'Absolutely. We don't pay him enough. He couldn't afford to buy them. Unless he's dealing.' He drew back and looked at Cassie. 'You knew about Roger, didn't you?'

Cassie picked up her wine glass and took a gulp. 'I knew what he told the police. I didn't know someone in chambers was taking drugs. I'm not surprised, but I've never seen any sign. Do you think he's supplying drugs? Alex Seymour came to see me. She told me the drugs are contaminated and the police want to find the supplier quickly. Trying to prevent further harm. I said I'd help. We don't want police officers crawling all over chambers.'

'Definitely not.' He pushed his hand over his face. 'No one is going to admit taking drugs. It's mainly the youngsters, although well … country house parties. But not your scene. You don't go to the clubs some of the younger ones go to. That's where they get them. But I've never heard of anyone having drugs in chambers.'

'Do you have any idea who might have dropped them?'

'Maybe. I think, possibly. I don't want to get anyone in trouble. On the other hand …'

'They're dangerous. Whoever it is should be warned.'

'You could introduce me to the beautiful detective. I'd be quite happy being her snout.'

Cassie laughed. 'You're incorrigible.'

'Don't use dirty words to me.'

Chapter 14

Cassie made her way up to the fourth floor and pushed open the door of her room. As usual, it looked like a rubbish tip. She sighed in despair as she picked her way through the bundles of papers on the floor, and then pushed half-empty coffee cups to one side of her desk to create a space for the two rather slender briefs and the letters she had just picked up from her pigeonhole. She promised herself, not for the first time, that she would spend an afternoon decluttering her desk and the space around it, but it would have to wait. There were more pressing things to do. Amongst the official correspondence, reminders about VAT and the advertisements from the numerous suppliers of legal books and equipment, there was a blue envelope with the address in an elegant script. She turned it over in her hand, but before she could open it, a face topped by a thatch of red hair appeared round the door.

'You are in – Hamish thought you might have gone home,' James Callan said. 'I've just been told about this Montgomery case. Thanks for suggesting me for the junior brief.'

'That's ok. Mind you, I didn't ask for you because of your brilliant mind …'

'Or my beautiful body?'

Cassie laughed, although she did think he was a rather good-looking man, if a bit too young for her.

‘Afraid not. Really, it would have been better if the client had agreed to have Sayeed or Aysha, but he refuses to be represented by anyone who isn’t white. He’s already sacked two leading counsel and Tim’s only concern is that we get through the trial. We’ve got Judge Crabtree and he doesn’t want an unrepresented defendant.’

James nodded in agreement. ‘Does this guy have a defence?’

‘Yes, I think so – self-defence. I take it you haven’t read the statements yet?’

‘No, I’ve only just got them.’

She described how the incident had started and how, under provocation from the three youths, Montgomery had picked up a golf club he kept for just such an event. ‘Then one of them drew a knife and threatened him. That’s when he struck out, but instead of hitting the boy with the knife he caught one of the others on his head. The force of the blow damaged the brain.’

‘Some blow. What number iron was it?’

‘No idea. Not relevant. The Crown will say Montgomery is a racist, which is true, and he struck out in revenge not self-defence. There’s a video of some of the incident, but the police haven’t let Tim have a copy yet. Anyway read through the papers, and when we get the DVD we’ll get together and watch it. The case may turn on how many steps our client took before he struck out.’

‘You said he was provoked, so what about running loss of control? Doesn’t that provide a defence?’

'To murder but not manslaughter. He'd have to plead and I don't think he will.'

'Do we know who's prosecuting yet?'

Cassie grinned. 'Yes, Marcus Pike.'

'The Silk who led you in the Barker case?'

'That's the one. He's very sharp but hides it well. Tries to make out he's just your average bloke.'

'And his junior?'

'I think it's Robin Tasker.'

'Right, I'd better start reading.'

After he left she sat for a few moments; she thought again that James Callan wouldn't have been her first choice. He was an able young barrister but he couldn't provide any insight into the young witnesses' minds. She would have to do the best she could. As her mind wandered over the evidence in the Montgomery case, she noticed the unopened letter. She picked it up and slid her finger underneath the flap; some instinct told her this was from Delaney. She pulled out the sheet of pale blue notepaper and unfolded it. The note, printed from a computer, read, 'You really shouldn't spend so much time working. Every girl deserves a little fun. Come fly with me.'

Cassie threw the note across her desk. Who was it continuing this unwanted intrusion into her life? And why? She picked up the envelope again and looked at the postage stamp. *Pity it's self-stick*, she thought; licking either the stamp or the envelope would leave saliva that could be matched with DNA, if the writer was ever caught. She wondered whether she should make a complaint of harassment against Delaney, but he wasn't threatening her, at least so far. For a moment she considered talking to Alex again and asking her to try and trace the man. Perhaps warn him off. But Cassie knew Alex would repeat her earlier advice and tell her to make a formal complaint. She wasn't ready for that. The notes were creepy but not abusive. Anyway, she didn't want to have the hassle of reporting the matter to the police, hanging around some police station to provide a witness statement, and then, months from now, perhaps having to attend court to give evidence. She opened the drawer of her desk and shoved the note and the envelope to the back, but she couldn't stop thinking about the Sadler trial.

Chapter 15

Cassie had left home soon after eight thirty so she would have time for a cup of coffee in the Bar Mess and compose herself before the trial of Paul Sadler started. She needed that time; the journey by Tube didn't take long on the Central Line from Notting Hill Gate to St Paul's, but it was never comfortable, the carriages packed as workers made their way into the heart of the City. Then there was always a queue at the entrance to the courts as the assortment of people – defendants, lawyers, police officers, witnesses and jurors – waited their turn to go through the security barriers in the front hall.

When she was at the front of the queue, the security officer recognised her and greeted her by name; she was warmed by that acknowledgement – it confirmed she was a regular at the Bailey. She walked through the glass tubes, which looked like something from a spaceship and were the equivalent of a sniffer dog able to detect anything untoward. She placed her bags on the X-ray machine, waited for the police officer to wave her through and then she made her way to the top floor. There was still enough time for that cup of coffee.

In the Bar Mess she saw the bald head of her opponent, Hugh Palmer. He waved her over and after getting her caffeine fix, she sat down opposite him. She was fond of Hugh. He was mild mannered and scrupulously fair; it helped when dealing with these difficult cases. Today he didn't look as calm as usual, constantly pushing his half-moon glasses back onto his nose. He grinned at her. 'I thought you'd stopped doing rapes?'

'I've agreed to do this one.'

'New solicitors?'

'Something like that. Lee Shaw – do you know her?'

'Not really. She represented a kid accused of taking part in a gang rape I prosecuted a while back. Came to court some of the time. Quite pushy, I thought.'

'She thinks this guy's innocent.'

'And you?'

'The case seems weak, but … Have the police taken statements from the other women he contacted?'

'Your solicitor got there first. They confirm his story.'

'So the other Rush Hour Crush notices aren't relevant. I think that part of Sadler's interview shouldn't be given in evidence. Crawford's assumption is not supported.'

'I can't agree. Crawford's insisting it goes in. Sadler lied about them and the jury are entitled to ask themselves why he did so.'

'You don't need to refer to it in opening do you?'

'I needn't if that's what you want.'

'I'll make my application before we begin if you do, otherwise I can leave it until we get to the interviews. We'll still have time to get the women to give evidence if Judge Tyte allows it in.'

'You'd call them?'

'Why not? They confirm what Sadler says.'

'I guess so. Ok, I'll not use it in opening.'

Cassie nodded. 'Right, I'll go and see if my client has arrived.'

Outside Court 11, standing by a window in the broad corridor that served as a waiting area for the courts on that floor, Cassie saw Lee Shaw and her client Paul Sadler. Sadler had taken her advice and dressed in a dark grey suit, pale blue shirt but no tie. Lee by contrast was wearing jeans and a T-shirt covered by a navy blue jacket. 'They can't see what I'm wearing when I'm sitting down,' she said when Cassie raised her eyebrows. Cassie explained to Sadler that he would have to surrender to the prison staff and he would be brought back into the dock at the beginning of the trial. 'I'll ask for bail to continue at all the adjournments. I'm sure he'll grant bail overnight, but sometimes judges prefer defendants to remain in custody during lunch. It avoids any risk of meeting witnesses or jurors.' Sadler swallowed hard but said he understood.

'You'll plead not guilty when the clerk of the court puts the charge of rape to you. Then a jury panel will be brought into court. We can only object to anyone being on the jury if they know you. If there is anyone you think you do know, tell Lee straight away. It's very unlikely but it does happen.'

'What happens if there are a lot of women on the jury? Won't they be prejudiced against me?'

'I wouldn't worry about that. It's my experience that women can be quite harsh on other women. The difficult ones are men who have daughters.' She had just finished speaking when the usher asked Sadler to surrender.

Cassie walked into court and across to the end of the benches closest to the jury, the position the defence team traditionally took. She put all her files on the front row and rearranged the chairs so that there was sufficient room for all the papers in the case in front of her, and then she placed her copy of Archbold to her right. She pulled out a green leather pencil case and placed that next to an unused counsel's notebook; she wrote her name on the cover and underlined it with a flourish. Finally, she fished a packet of mints from her handbag and placed it to the left of the notebook. These arrangements were part of a ritual she repeated before every trial, making sure everything was in reach. Normally this habit calmed her and made her feel comfortable but not today, not in a rape trial.

A few minutes later Hugh arrived in court followed by a woman who looked like a forty-year-old harassed housewife. He rolled his eyes skywards and waved his arm behind him. 'Detective Constable Leanne Pomfrey. Miss Hardman is defending.'

The officer nodded in her direction and then turned to Hugh. 'Can we have a word, sir?'

'Can't it wait? The judge is about to come into court.'

'It's quite important and …' Hugh put his file on the bench and walked back towards the door underneath the public gallery.

Cassie tried to ignore them and busied herself with her papers. She could hear odd words from the conversation between Hugh and the officer. 'Mrs Gilbrook … not … daughter …'

And then Hugh quite clearly: 'It's the daughter alleging rape.' Cassie kept looking at her documents. Hugh moved over to counsels' bench, pulled the hem of his robes round him and plonked himself down.

A moment later Judge Tyte trotted into court. He was a small man with a teddy bear figure inconsistent with his reputation. He acknowledged counsel then took a hard look at Lee. 'Bring the defendant up.'

Cassie turned round in her seat and watched Paul Sadler walk into the dock. It was such a long way from where she was sitting. Nothing like an American courtroom where defendants sat with their defence team. Lee got up and went to stand below him. The court clerk read out the indictment – one charge of rape to which Sadler pleaded not guilty.

'Now, before the jury panel is brought into court … it is my usual practice in cases of this type to give a direction to the jury about the risk of making assumptions about the behaviour of victims, before the case is opened. Do you either of you have any objection to that course?'

Cassie indicated she was happy with that. She had no intention of suggesting there had been any delay in Emma Gilbrook making the complaint, but Hugh said, 'May it not be better if it is given during the summing up?'

The judge pursed his lips. 'I prefer to give that direction at the beginning.' Before Hugh could say anything else he asked for the jury panel to be brought into court.

As they were called to take their place in the jury box, Cassie made a note of their names. When the twelfth was making his way across the courtroom, she looked at Lee to see if she needed to challenge any of them. She knew her solicitor would have asked Sadler if he did know any of them. Lee shook her head.

One by one the jurors took hold of the bible and read the oath to try the case on the evidence. Cassie watched them and tried to make some assessment of their personalities – who they were, where they came from, their occupations and more significantly their prejudices. She wanted to feel at least some of them were open-minded, ready to listen to all the evidence and arguments, but how could she tell? There were a few signs all barristers looked for – the newspapers they were carrying, the clothes they were wearing – but she wasn't sure they were of any value.

She became aware that one of the men on the panel was staring at Sadler. The man then beckoned to the usher and whispered to her. The usher turned towards Judge Tyte. 'My Lord. The juror says he believes he knows the defendant.'

Judge Tyte looked at Cassie, who got to her feet. 'I don't think …'

Lee came and stood by her. 'He doesn't recognise him,' she said.

'How do you think you know the defendant?' Judge Tyte asked.

'I work at Heathrow, sir, and I think he does too.' The juror nodded in the direction of the dock. 'We've never spoken, or anything.'

'Miss Hardman, I'll excuse this juror rather than there be any hint of outside knowledge, unless you have anything to say.'

'No, My Lord.'

Another juror was called into the jury box and took the oath.

The clerk to the court asked the defendant to stand and then turned to the jury. 'Paul Sadler is charged that in March this year he raped Emma Gilbrook. It is your duty having heard all the evidence to say if he is guilty or not guilty.'

Judge Tyte began by explaining the hours the court would sit and asked them to try and be punctual.

'Now there are two directions I want to give you right at the start of this case. It is important that you try the case on the evidence you hear in this court, not on something from any other source. It is easy in today's world to search for information on the internet, but I am instructing you not to do any such searches in respect of this case. It wouldn't be fair to either the complainant or the defendant if you brought into the jury room information of which they are unaware and which they cannot confirm or deny.

'Secondly, the case you are to try, as you have heard, is an allegation of rape. Experience in these courts shows there is a risk of stereotypes and assumptions being made about sexual behaviour and reactions to non-consensual sexual conduct. I would ask you to put out of your mind any such stereotypes or assumptions you might have. In particular you should bear in mind that there is no one classic response to the trauma of a serious sexual assault. Some may complain immediately whilst others feel shame and shock and may not complain for some time. A late complaint does not mean it is a false complaint.'

What did that direction mean? Cassie thought. What stereotypes did jurors have, and what assumptions would they make? Surely all they could do or would do was think about their own sexual experiences. Just as she did.

Chapter 16

The entry bell sounded twice as Cassie pulled the cork out of a bottle of Australian chardonnay. She went to the phone and pressed it. 'It's James,' said the voice over the intercom.

'Come up, top floor.' Cassie pushed the button to release the door catch and opened the door to her flat. She heard the sound of heavy footsteps dashing up the stairs as she went to the kitchen, then James was asking her how many steps there were.

'Only forty-two. Will a glass of wine help you get your breath back?' she said as she returned to the living room carrying two wine glasses. She sniffed the golden coloured liquid and said, 'It's a bit over-oaked for my taste, but tell me what you think. It should be ok.'

Cassie watched James as he held the glass to his nose and inhaled the scent of the contents, before taking a mouthful. 'I like this,' he said, then took another sip of the wine. 'Nice place. How long have you lived here?'

She saw his eyes flick over her and the thought crossed her mind that she should have worn something more flattering than an old pair of jeans and a faded T-shirt, before dismissing the idea. This wasn't a social visit, they were here to work; nevertheless, she answered his question. 'About ten years. Prices weren't quite as steep as they are now, and it was easier to get a mortgage. Anyway, let's play this DVD.' She motioned James to sit down on a chair facing the television, and then she put the disc into the player, walked back to the green velvet settee and sat down.

'Ok. I don't know how much of the recording we've been sent. Montgomery says he turned it off when he went back into the shop to call the police. It records about eight hours before the machine wipes the disc and re-uses it.' She pushed the play button on the remote and the screen came to life. On the lower right-hand side, the time was shown as fifteen thirty-three.

Cassie recognised the inside of the newsagent's even though the camera was filming from the rear of the counter. It took her a second or so to relocate the shelves from left to right, as she reminded herself she was looking at the mirror image to the one she had seen on her visit. The recording was jerky because the camera took pictures every few seconds as it swivelled round the shop, and the focus moved backwards and forwards.

'At least the pictures are in focus,' James said.

Cassie nodded, watching the screen intently, taking note of the position of the magazines and the displays of chocolate bars. For a few minutes nothing happened, and then a figure appeared behind the advertisements stuck on the window pane of the front door, which opened and a bell rang. At that moment the camera swung round towards the right and when it returned to centre there was no one in view. As it moved to the left three figures were standing by the racks of newspapers and magazines. The young men were all quite tall and dressed identically in what was clearly a uniform of some kind – pale brown jumpers, dark coloured slacks, white shirts and striped ties in brown and gold. The top buttons of their shirts were undone and their ties hung loosely.

'I'd have been in detention if I'd gone out of school dressed like that,' said James.

'I think this school's just glad they turn up.'

Cassie wondered which school he had attended. He still had a faint Irish accent, which made her think he might have gone to some posh school. James must have guessed what she was thinking. 'Rathmore Grammar School in Belfast. It's a mixed Catholic school. And I got a scholarship,' he said.

The camera moved back and this time the bald patch on the back of a head was visible and a voice said, 'What do you want, boys?'

'That's our client,' Cassie said.

'Bit brusque.'

They continued to watch the video in silence. Cassie could see James grimacing at their client's language. She too was disgusted by his racism but she had agreed to defend the case, indeed under the cab rank rule she had no option. Montgomery was entitled to a defence no matter how obnoxious he was.

During a sequence when there was a lot of shouting, Cassie heard the sound of a mobile. For a moment she thought it was something on the recording, but then she picked up her phone and answered it, while motioning to James to put the DVD on pause.

'Ben,' she said and then she stood up, walked across the room and looked out of the window towards the gardens below. 'Where are you? I thought you weren't back for another fortnight?'

'I'm still in Washington. I've been trying to contact you on Skype, but you're not responding.'

'I know. Every time you've been online, I've been in the middle of something.' It was a lame excuse, but if she was concentrating on her work she did find it difficult to suddenly switch to idle chatter, even with the man she thought she was in love with.

'I've been worried about those emails you've been getting. Have you been to the police?'

Cassie was touched by his concern. 'No, it's just some crank, one of the groupies at the Bailey. I'm sure it's nothing to worry about. He hasn't threatened to hurt me, or anything like that.' She didn't want him to know how upset she was. 'How's the conference going?'

'Good, but I've been rushing around attending different groups. Look, I'll tell you all about it when I get back.'

'Ben, I start this murder trial next week. I'll be tied up while that's on. Call me when you've recovered from your jet lag,' she said. James was standing next to her and poured some more of the wine into her glass.

'Is there somebody with you?' said Ben.

'No. I'm working on this case. Ben, I have to go. See you soon. Bye.' She disconnected the call and immediately regretted the lie. She should have said the junior barrister for Montgomery was with her. There was nothing wrong with that, but she wasn't sure Ben would understand.

Neither she nor James spoke, but they both returned to their seats, and James pushed the remote to start the CCTV recording. Now the door of the shop was wide open, Montgomery was either on the step or just outside on the pavement with his arm aloft. There was a movement on the left of the shopkeeper and then the arm holding the golf club descended. The camera began to pan round the shop. Cassie and James waited for it to pick up any of the action again, but by the time it did, Montgomery was running back towards the camera. The time was fifteen thirty-seven and then the screen went blank.

'Four minutes. The whole incident took four minutes,' said James, 'and the kid was dead.'

'Seriously injured. He was taken to hospital but there wasn't anything the doctors could do. He was in a coma when his parents arrived. His mother was distraught. The medics talked it over with them. They didn't understand or didn't want to accept how badly he was injured. He wasn't going to survive and they had to make the decision to turn off the life-support machine. That's a terrible thing to have to do.'

James said nothing but his face was set and his eyes stony.

Cassie broke the silence. ‘I’d like you to play the DVD over again and make a note of the times when anything significant happens. Jas says Loveday yelled but the camera doesn’t appear to have caught that. Can you check that out? Is that ok?’

‘How far out of the shop do you think Montgomery was?’

‘It was difficult to tell, but I guess the boy coming from the left was Young, so we could argue the group were still crowded round him,’ Cassie said.

‘He could have closed the door on them, couldn’t he?’

‘He’s entitled to make sure they leave his property. Then he says one of them pulled the knife out and threatened him with it. That’s when he struck out.’

‘I don’t think the CCTV is much help. It proves the events take place quickly, but there are too many breaks to give a clear story.’

‘Clear account. Never say story.’

‘Sorry. I was sort of thinking the recording supports the prosecution version. Montgomery chasing them out, brandishing a golf club and then hitting out at Young. Would you want the jury to see it?’

‘I don’t know. I’ll have to think about that. Can you ask Tim to get another copy?’

Cassie picked up the bottle of wine and held it towards James. ‘Let’s finish the bottle.’

He held his glass out for her to refill it. ‘What’s with the Bailey groupies and emails?’

Cassie twisted her hands as she told him about both the emails and the envelope containing the postcard.

'It seems a bit more threatening than some old boy who sits in the public gallery. Shouldn't you tell the police?'

'We've this murder trial to get through. I can't get tied up with making statements at the moment. Anyway, as I told Ben, I don't think it's anything to worry about yet.'

'I gather Ben is a scientist. A bit of a genius, I'm told. Is it serious?'

'I don't know what you've been told, but I keep my private life out of chambers. It works best that way.'

'You mean you don't want anyone to think you're vulnerable. Not tough enough.'

'Something like that.' Cassie frowned.

'I think I'll go,' said James, putting his glass down.

'Sure, we'll speak soon, arrange for you to meet the client before the trial.'

James put his hand up to her face and stroked her cheek.

'Don't – this is a professional relationship. It doesn't work, other tenants … and there's Ben.'

'Sure there's Ben.'

After James had left, she sat in front of her computer, thinking about Ben. They had been in a relationship for over two years now and she knew the time was fast approaching when she would have to make a decision about him. Although they spent most weekends together, Ben had recently hinted at moving in with her and leaving the flat in South Kensington he shared with two of his friends. She had taken him home to meet her parents. Her father said very little, but she thought he had approved of Ben. Her mother had been more forthright. 'So much nicer than Tony. I knew that was a mistake from the beginning. But you'll make your own mind up, you always do. Just remember time is slipping past.'

Cassie shook her head, closed the computer down and put the thoughts of her ex-husband and his behaviour out of her head. Her future: she'd think about that some other time.

Chapter17

Cassie spent the Thursday before the Montgomery trial was due to begin at home working on the papers and planning her tactics for the trial. A conference had been arranged for the next day at the offices of Durrant and Smyth in Shepherds Bush. Later that afternoon a telephone call from Hamish had sent her into chambers to advise on a case of incest listed for the autumn. When she finished working on the papers, she went down the darkened stairwell into the clerks' room. Some time before Cassie joined 3 Burke Court it had been two rooms, and it still had the high ceilings and ornate cornices. She had been told by her pupil mistress that there had been a row with their landlord, Middle Temple, and English Heritage about the alterations, but in the end the wall had been demolished. Rumours had circulated around chambers that these were the rooms in which the notorious Judge Jeffreys had lived and worked in the seventeenth century. Cassie hoped his malignant influence had not reached out across the centuries.

The single lamp in the courtyard at the rear threw shadows across the desks and the computers, whose own lights flickered. Towards the back of the room a lamp on one of the desks was illuminated. Cassie stepped forward and put out her hand to the switch, but before she flicked it off, a voice said, 'Who's that?' Cassie recognised it as

Eleanor and walked into the hidden interior of the room.

'Just me,' she said. 'I had to come in to do an advice for a solicitor who's screaming, even though the trial isn't for months.'

Eleanor came towards her. 'Sure, sure, some of them are impossible. As if one hadn't enough to do with one's current trial. I thought everyone had gone home.'

'I'm on my way, I'm just picking up some papers.' Cassie moved towards her pigeonhole which was at the far end of the row.

'How are you getting on with that murder brief? I understand the man has a defence.' Eleanor backed a few paces, putting herself between Cassie and the desks at the rear of the room.

'He has a run on self-defence, but he's such a racist, he'll say something that will lead to his conviction. Marcus Pike is prosecuting and he won't let him get away without a fight.'

'Cassie, I suppose you know Richard knows about Hales being arrested. I thought it best to tell him. I hope you don't mind.'

'No, no … of course not. He would have to know eventually. And Jack knows as well.'

'Have you succeeded in keeping the police at bay?'

'For the moment. They're very anxious to trace the supplier.'

'What puzzles me about Roger's story is that he just left it in his pocket until it was found by the police. Would he go clubbing in a dark grey suit?'

'You're right. He was described as wearing jeans at the time of his arrest. He was asked about it during the police interview but he couldn't explain it. Afterwards he told me he wasn't sure but it may have been the day he was clearing out that cubby hole on the third floor. He'd put the same jeans on to go out on the Friday night – the night he was arrested.'

Eleanor nodded, but Cassie thought she wasn't convinced. 'Has Jack confirmed that?'

'I haven't asked him. At the time I assumed he didn't know Roger had been arrested.'

'Richard told him and said to hold his fire until we're sure we've got the police off our backs.'

Cassie turned away and pulled all the letters and papers from her pigeonhole. She stuffed them in her briefcase without looking at them. If there were circulars and advertising material she would sort them out at home. As she turned to leave, Eleanor said, 'Did Jack tell you how clever he was to get you the Montgomery brief?'

Cassie thought there was an edge in Eleanor's voice. 'Of course, he wouldn't pass up the opportunity.'

'How much are you dependent on the clerks for work? I know Tim Durrant sends you some good work, but is he the only one?'

'I'm getting some work from Alison's husband, as you said.' Cassie had opposed Alison being given a tenancy at 3 Burke Court, but Eleanor had suggested she might benefit from work sent from the firm where Alison's husband was a partner. In the end she had been too wrapped up in the Barker case to spend any more energy fighting about who would be offered a tenancy. Now she was glad she had dropped her opposition.

'And I've just done a case for Lee Shaw.'

'Shaw and Winter. Good firm. I'd suggest you don't rely on Jack too much. See what you can do to broaden the number of solicitors.'

Cassie didn't know what to say. She appreciated how fickle Jack could be, but she had always relied on getting work on the basis of her ability as an advocate, not on cultivating solicitors by entertaining them to drinks or dinner. On the one occasion she had taken a solicitor out to lunch, he had made it clear he sent his work, which was mainly large fraud cases, to barristers who introduced clients to him. As she didn't know anyone who was likely to be involved in running companies where opportunities for dishonesty arose, she had come to the conclusion that she wouldn't be instructed by him or his firm.

'You might think about doing a little more prosecuting,' Eleanor said, and then she turned away, checked her watch and switched off the computer.

'I'm dining in Middle Temple Hall, and if I don't leave now I'll be late.' Eleanor smiled at Cassie, her eyes warm and her usual charm restored.

Cassie turned off the lights and followed Eleanor out. They parted at the bottom of the steps into Middle Temple Lane, Eleanor crossing towards the entrance to the Hall and Cassie turning north towards Fleet Street. She had been startled by

Eleanor's advice and was trying to work out why Eleanor had chosen that moment to offer such guidance, when she saw the well-dressed figure of Marcus Pike coming towards her.

'Cassie, just the person I wanted to see. Come and have a drink. We can talk about this case we're doing.'

He took her arm and led her back along the lane and across Fountain Court, where a large stone bowl had water bubbling up from its centre and from which the square got its name, out through the narrow gate into a crooked passageway and then into the door of the Devereux Arms. The bar was full with the barristers, solicitors and their clerks who comprised the Victorian pub's clientele. The dark clothes, unrelieved by any hint of colour, made the scene look like it was from an early movie. Cassie saw a number of pupils from her chambers and she spoke briefly to them. Marcus too nodded at some of the people standing in the room. He pushed his way through to a table by a window which looked out onto the narrow pedestrian walk, and invited her to sit down while he got some drinks. She watched him as, despite his small stature, he elbowed his way through the crowd to the bar. He soon returned carrying a bottle of red wine and two glasses which he placed in front of her. Seating himself opposite her, he poured out the wine.

'Now, young lady, I thought we might talk a bit about this case you're defending. See if we can come to some solution. You don't want to fight this, do you? I'm told your client will not be able to resist putting his foot in it.' He waited for Cassie to respond, but she said nothing, her eyes steady.

'I do have some sympathy with him. Lads coming in every day making a nuisance of themselves. Damaging his property, stealing from him. But he went a bit over the top. Lost his rag. I'd advise the CPS to take a plea to manslaughter, on the basis of provocation – or is it loss of self-control now? Sometimes I can't keep up with all the changes.' Cassie shook her head in denial at his comment. He was a good lawyer. He continued, 'I don't know if they'll accept it, but I think I can persuade them.'

'Got another case to go to then?'

'Oh, Cassie, when did you become so cynical?'

'Come on, either you have something else you'd rather do, or you think you'll lose the case. Montgomery has a good defence.'

'Maybe he does, but you know how even the best conducted cases can go wrong, particularly with a difficult client.'

She smiled at him. 'I'll do my best.'

'Yes, you will, and your best is very good.' He leant over and patted her hand, and then looked at his watch. 'Didn't realise that was the time. I'm dining at the Garrick, summoned by one of Her Majesty's High Court judges, and I'm late already.' He drained his glass and vanished through the crowded bar, leaving Cassie sitting alone with most of the contents of the bottle of wine.

'Drinking alone?' Cassie looked up and saw Stephen Burnett. They were good friends who had obtained their tenancies at 3 Burke Court at the same time and now their careers were following similar tracks. Cassie was sure that if Stephen was not so nonchalant about his cases he would be treated more seriously by the clerks, but she assumed he was not dependent on his income from the Bar.

'No. Marcus Pike has left me for a better date. Meeting some High Court judge at the Garrick. I'm not quite in that league,' she said and laughed. 'Not sure I want to be, bit stuffy for me. Anyway, I assume it's a men only club. Sit down and help me finish the bottle.'

Stephen settled onto the chair Marcus Pike had vacated and stretched his long legs out, revealing yellow socks below the trousers of his dark grey suit. He was curious about Marcus Pike and the Montgomery case, and Cassie told him Marcus had indicated he would accept a plea to manslaughter. They discussed the pros and cons of taking that course, although Cassie was certain her client would not want to plead guilty to anything.

Cassie poured the last of the wine into their glasses. When she turned her attention back to Stephen, he was looking across the room towards a group of young men; one of them was their junior clerk, Hamish, and with him was Roger Hales. She waved at them. Hamish nodded in reply, but Roger turned away.

'Clerks,' said Stephen. 'I sometimes wonder what they do. I'm sure they're behind with fee notes. I don't seem to have been paid for ages. Changing the subject – that wrap Roger found. I heard a little whisper that whoever bought it, and I'm not at liberty to say who, got it from somewhere off Ladbroke Grove, Cotburn Mews?'

'Isn't that where Oscar lives?'

Stephen looked away. 'Is it? Somewhere … Talk of the devil.'

Cassie looked in the same direction as Stephen. Oscar Davenport was leaning against the bar and standing next to him was Roger Hales. Hamish was not with them. She watched them as Stephen continued talking. 'It seems harder to earn a decent living out of crime these days.'

She saw Davenport hand something to Hales. 'What did you say? Oscar has …'

'Roger's brought Oscar's brief,' Stephen said. As he spoke, Cassie saw Davenport pick up a set of papers from the top of the bar and push them into his holdall.

'Sorry, I was …'

Stephen reiterated that he was finding it more difficult to sustain a reasonable income.

'What are you thinking of, committing an armed robbery?'

'You know what I mean. Legal Aid being cut. Even I can see there's an argument for looking after the pennies.'

'I suppose so.'

'You don't sound very sure. You're usually quite keen on keeping a proper check on where our rent is going. Although we all know the clerks cost us a tidy packet. Some people are struggling with paying the rent as well.' Stephen looked across the bar to where Oscar and Hales were standing.

'Yes, you're probably right.' Chambers' finances were a distraction. She would have to think over the information about the wrap of cocaine.

Chapter 18

Cassie arranged to meet James Callan at Shepherds Bush Tube station before the conference with Montgomery at his solicitor's office. She'd worked at home in the morning and, as it was a sunny day, she decided to walk. James, she knew, was at Kingston Crown Court and would make his own way there. He had texted her when he had completed the plea in mitigation for his client to reassure her he would not be late. By the time she arrived at the entrance to the station he was already waiting for her and they strolled along the north side of the Green past the array of independent shops, a French patisserie, then a shop selling hardware where piles of plastic crates spilled out onto the pavement, a clothes shop with vivid-coloured saris in the window, tucked in between the usual high street names. A couple of hundred metres along the Uxbridge Road was the solicitor's office in a former shop, the interior screened by venetian blinds across the plate-glass window.

Inside, the receptionist, a well-built woman with a Welsh accent, whose complexion indicated to Cassie she clearly liked a drink or more, ushered them into Tim Durrant's room. He was standing up listening to someone on the phone. On the shabby desk was a half-eaten sandwich surrounded by an accumulation of files, and a computer that had been swivelled round so the screen was visible. The screen saver was of two young girls, twins, who Cassie assumed were Tim's daughters. The lights were on even though it was sunny outside, and they illuminated the dust on the rows of dark grey filing cabinets lining one wall of the office.

Tim Durrant was one of her most supportive professional clients; he had instructed her in a number of serious cases and had made clear how much he admired her abilities. During that time, however, he had disclosed very little about his personal life. She knew he was married, rather unhappily she thought; he rarely mentioned his wife. The family lived somewhere in Kent and from time to time arrangements for conferences had been changed to enable him to go to a parents' evening at the twins' school. There did not seem to be any question of the girls' mother going alone.

Tim waved at two upright chairs as he continued to listen to whoever was on the other end of the phone. From time to time he interjected, saying either yes or no, and rolling his eyes up to the ceiling, stained as a result of clients who insisted on smoking however much Tim objected. As he put the phone down, an intercom buzzed and the receptionist said Montgomery had arrived. He swept the remains of the sandwiches from his desk, and explained he had been delayed in West London Magistrates Court. 'When I got back there was a long list of telephone calls to make and I've managed to speak to about three,' he said.

Montgomery was directed into the room by the same receptionist, who smiled at Cassie as if they shared a secret, and then she closed the door behind him. He took a couple of paces towards Tim, who had come out from behind his desk, his hand out to welcome his client. Montgomery ignored him, but nodded at Cassie, and then said, 'Who's this?' waving his hand towards James. Tim introduced James Callan to his client, who said, 'I suppose you'll do.'

'Mr Callan is very able. You're lucky he was available at such short notice,' Cassie said. She had to remind herself to be polite. She knew he was under a great deal of stress and she tried to make allowances, but Montgomery was repugnant. Whatever she said or did, she must not get the sack.

Tim directed Cassie towards his office chair behind the desk. She would be the one asking the questions and directing the conference, while Tim and James made notes. She liked to begin a conference by getting the client to talk about their personal circumstances, hoping it would ease any tension before they came to the evidence in the case.

She asked Montgomery about his life in the navy. He wouldn't say too much at first, but after a few questions he said, 'Travelled the world … nowhere like home. Always saw England as, well, cosy. What was it that prime minister said – cricket on the village green, old ladies cycling on country lanes, warm beer? Thought Dad would sell the shop and we'd go, him, me and Val, and live in a quiet village – Norfolk, Suffolk. Go down the pub with my mates, talk about football – but costs too much now. Stuck in this dirty noisy city.'

Cassie didn't know what to say. She loved London; it was a city of opportunity, a city where the unexpected was a certainty, the city where she had found success.

'Small villages have their downside too,' Tim said. 'Nosy parkers and mud.'

His comment broke the tension and they spent the rest of the afternoon reviewing the evidence for the prosecution. Montgomery seemed largely indifferent, apart from calling the witnesses 'lying bastards', or 'those black buggers'.

She knew she had to tell him about her conversation with Marcus Pike; it was her duty to do so, despite being worried he would sack her on the spot.

'I saw the QC who's prosecuting this case the other night. He did say to me that he had every sympathy with your position.'

'Quite right too. He ought to stop them prosecuting me.'

'I don't think that was what he had in mind. He suggested, if you pleaded guilty to manslaughter, he would try to persuade the Crown Prosecution Service to accept that.'

She was about to explain what that meant, but Montgomery got to his feet and said, 'Tell the fucking prosecution I'm not pleading guilty to anything. They were stealing from me. The silly nigger got what was coming to him.'

Tim tried to calm him down, but Montgomery turned on him and said, 'I'm not staying any longer to hear this shit. Stupid buggers.' With that he rushed out of the office. The three lawyers sat in silence for a moment before

Tim said, 'I'm sorry to land you in this. He's an impossible client.'

'At least he didn't sack us,' Cassie said. 'I hope he'll be a little less excitable on Wednesday. If he goes on like that he'll be convicted. As you say – an impossible client.' She began to gather her papers together but some of them fell from her grasp towards the floor. James leant forward to pick them up. She struggled to grasp them as he handed them to her. He kept hold of them and touched her hand, letting it linger there. She acknowledged his help with a faint smile.

'Was he so aggressive when you saw him earlier?' James said.

'No, he wasn't. I suppose it's getting to him. Hanging over his head. Although I don't know why I'm making excuses for him. He's a very offensive man.'

There were a few moments' silence. Cassie contemplated the trial ahead and then shrugged her shoulders. 'Will we see you on Wednesday?' she said to Tim.

'No. I have a major fraud case at Mansion House Magistrates. Privately paid so I need to be there. I'll send a clerk along to sit behind you.'

'Any idea who?'

'Not yet, probably some out-of-work actor.'

Cassie was a little surprised Tim didn't know who the outdoor clerk would be. Most solicitors had a circle of people who were happy to have this kind of casual employment, and would have sorted out who was covering a murder trial at the Old Bailey by the Friday before the trial was due to begin.

Once outside, James said he wasn't surprised Montgomery had rejected his previous legal advisers. 'I'm not sure I really want to represent him.'

'We don't have a choice. That's the deal. However unpleasant the defendant or the offence alleged against him, he is entitled to have a lawyer defend him. But this guy is his own worst enemy.'

Chapter 19

Alex attended another meeting of the drugs squad with Chris Dundy. Each of the team reported on the further interviews with the men and women who had been found in possession of the contaminated drugs. There had been no solid information on which they could rely. Some said they had bought the drugs in a nightclub called Peaches, which was under the Westway, others talked about a café on the Portobello Road. The only common thread was the area. DCI Saltburn asked Mel Haskins if there was any other information coming from the woodentops.

'No, nothing from uniform. But … although on the face of it the drugs seem to be spread around West London, most of those arrested had been to Peaches within a day or two of them being caught.'

'Are you suggesting the club is where the drugs are sold?'

'Possibly. But not where they're cut and bagged. That has to be somewhere else. It stands to reason it's somewhere near the club.'

'Any ideas?' said the DCI. Everyone shook their heads. 'Ok. Let's keep digging. Something'll turn up.'

Alex decided to ring Cassie and see if she had any further information about Hales and the wrap of cocaine. She tried Cassie's mobile but it was turned off. She saw the time was two thirty. Of course, Cassie would be in court. She would have to wait until after four at the earliest.

When she did make contact with her friend, she thought Cassie was a little reluctant to talk. Alex asked if she had spoken to Hales again or not.

'No. I haven't. I can't ... I don't want to get involved in this. I feel I'm betraying my colleagues. No one will admit taking cocaine to me.'

'I realise it's hard for you, but my governor's breathing down our necks to get this investigation wrapped up. I promise no one will know you told me anything.'

'Cotburn Mews. I've been told that's where the drugs were bought.'

'Nothing more?'

Alex heard Cassie take a deep breath. 'One of the tenants lives in the mews and ...'

'And?'

'I've seen him and Hales in some transaction in a pub. It was probably completely innocent.'

'The name of the tenant.'

'Oscar Davenport. But, Alex, please don't ask me anything anymore.'

Alex thanked her and rang off.

Back at home Alex turned on her computer and found the website for 3 Burke Court. It didn't take long to find the name of Oscar Davenport amongst the tenants. She recognised the face as the man she had seen on the staircase when she visited Cassie. She tapped the name into the search engine and found entries in the legal directories. From those she discovered he was twenty-seven, a graduate of LSE. He hadn't been qualified long enough to figure in the top echelons of his chosen profession, but the set headed by Richard Jago was in the top twenty for crime and commercial fraud. She found his Facebook page. There were a number of posts of what appeared to be parties in a country house – girls in ballgowns and young men in dinner jackets. The sort of events her mother had encouraged her to attend. She printed one of the photographs having edited it to show Davenport clearly. What was it Cassie had said about not moving in the same circles as some of her fellow lawyers? Alex pondered if it was a coincidence Davenport went to the same club as Hales. Peaches was in North Kensington and was popular with the residents of the expensive flats in the area as well as the social housing. It could just be a coincidence.

Alex reported her conversation with Cassie to DCI Saltburn, keeping her promise not to reveal who had told her about Cotburn Mews. To her relief, he didn't push her on the source of the information.

'You're local, do you know it?'

'Yes, I do. It's to the south of Cotburn Square. It's a large garden square, big properties and behind them on the south side are mews cottages converted from what were the coach houses. I'm not sure if there are any garages left, but I think there are a couple of offices or workshops.'

'I suppose it's a long shot but it's the best we've got. There've been too many seizures of contaminated drugs. We've got nowhere with interviewing the other buyers.' DCI Saltburn tapped his fingers on the table. 'I'm not authorising any overtime, but if you get the opportunity to wander up there … you're still investigating street robberies, aren't you? It's probably worth a look.'

The next day, Alex walked to Cotburn Mews. The street was cobbled and just wide enough for vehicles to be parked on one side without blocking access along it. There were about forty properties in the cul de sac; most of the cottages were painted in ice-cream colours. Some retained the original garage doors, although Alex guessed they weren't used for cars.

She walked a little way into the mews, wondering which one Oscar Davenport lived in, before choosing one of the houses and knocking on the door. Early evening was not the best time to visit homes inhabited by young professionals who worked long hours. There was no reply at the first door she knocked on and she moved a couple of houses along. As she waited by the door, she noticed a young woman dressed in a black leggings and orange running shoes pushing a stroller.

'Can I help?' the woman said.

'I'm DC Seymour from Notting Hill. I'm making enquiries about some kids making a nuisance of themselves in the area.'

'I can't say I've noticed anything.'

'Nothing unusual? Lot of noise at night? Anything like that?'

The woman shrugged and repeated she'd heard nothing of any concern. The child began to sob and the women bent over and put a dummy in his mouth. While she was distracted Alex pulled two photographs out of her pocket. 'Do you know either of these two men?'

The woman laughed. 'Of course. That's Oscar. He lives …' She pointed to a blue-painted house about three doors way.

'Does he live there alone?'

'Most of the time. Sometimes there's a girlfriend, not often the same one.' She smiled and Alex felt a strange sense of relief. 'Then his father comes as well. Can be a bit of a nuisance. Turns up in his chauffeur-driven Rolls. Blocks the street.'

'The other man?'

'Don't recognise him. Sorry.'

'Thanks anyway.' Alex turned away as the young woman opened the door of her home.

Towards the end of the mews there were still a couple of buildings occupied by small businesses. She saw the premises of a print works, but the door was closed and there was no sign of any one working there. Next door the large plate-glass window was etched with the name of an architects' practice. In the room visible from the street, Alex could see a large computer screen and the hair and eyes of the woman sitting behind it. She went in.

'Can you help me?' she said.

'Sorry, I didn't see you there.' An elegantly dressed woman stood up and came around the side of the desk. 'What is it?'

'I was looking for the print shop.' Alex nodded in the direction of the property next door.'

'That's not been open for a couple of years.'

‘Does anybody come to the shop? Collect post?’

‘From time to time a van turns up. Somebody uses it for storage.’

‘Frequently?’

‘Not sure. Not regularly. I’ve seen lights on sometimes. Why do you want to know?’

Alex produced her warrant card. ‘Police. There’s nothing to worry about. Just making some routine enquires.’

The woman shook her head. ‘Do you want to ask any of the partners about it? They tend to stay late.’

‘That’s ok. How long have you worked here?’

‘Five years. The print shop was open when I started. We had some stuff printed.’

Alex produced the two photographs again. The woman recognised Davenport; she’d seen him frequently and assumed he lived in the mews, but she said she had never seen Hales. Alex thanked her and told her she may call back.

She walked back to her car musing on who and for what the print shop was used. Renting a property in this location wasn’t cheap; why would it be left empty?

Checking her mobile there was a call for her to go to the station and a text from her mother asking her to have lunch at her home in Richmond. The message said her mother wanted her to meet someone. There was a time when that had meant she had invited some man who she thought would be a suitable husband for her only daughter, but this time Alex knew the man was the one her mother was seeing. She wasn't ready for that, she wasn't ready to accept someone else in her mother's life. She texted her refusal, using pressure of work as an excuse.

Alex was the last to arrive at the briefing meeting. Chris was already there. He pushed the chair next to him back for her and produced a coffee in a takeaway cup. She took it gratefully.

DCI Saltburn was looking grim. 'I've had a call from on high – they want a result. Anybody got any ideas on where we go from here?'

'Doesn't the information we're getting point to the drugs being supplied from Cotburn Mews?' someone said.

There was a murmur of assent in the room. 'The mews has come up a lot.'

'Every time you ask about the mews, they hesitate.'

'We could stake it out,' another officer said.

'Alex, you live locally. You know the place?' DCI Saltburn said.

'A cobbled mews. Most of them are houses now, but there's an architects' practice in one of them and next door there's a print shop. It's been closed about two years. I did speak to the receptionist at the architects' and she told me there was some activity there from time to time.'

'So it's possible that's where the cocaine is distributed from. It's got to be worth a try. Let's start by seeing if we can get into the premises.'

'Search warrant?' someone said.

'Fine. Let's do that.'

'What about surveillance on the place?' Mel Haskins said. 'It'll take at least twenty-four hours to get a warrant.'

A day later a team of detectives and SOCOs forced an entry into the print works. The room behind the garage doors was divided by a counter from what had been the hallway. The forensic team began to take samples from the large table in the centre of the room. Alex walked to the far end of the short corridor towards a closed door on the left. Wearing plastic gloves she opened it. The room was dark, the windows boarded to prevent daylight from entering. Alex fumbled along the wall for a light switch and when she found it, turned it on. This room too was empty save for another table, a couple of old chairs and a tall metal filing cabinet. One of the forensic boys followed her, took one look at the tabletop and said, 'I think you've got the right place.' He pointed to a thin layer of white powder. Alex opened the filing cabinet with her little finger. Inside was a roll of small plastic bags similar to the one found in Roger Hales's pocket. She asked the SOCO to bag them.

'Fingerprints?' she said.

'Not much chance. I'll dust the filing cabinet but it's unlikely.'

The search was soon over. As the team of detectives walked back to their cars a man carrying a large holdall and wearing a pinstriped suit came towards them. He was fumbling in his pocket, no doubt looking for the keys to his home. She thought he was too preoccupied to notice her, but although she didn't get a good look at his face she was certain it was Oscar Davenport. She dropped back level with Chris. 'Don't look round. That guy is from the chambers where Hales works.'

Chapter 20

On the first day of the Montgomery trial Cassie arrived at the Old Bailey well ahead of time. She was struggling to sleep, getting up to check her emails, wondering where and who Delaney was and when he would contact her again. In the robing room she pulled out her gown, and shook it to straighten out the creases, fixed the lace collar with the tabs round her neck and went over to the mirror to check her make-up, making sure the dark shadows under her eyes were not too obvious. In the mirror she saw Ayesha Khan come into the room and throw her bags onto the table between them.

'Ayesha, what brings you here?' Cassie said.

'A plea on a burglary. I'm in front of Judge Baxter – he's the Common Serjeant, isn't he?'

'Yes, and can be difficult.'

'Great. The client has no mitigation at all. I'm going to make a fool of myself and I'll be lucky if I get paid.'

'I wouldn't worry too much. Making a fool of yourself – well, no one would do this job if they weren't prepared to do that. The money will turn up eventually.'

'I'm not so sure. I seem to be working for nothing most of the time. My overdraft is increasing day by day, and I've still got my student loan to pay off. I was doing better when I was working as a sales assistant.'

‘Have you asked Jack about it?’

‘Yes, but he shrugs his shoulders and says some people are very bad at putting their claims in.’ Ayesha paused and then said, ‘I find him unapproachable. He brushes me off. Sometimes I think he’s not that interested in the baby barristers, particularly the women. That’s apart from you.’

Before Cassie could ask her what she meant, she heard her name being called over the public address system, asking her to go to Court 10. She grabbed her files, her copy of Archbold, the criminal lawyers’ bible, and her wig and tucked them under her arm. On the way down the flights of stairs to the first floor, she pondered on Ayesha’s comments. Did Jack really help her more than the others? She didn’t think he did; she had fought hard with him about the type of work she was sent. It was true that recently he had found her more serious cases, more like those the young men were instructed in. Eleanor’s words about not relying on him too much came back to her, but there was nothing she could do about it at the moment; she had a trial to conduct.

Outside Court 10, in the wide marble-floored hallway that overlooked the street from which the courthouse got its name, she found David Montgomery waiting for her. He was standing stiffly, his face rigid, barely acknowledging her; he was wearing the same clothes, the blue tweed jacket and dark shirt he had worn at the first conference with the addition of a navy tie bearing a small gold crest. She was dismayed by his disinterest; normally clients were eager for their barrister to turn up and provide reassurance. James had not arrived yet. Nor did there appear to be a clerk from the solicitors. Normally she would not be too concerned about seeing a client on her own, but Montgomery was so difficult she was reluctant to talk to him without a witness to their conversation.

She was relieved when her mobile vibrated in her pocket. She motioned to her client to wait by the door to the courtroom while she took the call. Her relief turned to panic when she saw the name Delaney and the message:

'*Back at the Bailey. Another vulnerable witness. Take care.*'

She closed her eyes and then pressed the delete button on her phone. She gritted her teeth and took a deep breath. She had to concentrate on this trial. A moment later James came loping along the hall towards them hugging his papers to his body. Montgomery appeared to relax a little at the sight of James. *Another man*, she thought.

As Cassie explained to Montgomery how the jury panel would be selected, instead of looking at her, he began to brush at the beige mac he was holding over his arm.

'I don't want any black men on the jury,' he said. He looked up at her, his face set and his eyes fixed.

'We can't challenge someone just because of their colour. We have to give reasons, such as you know them.'

The court usher came to the door and said, 'Miss Hardman, your client needs to surrender.'

‘Of course. Shall we all go into court.’ Cassie put her wig on and led the way through the double doors and into the pine-panelled courtroom. Montgomery was directed towards the dock where the security staff took him out of her sight behind the door from which were the stairs down to the cells.

Cassie dumped her papers on the front row, James behind her. She turned round to speak to him and at that moment Marcus Pike swept into court and dropped his papers onto the opposite end of the bench.

‘Good morning, Cassie. Ready to change your plea?’ he said.

‘Sorry, Marcus. It’s a shame but I don’t think we can oblige. Have you got somewhere else to go?’ Cassie said, lifting her eyebrows.

Marcus looked round at his junior, Robin Tasker. ‘I told you she was a challenge. You know Robin, don’t you? And your junior. I don’t think we’ve met.’

‘No, I’m James Callan.’ James moved towards Marcus as if to shake hands then withdrew. Cassie smiled; James had remembered barristers don’t.

A knock on the judge’s door prevented any further exchange; all four turned to face the front of the court as Judge Crabtree strode across the upraised platform to his chair decorated with the coat of arms of the City of London engraved in gold on the green leather. He opened the red notebook on the bench in front of him and looked round the room.

The doors to the gallery were opened and a trickle of men and women took their seats. Cassie saw Mrs Montgomery move forward to the front row closest to the dock. A group of older men dressed in dark overcoats sat together towards the rear. For a moment, Cassie wondered if one of them was the mysterious Malcolm Delaney, but dismissed the thought quickly. She had no time now to dwell on her own problems.

The jury selection continued without interruption. Nevertheless, Cassie scrutinised each one of them, knowing she would need all her skills to keep her client under control and the jury on her side.

She turned to glance along the bench at Marcus, who was also scanning the members of the jury. She was glad he was leading for the prosecution; having been his junior in the Barker case she knew something of his strengths and weaknesses as an advocate and, most importantly, she trusted him. He would play it straight with her.

Once the jury was sworn, Judge Crabtree asked Marcus Pike to open the case to the jury. Marcus had placed his small folding wooden lectern on the bench in front of him. He put his opened notebook on it, and then took a black pen out of his waistcoat pocket which he placed with precision in the remaining space at the top edge. He looked up and turned so that he was standing looking at the jury. He took a few moments, running his eyes along the two rows, smiling at them, trying to establish some rapport with a least one or two of them. Cassie would do the same as the trial progressed, but for now Marcus had centre stage. She leant back in her chair and listened to him outline the prosecution case in his plummy voice. As she had anticipated, he dealt cleverly with the behaviour of the two main prosecution witnesses who, he said, had nothing to be proud of. They had played their own part in the events that led to the death of Albie Young, and, he said, they would have to live with that for the rest of their lives. But even so, whatever they had done, they could be relied on to be truthful. Their evidence would show that David Montgomery had acted out of revenge fuelled by his hatred of black youths, not in self-defence. He had put the case in a nutshell. She would have to combat that view of events.

After Marcus had finished his opening speech to the jury, he asked for a short adjournment and Judge Crabtree agreed. The jury were escorted outside the courtroom and, once the door had closed on them, Marcus switched on the monitor on the bench beside his lectern. At first the screen didn't come to life and Marcus turned to Robin and asked him if it had been tested before the trial had begun. Robin said he understood that to be the case. Cassie pressed the controls to see if the monitor she would be using was working or not. It wasn't.

'It may be that the judge has turned them all off,' she said. Marcus asked one of the court staff to fetch the court clerk or someone who could check the video link was working. He then began firing questions at Robin about the witnesses. Cassie didn't want to listen and left, followed by

James. The jurors were corralled by the usher close to the doors, so Cassie and James drifted towards the staircase.

'He's making a bit of a fuss about the video link, isn't he?' James said.

'He wants it to work straight away – it shows he's in control.' As they reached the flight of stairs and were about to turn to go up, Cassie saw the auburn head of the court reporter, Ruth Pymlott, coming up towards them. She was dressed in a dark suit and her hair was cut to a short bob, which would have made her look very serious if it wasn't for the freckles across her nose.

'Miss Hardman, I gather you are defending in this shopkeeper case. Leading brief as well.'

Cassie smiled at the reporter. She admired Ruth, who was a capable woman; she had a first-rate knowledge of the legal system and fought ferociously when journalists were excluded from reporting parts of cases, but she knew it was better not to be too open with her.

'I suppose he's running self-defence. Quite right too, in my view,' Ruth said.

'And I assume your newspaper's as well?' Cassie said.

Ruth laughed. 'Always on the side of the working man.'

'Rather an overworked expression these days.'

'Yes, yes it is. That case you did a few weeks ago, Sadler, wasn't it? You handled it well.' Cassie didn't want to be reminded of the Sadler case at this time but she enjoyed praise from such a knowledgeable source. 'He was such a good-looking bloke though.'

Cassie tried to smile. Paul Sadler had been a very attractive man.

Chapter 21

Once the video was working, Christopher Young's evidence was played to the jury. As soon as the video was finished Cassie began her cross examination. She didn't want Christopher to cry so she tiptoed through her questioning, but just before the luncheon adjournment he blurted out that he had never seen a knife.

As the jury filed into court an hour later, Cassie looked up at the public gallery. She wanted to believe the man who had emailed her and sent the postcard was one of the group of older men who came to the Bailey as a hobby, following any case they found interesting, or a barrister they thought was entertaining. Only six people were occupying the seats in the gallery set high above the court where they could observe the judge, the jury and the defendant, but they only had a back view of the witnesses. Of the six, two were women; Delaney was not one of those unless the name was a pseudonym. She didn't recognise any of the men and there was no indication of any unusual interest in her. Whoever Malcolm Delaney was, she began to doubt he was one of the men currently watching the trial.

Cassie turned back to her papers and then felt a touch on her shoulder. She looked up; James was standing in the row behind her. He motioned behind him. 'Tim's found a clerk for us,' he said. He was pursing his lips, trying not to laugh. Then he moved slightly to his right so she could see behind him.

Sitting at the bench was a young man wearing a dark grey jacket over a black open-necked shirt. The solicitor's clerk rose slightly from his seat and nodded at her. 'Miss Hardman. Tim's asked me to clerk for him. My name is Zachariah Rose. Most people call me Zac.'

'I'll introduce you to the client later,' Cassie said. She swallowed hard and put her head down; she didn't want Zac to know she was worried about Montgomery's reaction. Tim had been a bit underhand, selecting a clerk who would give the defence some racial balance. She hoped her client would accept it; she didn't want a fight with him at this stage. It was something she would have to worry about later; there were a few more questions for Christopher Young.

'Chris, you said this morning "I never saw a knife". Do you remember saying that?'

'Yes, miss.'

'You hadn't seen a knife?'

'No. I don't think I did.' Chris spoke slowly, as if he wasn't sure what to say.

'So why did you say you hadn't seen a knife?' He looked straight at her. Something in his eyes made her think he'd changed over the adjournment and now was more resilient. For a moment she wondered if he had spoken to Jas or Loveday, but then remembered they were not in the building.

‘Because I hadn’t.’ It was the obvious answer, but it wasn’t what Cassie was hoping to establish.

‘But you hadn’t seen a gun or a baseball bat had you?’

‘Golf club. Saw a golf club.’ He continued to stare at her, defying her to continue with her questions.

‘Mr Montgomery had the golf club, but you were referring to your brother and his friends. Did one of them have a knife?’

‘I never saw one.’ Chris thumped his fist down on the arm of his chair. ‘I never saw a knife.’

‘Did your brother have a knife?’

‘No. No.’ He wiped his face with his hand and looked away. His defiance was crumbling; Cassie knew he was beginning to weaken as she got close to the truth.

‘What about Jas or Loveday?’

‘I never saw a knife.’ Now there was truculence in his eyes; there was no point in pursuing that line of questions. She would try a different approach.

‘Did either Jas or Loveday ever carry a knife?’

‘I don’t know. I didn’t see one.’ He began to sob; Cassie waited for him to calm down.

‘Have you talked to either Jas or Loveday about what happened that day?’

‘A bit.’

‘Did one of them say anything about a knife?’

Chris put his head down again; his voice so low she could only just hear him. 'I can't remember.' If he had been an adult she would have repeated the question, implying she didn't believe the witness couldn't remember, but not this traumatised boy. Instead she would take another tack.

'Had you seen either of them with a knife before?'

He lifted his tear-stained face towards her. Cassie hoped he would answer and she wouldn't have to persist in questioning him, hurting him.

'I think Loveday usually had one.'

'Thank you. I've no more questions, My Lord.'

She sat down, leant back in her chair and took a deep breath.

Judge Crabtree told Christopher he was free to go but he must not talk to any of the other witnesses about the case. 'I know Jonathan Wilding and Leon Campbell may want to know what you were asked today, but don't tell them anything. Do you understand?' Chris said he did, and then the court clerk switched off the TV screens, cameras and microphones.

'I think that's enough for today,' Judge Crabtree said as he left the bench.

Cassie asked James how he thought the jury had reacted to Christopher Young, but before he could answer the court usher came towards her and said, 'This has been left for you at the front desk,' handing Cassie a white envelope with the words M/s Hardman typed on the front. Cassie thanked the man and moved over to some seats where she could put her papers down and open the note.

'Oh no.' She handed the piece of paper to James. After he had read it he gave it back to her.

'You weren't being hard on him at all. Anyway, whoever it is can't see the screens very well so he doesn't know how the kid took your questions.'

'He must have been here in court. What does he want?' she said. She wasn't expecting a reply, but there was no opportunity as Montgomery came towards them. His face was red and his lips were clamped together.

'Mr Montgomery, this is Zac.'

'Who the hell …' Montgomery said.

Cassie grabbed his arm and pulled him to one side. 'He's going to be with us, making notes and generally there to make sure our case goes smoothly. Please, I don't want an argument about it. He's here to help.' She scowled at him. Montgomery opened his mouth as if to comment. She said, 'I think that went very well. Christopher couldn't see clearly what happened and he says Loveday carried a knife.'

She turned away and walked towards the staircase, clutching the white envelope. Whoever Delaney was he had managed to get past the initial scrutiny of the security staff. She didn't want to think about him anymore.

Chapter 22

Cassie was relieved the trial had finally started and the first day was over without her being given the sack by Montgomery. Back in the safety of her top-floor flat, she unpacked her briefcase and took out the envelope she guessed was from the inscrutable Delaney. She pulled out the printed note and read it again. '*You appear to enjoy making vulnerable witnesses cry. Like Emma.*'

She screwed the paper up into a ball and then opened it again and straightened it out as best she could, stuffed it back into the envelope and threw it into the drawer of her desk. For a moment she stood by the desk and stroked the polished oak. She felt exhausted and wanted to close her eyes. She was finding this trial particularly hard. She disliked the defendant. His racism upset her; only her professionalism kept her working on the case. She walked into the bedroom and dropped onto her bed. The room was cool and there was the faint smell of her perfume.

Cassie lay stretched out but her hands made tight fists and every time she closed her eyes the words *enjoying, vulnerable witnesses* and *crying* seemed to be etched on the inside of her eyelids. Yet she knew her cross examination of Christopher Young had been considerate, some might say too considerate. She hadn't needed to accuse him of lying because he really hadn't seen anything, and he'd volunteered the piece of evidence that enabled her to establish Loveday carried a knife. Delaney's real interest was in the Sadler case and he'd referred to Emma, the complainant in that case. Emma Gilbrook had been tearful and distressed, but she hadn't broken down during cross examination.

She wouldn't think about the Sadler case. She'd think about the witnesses who would be called the next day. Could she get Jas Wilding to admit his friend had a knife? Had the two boys got together the evening of the incident and agreed to deny any knowledge of the knife Loveday had used to threaten Montgomery? She sighed and roused herself; she needed to go over the statements again, but first she would have supper. Since childhood, she had always enjoyed cooking. She had spent many hours in the kitchen of their terraced home in Lancaster helping with family meals as well as with the cakes her mother baked and decorated as a way of adding to their income. It had been her ambition to be a chef until her headmistress had told her she should set her sights on university. She took a piece of salmon from the fridge, wrapped it in foil with some lime juice, coriander and ginger and placed it in the oven. Then she pulled the cork from a bottle of Pinot Grigio and poured herself a large glass. The fish would take about twenty minutes. While she waited she turned on her computer and opened her Facebook page. There was an update from her sister about a satisfactory Ofsted inspection at the school where she taught. Cassie clicked the Like button and added her congratulations. Then she turned to her emails. Amongst them was one from her Head of Chambers, Richard Jago. He had sent a copy to every member informing them there would be a chambers meeting on the following Friday. Cassie was immediately suspicious.

She checked the salmon and decided it needed a little longer so, while she waited for her supper to cook, she settled down at her desk. From the window she could see, level with the sill, the pale green canopy of the London plane that grew in the next-door garden. The light was fading but for a moment she watched the leaves sway in the light breeze. She thought of summers at home, family outings to Glasson Dock or the Trough of Bowland, before reprimanding herself for procrastinating. She turned back to her files and began working on the statements of the two boys. Jas, she mused, was more likely to admit to the knife being wielded because it wasn't his, but even if the jury believed Loveday had a knife, would they think that was a sufficient reason to strike any one of the boys? Would they ask themselves why Montgomery hadn't gone back into the shop and called the police? She hadn't got very far in analysing the documents when she was interrupted by the sound of xylophone notes from her mobile. She picked up the phone. The caller was Alex Seymour. She didn't really want to answer; she had passed on the information Stephen had provided even though she felt she was betraying a confidence. Nevertheless, she pressed the button to answer the call.

'Cassie, I've been looking at the CRIS report on Hales. I'm puzzled by him wearing jeans when he was arrested. Doesn't he wear a suit to work? I know I asked him in interview but he didn't explain …'

'He told me he'd been clearing up one of our rooms. One we use for storage. He didn't want his suit messed up.'

'Is that true?'

'The room was tidied up recently. I can't say when but I have no reason to doubt Roger.'

'I think we may have to start interviewing some of your colleagues. Trying to trace the drugs back to the supplier.'

'Have you been to Cotburn Mews?'

'Can you tell us who suggested the mews was where the drugs were supplied from?'

'One of my friends told me, but I'm sure the drugs were not his.'

'Sure they were not his?'

'He was working on a case in Liverpool at the time so wasn't in chambers.'

'Ok. Cotburn …'

Cassie's attention shifted away as she heard something that sounded like movement in the hallway. She dropped her voice to a whisper. 'Alex.'

'What?'

'I think I can hear something in the hall.' Cassie was silent, hardly breathing so that she didn't miss any sound. She could hear the slow tap of one foot being placed in front of the other outside the sitting room door. Cupping her hand round the mobile, she placed her mouth close to it and said, 'Stay on the line.' She put her mobile down on the green Chesterfield sofa. She could still hear Alex's voice and guessed she was asking what was going on. Her stockinged feet made no noise as she crept towards the door. She put out her hand to open it. As the tip of her fingers closed on the handle, the timer rang. Cassie flung open the door into the small hallway of her flat but there was no one there. The carpets on the stairs she shared with other occupants were thick to deaden any sound; nevertheless, she thought she could hear footsteps going down the four flights, then the front door closing. She ran to her bedroom window and looked down onto the street. It must have started to rain as the pavement gleamed, but there was no sign of anyone walking away from the house. She tried to see if there was someone in one of the vehicles parked along the road, but all she saw was either their roofs or the glint of light reflected from their windscreens. She went back to the phone and told Alex what had occurred. As she explained she walked back into her bedroom and over to the window and to see if any of the cars moved away.

'Is there anyone in the street?' Alex said.

'No, no. There's no one about, but I'm sure there was someone in the hall. I'm certain.' She walked into the small corridor. 'The door isn't closed.' She pushed it to and the latch clicked. 'I didn't leave it open.'

'Are you sure? Is there any sign of a forced entry?'

'Not that I can see. Oh wait. There are some scratches by the lock. I don't remember seeing them before.'

'Cassie, what is this about?'

'I don't know, but … those strange emails and today a note was left at court accusing me of making a witness cry.'

'Some crank? You must report it.'

'No. I can't. I can't spend the time going to the police station, making a statement. For what? I have no idea who was there. We're not the most popular of people with the police, as you well know. They'll think I'm mad, hearing things.'

'Look, I really think you need to make a formal complaint. If you are being watched and an officer comes round, whoever it is will hopefully back off.'

Cassie knew she was right. She should report the break-in, if that's what it was.

'Ok. You're probably right. I'll do that.'

After she had spoken to the police, she went into the kitchen and pulled the overcooked salmon from the oven, decided she didn't want it and put it in the kitchen bin.

The policeman who arrived in response to her call listened to her account of hearing someone in the hall. He was, she thought, a new recruit. He was sympathetic, although she was sure he didn't believe her. She saw him look at the almost empty wine bottle on the table. He clearly thought she had been drinking. She wondered about telling him she had only had two glasses and the rest she had drunk the night before, but instead she pointed out the mark on the door to her flat. He looked at it before moving back to the sitting room. He sat down on the sofa and took out his notebook and pen, made a few notes, then flipped it shut and said, 'Are you sure there was someone in the flat? Could it have been one of the occupants of the other properties? Who lives in the one below you?'

'She's an air stewardess and is away a lot of the time.'

She had just finished explaining that she hadn't seen or heard her neighbour for a few days when the sound of what was probably a television programme floated up from the flat below.

The young officer got up. 'I'll make a note at the station and arrange for the patrol car to sweep past later on. Just in case.'

Cassie ushered him out of the door, convinced he thought she was a neurotic female.

Chapter 23

The next day Cassie was the first person into the courtroom. She put her papers down on the wooden bench and opened the file of witness statements. When she was about halfway through reading the two boys' statements, she heard the double doors of the courtroom being thrust open and Marcus strode into the room to his place on counsels' bench.

'Cassie. How are you this morning?' He looked over the top of his dark-rimmed spectacles. 'You look a little tired. Not your usual perky self.'

'I'm fine. Are your two heroes here fighting to give evidence?'

'Why wouldn't they be? They have only to tell the truth.'

'Whatever that may be.'

'Cassie, Cassie don't go all cynical on me. You're much too sweet a girl for that.'

'I'm …' At that moment there was a rap on the judge's door and they all rose to their feet.

Once the judge and jury were in place, Marcus called Jas Wilding to give evidence. Jas was a tall, muscular, sixteen-year-old. His hair had been cut much shorter than in the shots of him taken by the security camera. He was dressed in navy trousers and a white shirt with the green and gold tie of his school. Today the knot was properly secured around his neck rather than hanging on his chest as it had been in the CCTV recording.

Marcus established Jas was at the same school as Leon Campbell, who he called Loveday, and Albie Young, and then question by question got Jas to give his account of the incident at the sweet shop.

Part way through, Marcus put one elbow on his lectern and turned to face the jury so that Wilding could not see his face. Wilding was addressing all his answers to the lawyer as if they were having a conversation. Cassie wasn't surprised by Marcus's move. Her experience was that this would make the witness speak out towards the jury. Marcus, certainly, would be hoping so. For a moment the Wilding seemed puzzled by the manoeuvre, but then began to give his account of the incident. Cassie now looked towards the jury box, and caught the eye of a woman in her forties wearing a pink shirt with the collar turned up.

Cassie grinned when Marcus asked Wilding what they had done with the magazines they had taken from the top shelf and Wilding said, 'You couldn't do anything with them. They were wrapped in that plastic stuff.'

Marcus had persisted. 'What did you do then?'

'Took the wrappers off.'

'Why did you do that?'

'To see what was inside.'

There were some hastily stifled sniggers from the jury benches and from the public gallery, but Cassie didn't see who had laughed. Judge Crabtree had looked up at the gallery and asked for silence.

Marcus continued questioning Wilding, drawing from him his version of the events that had led to the death of Albie Young. As he was asked about the way the incident had ended, Wilding's left hand was on the edge of the witness box, but with the other he reached for his tie and moved the knot a little. She was sure he was lying now they were getting to the real nub of the case.

'You walked away?' Marcus said.

'I didn't run, but left a bit, yeah, a bit smartish like.' He swayed slightly, shifting his weight from foot to foot.

'What about Loveday and Albie?'

'They were behind me, I think.'

'Did you leave the shop?'

'Had to. He came running from behind the counter, swinging this club thing.'

'Exhibit twenty-three, My Lord,' Robin Tasker said as he selected an item from where it lay with the others on a table to one side of the courtroom.

The usher held up a long plastic-wrapped package that was clearly a golf club. Marcus indicated she was to hand the item to Wilding. The witness held it at shoulder height away from the witness box.

'Is that the club?' Marcus said.

'It could be. I didn't look at it that closely at the time.'

'No, of course not. By this time you're outside the shop. What about Albie and Loveday?'

'We were all in the street.'

'How far away from the shop door?'

'Not sure. I looked round to see what Monty was doing. If he was coming after us.'

'And the two others?'

'They stopped as well. He said we'd taken chocolates and we should hand them back. He was going to call the police.'

'Had you stolen anything from the shop?'

Wilding looked towards the judge and then at Marcus before saying, 'I took a few bars of chocolate.'

'Did you give the bars back?'

'No. Loveday said to him, call the police. He said – that's Loveday – we'd tell them he was a pervert.'

'Where was Monty by this time?'

'At the door. Swinging that thing.' Jas pointed to the golf club which the usher had placed on the bench by Marcus Pike, who picked it up and held it by the handle. Cassie was reminded of the way he'd held the red high-heeled shoe of the murdered woman when she had been led by him in the Barker case.

'I kept out of his way, but I think he caught Loveday on the arm. Loveday shouted out. Then I heard Chris begin to cry.'

'Had you seen Chris before you heard him?'

'Yes. He's always hanging around and I'd seen him across the road earlier.'

'What happened when Chris shouted out?'

'That's when it happened. Albie rushed towards Chris and Monty hit him with the club. He fell to the floor. I ran away.'

'You ran away. Why did you do so?'

'I knew the police would come. I'd been stealing and …' He flicked his tongue over his lips. 'I had some weed in my pocket. Didn't want to get caught.'

'We'll take a short break, members of the jury. Mr Wilding is a young man and he's been in the witness box for quite some time. I'm sure he needs a few minutes, and you might like a coffee or something. So about twenty minutes,' Judge Crabtree said and then left the bench.

The room soon emptied and Cassie walked out to the broad corridor that served as a waiting area for the various courts. She turned on her mobile to check if there were any messages. She had a number of emails but her attention was caught by one with the subject line 'Paul Sadler'. That man again. *Don't open it*, she told herself. She put the phone in the pocket of her black jacket and walked to the window where the view over Seacoal Lane towards the spire of St Bride's had been replaced by the reflection of the court building in the gleaming windows of a new office block. She looked up. At least the sky was still visible. She watched white clouds scudding against a vivid blue. She blinked to ward off tears. *Don't open it.*

As Cassie went back into court her fingers closed on the phone – she could feel the weight of it in her hand. She let it go and then grasped it firmly, pulled it out of her pocket and opened the email. It read '*At it again, bitch!*'

She looked at the notes she had taken of Jas Wilding's evidence. She tried to concentrate on the words she had written but she kept thinking of the email message from the secretive Delaney. Her writing, like a doctor's, unreadable to anyone but her, seemed incomprehensible and the lines on the paper appeared to quiver. She muttered to herself to forget the email, forget the Sadler case, just get on with this trial. She picked up the carafe of water on the desk, poured some into the glass and sipped slowly. Her mind started to work on the questions she would ask the witness. The court began to reassemble around her, but she didn't look up until a knock on the judge's door brought her to her feet and Judge Crabtree made his way onto the bench.

'Mr Wilding, are you ready to start again?' He didn't wait for an answer before saying, 'Yes, Miss Hardman.'

Cassie rose from her seat and turned to face Jas Wilding, who glared at her across the room.

'Now, let's turn to the third of March. You left the scene of the incident without trying to find out what had happened to Albie Young?'

'Yes, miss. I didn't think he was hurt that bad.'

'You weren't interviewed by the police 'til later in the day, some time in the early evening. Where did you go between leaving the shop and going to the police station?'

'I went home and then … I didn't know Albie was dead.'

'So what did you do?'

'I went to play football.'

'Was Leon Campbell, Loveday I think you call him, there as well?'

'Yes. We both play for the same team.'

'Did you talk about the incident at the shop?'

'A bit.'

'You thought the police would want to hear about what happened?'

'Yes, sure. Albie had been hit with that club.' He pointed to the golf club that was still lying on the bench in front of Marcus's lectern.

'Did you compare what happened and decide on what you were going to say?'

'Not really. Anyway, when I found out how bad Albie was I knew I had to tell the truth about what we'd done.'

Cassie was annoyed; she had asked one question too many and given the witness the opportunity to emphasise he was an honest witness. She turned back to the incident.

'Were you going to steal cigarettes from Mr Montgomery?'

'Yes. We thought it would be easy if …' He stopped and looked up at the ceiling.

'It would be easy if you did what?'

Wilding didn't reply but looked at Cassie and then half turned towards the seats under the public gallery. She followed his gaze. Sitting on one of them was a tall well-built man dressed in a dark beige raincoat; his resemblance to the witness identified him as Wilding's father. The man raised his eyebrows and glared at his son, who swivelled back to face the jury.

'The cigarettes are kept behind the counter. How did you hope to get them while Mr

Montgomery was standing next to them?' Cassie said.

'We thought he would come out when we took the magazines down from the top shelf, and then one of us would've gone and got the smokes.'

'But he didn't come out from the counter?'

'He started to. I think he picked up one of the magazines, then he told us to leave and threatened us with that club.'

'Loveday called him a paedophile, didn't he?'

'Yeah. That made Monty really mad.'

'And threatened to tell the police he was a pervert, didn't he?'

There was no reply. Cassie didn't pause; she knew Wilding was feeling the pressure of her cross examination. 'But it wasn't true, was it?'

'No. No it wasn't. We made that up.' Wilding stared at Cassie and folded his arms across his chest.

'So you were prepared to lie in order to stop the police from arresting you?'

Wilding looked down towards his feet and let his hands hang by his side. 'Yes,' he said.

'Are you telling the truth now?' Cassie didn't wait for an answer. 'Let's go back to the cigarettes. Did you think Mr Montgomery would let you take some? He was going to do something to stop you, wasn't he? What were you going to do then?' She hoped that Wilding's insistence he was being honest and open about the events in the shop would push him towards telling the court the truth now.

'Loveday …' He stopped, turned to look at his father. 'Loveday was going to threaten him with his knife.'

'Loveday had a knife?'

'No. Yes, but he didn't use it in the shop.'

'Did you see him with the knife in his hand?' Wilding dropped his gaze and nodded. 'I assume that's yes. When did Loveday have the knife?'

'I saw it when we were outside the shop. When Monty was swinging that thing.'

'Where was Mr Montgomery when you saw the knife?'

'He was at the door of the shop.'

'In the doorway?'

'No, out on the pavement.'

'Albie ran across towards Chris between Mr Montgomery and Loveday?'

'Yes, he must've done.'

'I want to try and picture the scene. Chris is standing by the shop window, Loveday is about three feet away from the shop door with a knife in his hand, and you and Albie are the other side of Loveday. Is that right?'

'Yes, but I'm not sure about the knife. If he still had it in his hand.'

'Mr Montgomery was swinging the golf club at Loveday, wasn't he?'

'He was just swinging it.'

'Swinging it at Loveday who was shouting that if Mr Montgomery called the police he would say he was a paedophile?'

Jas lowered his head and shook it from side to side.

'Isn't that what happened,' Cassie said.

'Something like that.'

'Chris was crying, screaming, and Albie ran across between you and Loveday towards his brother, didn't he?'

Wilding stifled a sob. 'I don't know. One minute he's next to me, then he was lying on the ground bleeding from his head.'

Cassie waited until the sobbing stopped and then said, 'And Mr Montgomery dropped the golf club and ran inside the shop. A few minutes later the police and an ambulance arrived.'

'I didn't see them. I knew he would call the police so I ran.'

Cassie turned round to James and asked him if there was anything she'd missed. When he said no she looked back at Wilding and told the judge she had no more questions for the witness.

Marcus asked the usher to call Leon Campbell into the courtroom. He was a similar height to Wilding but not as muscular; his face was thin and his dark eyes were wide open. As he climbed into the witness box he was looking around so he missed the step and stumbled. He grabbed the sides of the pale wooden stand and regained his balance, but not before the bible lying on the side fell to the floor with a thud. Once he was upright he nodded at the judge, who asked the usher to administer the oath and, after Campbell had read with some hesitation the words on the card she handed him, Judge Crabtree invited Marcus to begin his examination in chief.

Campbell gave a similar account of the incident in Montgomery's shop to Jas Wilding's. He was very explicit about the language the defendant had used. 'He called us niggers and black bastards.'

Cassie turned round and leant over as if she wanted to speak to James, but really she was taking the opportunity to see if Montgomery had reacted to the witness's description of his language, but his face was impassive. There was nothing to indicate he was at all embarrassed or ashamed of his behaviour. She couldn't understand why he didn't realise how insulting he had been and show some contrition.

Marcus asked him if he had left the shop when Montgomery told him to do so. Before answering, Campbell half turned to where DS Kotzeva was sitting with a woman Cassie assumed was his mother. She was watching her son with a grim look on her face, unlike the police sergeant who was smiling at him. Cassie wondered if Mrs Campbell was less trusting of her son than the police officer. He was a difficult witness to read. Cassie was sure he wasn't telling the whole truth about this incident, but getting him to say what really happened was going to be a challenge. She didn't rate her chances with him. Although his age meant he was a vulnerable witness, Cassie thought there was nothing vulnerable about him at all.

He then described the incident. 'He was coming for us, for me. He caught me on my right arm. Jas and Albie were on his left and Chris was in front of the window. It was all very fast. And Albie was on the ground.'

Marcus thanked Campbell and asked him to wait as there would be some more questions.

Cassie took a deep breath and rose to her feet. 'Loveday, do you mind if I call you Loveday? I'm going to ask you some more questions on behalf of Mr Montgomery, do you understand?'

'Yes, miss. I've been in court before.'

'You have some previous convictions, don't you? Did you plead guilty to the four offences we've been told about?'

'Not all of them.'

'You were found guilty after a trial?'

'Yes.'

'Which offence did you deny?'

'The assault on another boy. He'd started it and so I hit him. Acted in self-defence. Protecting myself, like.'

'The magistrates didn't believe you, did they?'

'No, but it was the truth.'

'Now, let's go back to March the third. You waited until the police arrived but you didn't try to speak to them, tell them what had happened?'

'No. It was pretty obvious, what had happened.'

'Didn't you want to discover how your friend was, how badly he'd been hurt?'

Campbell stared at her, his jaw rigid. 'I knew it was bad. I wanted to get home.'

‘You didn’t go over to your friend and try and help him.’

Campbell shrugged his shoulders. ‘I wouldn’t know what to do. Better do nothing, I thought.’

‘Did you stay at home that evening until the police came to ask you to make a statement?’

‘No, no I didn’t. I play football and our team had a match that evening, well, after tea, not very late. I went to the game.’

‘Was Jas there?’

‘Yes, we both play.’

‘Did you discuss the incident at the sweet shop?’

‘Not really, we were playing football, a game. Then I went home and the police were there.’

‘Nothing was said at all about Albie, what had happened to him?’

‘I think I said it was bad. Jas had run straight away and had no idea.’

‘You didn’t agree on what to say to the police.’

Loveday began to chew on his lower lip. ‘It was terrible, we’d been stupid, but I knew we had to tell the truth about him and his racist remarks.’ He flung his arm out and pointed at the dock.

‘You didn’t agree that neither of you would say anything about you having a knife?’

The witness threw his head back. ‘I did not have a knife.’

Cassie continued questioning him about his behaviour in the shop. He agreed he had asked for cigarettes telling the defendant they were for his mother.

‘That wasn’t true, was it?’

‘No. I wanted some cigarettes.’

Cassie noticed Mrs Campbell lean forward towards her son. She was frowning. Cassie thought she probably didn’t smoke and hearing her son suggest she did was annoying her.

‘Does your mother smoke?’

Campbell turned away and looked towards his mother. She was shaking her head. He pivoted back and said, ‘No, she doesn’t.’

‘Another lie then?’

Campbell didn’t respond so Cassie continued. ‘Did you call Mr Montgomery a paedophile?’

The witness shrugged his shoulders. ‘I might have.’

‘You said earlier that Mr Montgomery was coming for you. Was that the three of you or just you?’

‘Just me. He was looking at me, evil in his eye, like he hated me.’

‘You threatened to tell the police he was pervert, a paedophile, didn’t you?’

‘Someone did.’

‘You did, didn’t you?’

Campbell did not reply until Judge Crabtree intervened and asked him to answer the question. The youth looked round the court towards the dock and said, ‘Yes, it was a joke.’

'Not a very pleasant joke, and had you told the police, then it was yet another untruth, wasn't it?'

'Yes, miss.'

'There was no reason to aim the golf club at you rather than any of the others, was there?'

'I don't know why he picked on me, but he did.'

'Was it because you had a knife?'

'No, I didn't. I had nothing.'

'You had a knife in your hand and you were pointing it at Mr Montgomery.'

'I did not have a knife. How often do I have to say it?'

'Do you carry a knife?'

Campbell grabbed the sides of the witness box and turned to look at his mother. Her lips were set and she was staring at her son. He swivelled back and said, 'I did not have a knife that day. Do I have to answer any more of these stupid questions?'

'One more. Was the reason you left the scene as soon as the police arrived because you had a knife with you?'

Campbell didn't reply.

'You had a knife, and what's more you and Jas agreed not to mention it when you made your statements. Isn't that the truth?'

Campbell stepped back out of the witness box and left the courtroom. His mother jumped up and hurried to follow her son. Cassie watched their retreating backs and heard a snatch of squabbling voices as the doors closed behind them. Then a movement in the public gallery caught her eye and she saw the back of a man as he mounted the steps and disappeared from her view. Was that Delaney?

Chapter 24

After Emma Gilbrook had given her evidence, the screens were removed; they were unnecessary for the remaining witnesses. Anita Connor was the first. Cassie had been expecting a severe-looking woman, the sort who supervised expensive dress shops and looked down their noses at her. Instead, a short woman with big hair bounced into the witness box. She took the oath in a breathy voice and then beamed at Hugh. He didn't need to call her for the prosecution, but Cassie had insisted she should attend. Hugh asked the witness to give her full name and to confirm she was a friend of Emma Gilbrook.

'Do you recognise the defendant, Paul Sadler?' Hugh waved his hand in the direction of the dock.

'Yes. He was at my flat when I got home that night.'

'You'd been out that evening?'

'I'd met a friend for dinner and gone back to his place afterwards.' Anita looked down and Cassie thought her cheeks looked flushed. When the witness lifted her head, she had regained her composure.

'Did you expect to find Sadler there?'

'Emma had said she was meeting him and asked if she could bring him back to my flat. I said that was fine.'

'Did you tell her you would be out?'

Anita hesitated. 'I – I said I was going out. I thought I would be back sooner than I was. I didn't know how the evening with my friend would go.' She tried to smile but couldn't quite manage it.

'Both Emma and Sadler were there?'

'He was sitting on the sofa, and Emma was on her feet. I assumed she had got up when she heard my key in the door.'

'What happened next?'

'Emma introduced us and then sat next to him on the sofa. We chatted for quite a short time and then he looked at his watch and said he had to go. He asked Emma if she wanted him to walk her home but she said she would stay.'

'Did he leave?'

'Yes. He did.'

'How long did Emma stay?'

'About half an hour.'

'Did she talk about Sadler and their evening?'

'I was expecting her to ask me what I thought about him, but she didn't. She didn't tell me what had happened that night.'

Hugh thanked her and sat down. Cassie got to her feet, and asked Anita Conner what they had talked about. It was evidence Hugh couldn't ask about but she could.

'She'd had another row with her mother,' Anita replied.

'They argued a lot?' Cassie said.

'They seemed to. Rose, that's Emma's mother, seemed very restrictive for a girl of

Emma's age. Not really wanting her to have friends she didn't know.'

'By friends do you mean boyfriends?'

'Yes. That was one of the reasons she came to me so much. She kept clothes she could wear on dates at mine.'

'Was this the first time she'd brought a man back to your flat?'

Again, Anita hesitated. 'No, no it wasn't.'

'Did she sometimes bring men to your flat without you being there?'

'I don't know … I don't think it was the first time.'

Judge Tyte intervened. 'Where is this going, Miss Hardman?'

'I'm not pursuing this any further, My Lord.' Cassie turned back to the witness. 'When Emma asked if she could bring Sadler to your flat, you told her you were going out. Did you say what time you expected to be back?'

'I didn't know myself.' She breathed deeply. 'Sometimes I stay the night with my friend. I didn't know.'

'Did Emma know you might be out all night?'

'She might have, but I don't think so. She would have expected me back.'

'You know Emma quite well. Did you get the impression anything was wrong?'

'I was surprised she didn't want to talk about him.' Anita looked towards the dock and then back at Cassie. 'If she's quite keen she does go on about them. She'd told me he was an attractive man and I expected her to be more enthusiastic.'

'But she had other things on her mind?'

'She was always tense when she and her mother argued.'

'She declined his offer of walking her home. Did that surprise you?'

'No. It didn't. She wouldn't risk her mother seeing her with a man.'

After Anita had left the courtroom, Hugh had asked the usher to bring the next witness, Rose Gilbrook, into court. The doors to the courtroom were held open as the usher called out the witness's name. Was an argument with her mother the reason Emma Gilbrook had alleged Paul Sadler had raped her? Diverting attention away from herself? There was always that question – why would any woman complain of rape if it wasn't true? Was falling out with your mother sufficient reason?

Instead of the witness coming into court, the usher returned and said there was no answer. Judge Tyte scowled but agreed on a short break for Hugh to find the witness and the court emptied. The usher, flapping around in her gown, said she knew he wanted to make a few telephone calls so they would have time for a coffee. Cassie made her way upstairs to the Bar Mess. She didn't enjoy these cases at all and any respite from thinking about them was welcome. She sipped her coffee and looked at the newspapers, but before too long the tannoy called her back into court.

As Cassie approached Court 11 along the marble-clad concourse she saw a woman wearing a bright red jacket hovering outside the courtroom doors. The women had her back towards Cassie but then she turned to face her. She was not as tall as her daughter and her hair was darker, but there was no doubt in Cassie's mind who she was. In order to avoid meeting the witness, Cassie changed direction and went to stand by the windows overlooking the street. She kept an eye on Rose Gilbrook as the woman looked around her, patting her head as if her hair was out of place. Rose Gilbrook started back along the gallery towards where Cassie was standing. Cassie didn't want to have any eye contact with the witness so she turned away. Then Cassie saw DC Pomfrey coming towards them. When Rose Gilbrook and DC Pomfrey met, they had a short conversation. Mrs Gilbrook turned and took a long look at Cassie, until DC Pomfrey took her arm and led her towards the courtroom doors.

'I'm just going to show Mrs Gilbrook the courtroom if that's ok,' DC Pomfrey said. Cassie assumed the comment was directed towards her although they were some distance apart. The court usher came through the door from the courtroom; she was frowning and pulling on her black gown. Cassie thought she was cross her break had been curtailed by the policewoman's request to show Mrs Gilbrook the court.

Cassie waited until Mrs Gilbrook was in the concourse again and made her way to her seat in the courtroom. Lee was already sitting in the seat behind her.

‘Did you see the mother? I’m sure she’s the problem. Can’t stand the thought of her baby having sex. What twenty-year-old hasn’t been at it for years?’ Lee said.

‘I suppose the argument with her mother was the start of the complaint.’

‘It was mum who phoned the police.’

‘It usually is somebody else though, isn’t it?’

‘I suppose so. But … did she ask her daughter if that’s what she wanted, rather than assume it was? Is that a reasonable line of questioning?’

Cassie made a note on the witness statement in front of her. ‘I think it is. Poor Emma doesn’t get asked what she wants.’

‘Sometimes you don’t need to ask. I think he’s innocent. Don’t you?’

Cassie turned away. It wasn’t her job to second guess the jury. Her own life had left her uncertain about making what might seem the obvious conclusion.

Rose Gilbrook looked towards the dock as soon as she came into the court. Of course, she’d never seen Paul Sadler before. Had she hesitated a little as she saw the man at the back of the court? What did she think a rapist looked like? Some hulk of a man throwing his weight around? That certainly didn’t fit Paul Sadler. What Marcus had said about ‘fair labelling’ flitted through Cassie’s thoughts.

Judge Tyte leant forward towards the witness box, making an unusual effort to put Rose

Gilbrook at ease. Hugh Palmer smiled at Rose too. He began his questioning by asking her to describe what had happened before her daughter had made the allegation of rape. Rose Glbrook told the court how her daughter had come home in the early hours of the morning. When the time came for her to leave for work she was still sound asleep. Emma's boss had phoned, asking where Emma was and saying something about a blouse she'd got. She had gone into Emma's bedroom and woken her up. The two had argued. Emma became upset, began to cry and screamed she had been raped. Rose had immediately called the police, and they had taken over.

Cassie found Rose Gilbrook formidable. Her mouth was set in a permanent grimace and her eyes were steely. She refused to look at Cassie, concentrating on the jury box.

'You've told the jury you argued that morning – did you argue frequently?' Cassie said.

'Yes.'

'What about?'

'What's it to do with him raping her? My daughter wouldn't lie.'

'Did you argue about things like sharing chores in the home?'

'She doesn't always pull her weight. I think she should do more.'

'Do you argue about her social life – does she go out too much?'

'If she wants to get on she needs to do more of her college work. Always the same at school – doesn't want to study. Always wants her own way.'

'And not afraid to say so?'

Rose Gilbrook had turned away from the jury and looked at Cassie. Cassie asked a few more questions about the argument in which Emma had made the allegation, but Mrs Gilbrook's replies became monosyllabic. Most of the time she repeated that her daughter would not lie. Just as Cassie was about to move on to the telephone call Sadler had made the next day, Rose Gilbrook said, 'My daughter wouldn't tell lies. She's innocent, a virgin.'

Although Cassie knew that was not true – Emma had told the medical examiner she had had sexual intercourse with other men before Paul Sadler – she ignored the comment. She and Hugh would sort that issue out without disabusing Rose Gilbrook about her daughter's sex life.

'When Emma said she had been raped, did you talk to her about what had happened?'

'No. I didn't. I phoned the police.'

'You didn't ask her if she wanted the police involved?'

'I wanted the police involved. Nobody does that to my daughter and gets away with it.'

Cassie looked at the jury; the woman with the bright green glasses was knitting her eyebrows together and one of the younger men looked perplexed.

Cassie then asked her about the phone call from Sadler the next day. She stared at Cassie, her eyes piercing. 'Cheek. He knew what he'd done and was going to try and talk her out of going to the police.'

‘Did he say that?’

‘Not those words.’

‘What words did he use?’

‘He asked to speak to Emma. I told him to get lost …’ Rose paused. ‘Actually I used stronger language than that. Wouldn’t you if your daughter had been raped?’

Judge Tyte had intervened. ‘Mrs Gilbrook, I understand you are finding this distressing, but Miss Hardman has to ask these questions. Do you understand?’

Rose Gilbrook said she did and the judge indicated Cassie was to continue.

‘Mrs Gilbrook, isn’t it right that when you found out who was phoning you swore at him and threatened him. He was unable to say very much at all.’

‘I was very angry. He was trying to arrange to see her. I didn’t want that.’

‘Didn’t he say something about his work shift?’

‘Something about work. Can’t really remember.’

‘You didn’t want to listen to him, did you?’

‘No, I didn’t.’

‘Did you at any time tell Emma he had phoned her?’

‘Of course not. I didn’t want to upset her anymore.’

Cassie thanked the witness and told the judge she had no more questions.

Chapter 25

Before the officer who had interviewed Paul Sadler was called, Cassie asked for the jury to be kept out of court as she had an application to make. She intended to object to part of the interviews. 'My Lord, in the course of the second interview by DI Crawford and DC Pomfrey, the defendant lied about placing other messages in the Rush Hour Crush column of the *Metro*. The police discovered these further messages when they searched his computer and his mobile phone. They believed he had placed those notices in order to meet other women who he could sexually assault. There is no evidence to support that allegation.'

'Have enquiries been made about these other approaches?' Judge Tyte said.

'Yes, they have. Both the police and those instructing me have spoken to those women who did contact the defendant and not one of them had been assaulted. There had been no attempt by the defendant to assault them or press his attentions on them.'

'Mr Palmer. Did the police take statements?'

'They did, My Lord.'

'I would like to see them please.'

DC Pomfrey rushed forward and handed a set of papers to the usher. Once they were in front of him, the judge told them to sit down while he read them. Cassie took her copies from the files and read through them.

Paul Sadler had placed six requests and had three replies, not counting Emma. The first woman described ringing him regularly but she'd not wanted to meet him because she was in a relationship already. Sadler had told Cassie during a conference some time before the trial he thought she was a bit of an oddball. The second woman said they had gone to a coffee bar in Hammersmith. Sadler was a perfect gentleman. They had spent about an hour in the coffee shop and then parted. She wasn't surprised when he didn't arrange to see her again. She wasn't really interested, she said. Lee had got the same message but said she wasn't sure the woman was telling the truth. She had been quite animated when she was talking about him. The third woman saw him twice, as he had told the police. She had said he was courteous at all times and she was disappointed when she realised he didn't want to continue to meet.

When he had finished reading, the judge looked up. 'Yes, Miss Hardman.'

'Furthermore, the officer put these further messages to the defendant without informing his solicitor about them. If Your Lordship looks at page five of the second interview …'

She gave him time to read the passage.

M/s Shaw. What are these? I've not been shown these. I don't think …

Sadler. I didn't place those notices.

M/s Shaw. I need some time with my client if you are going to persist in asking him questions about these notices.

DI Crawford. Do you want to speak to your solicitor?

Sadler. They're not mine.

DI Crawford. I have here a statement from an employee of the newspaper confirming the contact number is the same as your mobile.

Sadler. No comment.

M/s Shaw. I'd like to speak to my client alone.

Lee had told Cassie that DI Crawford and DC Pomfrey had turned off the recording machine and left the room. Once they had gone, Paul Sadler had admitted he had placed the other notices and had denied doing so because he felt embarrassed. He'd used the column in the newspaper like a dating agency.

Judge Tyte fingered the edges of the documents. 'I see. What do you have to say, Mr Palmer? It does seem to me that in the absence of any evidence to support the proposition that Sadler placed these … notices for the purpose of meeting women to assault the lie has no evidential value. I am mindful of the direction I should have to give the jury.'

'I would argue the lie shows he had something to hide.'

'I suspect Miss Hardman would then want to call the women the police interviewed. Miss Hardman, I'm going to allow your application. Do you need time to amend the jury transcripts, Mr Palmer?'

'Yes, My Lord.'

It took over an hour for the transcripts to be prepared. The six new copies were handed to Cassie and she and Lee checked them, making sure the correct part of the interviews had been redacted. The copies were then passed to the jury, some of whom searched for glasses in pockets or handbags. When they were ready, Hugh asked for DI Crawford to come into court.

The inspector had a hawk-like gaze and thin lips which he pressed together. Cassie thought he looked angry. She knew from the tapes of the interviews that he was a bit of a bully. Lee had said he was high on his own testosterone. Cassie wondered if he had daughters who he feared might be assaulted.

He read the transcript in a voice heavy with sarcasm. Cassie watched the jury when he came to the questions about the age difference between Sadler and Emma Gilbrook. Although there were some worried looks, she thought they didn't see the age gap as very important. Perhaps the witness's admission she had lied about her age diminished their concerns.

Throughout both interviews Paul Sadler had been insistent Emma had consented to have sexual intercourse with him. When Crawford was reading the last reply, he lowered his voice. Judge Tyte asked him to repeat the answer.

'Sadler said, "I would not have persisted if she had said she didn't want to. I liked her. I wanted to keep on seeing her, not blow it by forcing myself on her."'

It was a good note to end on for Sadler's defence.

Chapter 26

Immediately after DI Crawford had given his evidence, Hugh Palmer got to his feet. ‘My Lord, there is some housekeeping to deal with before I close the prosecution case. I don’t think we need to trouble the jury with it.’

‘Members of the jury, the prosecution case is nearly over, but there are a few matters to sort out before we move on to the defence case. They concern timing and other things like that, so if you’d like to go now. We’ll start again tomorrow morning. Thank you,’ Judge Tyte said.

The jury filed out and when the last one had left the court and the door was closed behind them, Hugh said, ‘There is the matter of Mrs Gilbrook’s evidence that her daughter had not have sexual intercourse before. If one looks at the forensic examiner’s statement, Miss Gilbrook told him she’d had sexual relations with other men. The jury have been left with the impression that the complainant was a virgin. Not surprisingly Miss Hardman wants that to be corrected.’

‘I suppose she is entitled to ask for that. What do you propose? Do you want to recall the daughter?’

Cassie stood up. ‘If my learned friend would make an admission in similar terms to the information Miss Gilbrook gave to the doctor that will suffice. Otherwise the complainant will have to be recalled.’

‘You’d have to ask for consent to put questions to her about her previous sexual history,’ Judge Tyte said.

‘I am aware of that. I would argue that it would be unfair to allow the jury to believe the young woman had not had sexual intercourse before.’

‘I think I would have to grant such an application. Mr Palmer, what do you have to say about this?’

‘I am prepared to make a suitable admission, My Lord.’

‘You should have kept more control of your witness, Mr Palmer. Now, before we adjourn, Miss Hardman, are you planning to call your client?’

‘Yes, My Lord. I should also say that I plan to call at least one character witness.’

‘Are you intending to assert Miss Gilbrook should have made her allegation to Miss Connor and the delay to the next morning suggests it is not true?’ Judge Tyte said.

‘I am not relying on the delay, but I do intend to comment on the circumstances in which the complaint arose.’

‘The argument with her mother?’

‘Yes, My Lord.’

‘Tomorrow morning.’

Cassie asked Lee to tell their client to wait for her outside the courtroom and began to gather her papers together. Hugh was stomping around at the other end of the bench. ‘It wasn’t your fault. She was answering my questions,’ she said.

'There'll be grumbles about the admission, but I can't see any way round it. What do you want me to say?'

Sadler and Lee Shaw were waiting outside on the concourse. 'Right, it won't take long for the prosecution to close their case tomorrow and then you'll be giving evidence. Do you have a copy of the statement you gave to Lee?'

Sadler nodded to indicate he had.

'Ok. Now read it through carefully to remind yourself what you said when the events were much fresher. Keep your answers short. I can't lead you …' Sadler frowned. 'I can't ask you questions that suggest the answer. If I want you to elaborate I'll ask further questions. When Mr Palmer starts to question you again keep your answers short.'

'What's he going to ask me about?'

'My guess is he'll ask about the age difference, implying you are quite a few years older and more experienced. Also, why you didn't ask if she wanted to have intercourse. He'll probably play a lot on her saying no at one point and pushing your hand away when you tried to place it in her vagina …'

'But that was right at the beginning.'

'Don't argue with him. Agree she said no at one point. I can ask further questions after Mr Palmer has finished and I'll deal with that if I have to. It's important the jury don't see you getting angry. Do you understand?'

'I do. I didn't do it. I can't understand why she would say I did. I was looking forward to seeing her again. She was lovely and she laughed at my jokes.'

'I'm telling you this now because when you start giving evidence neither I nor Lee can speak to you until you've completed it. Have you got any family here?'

'My mother's been waiting for me. She couldn't bear watching the trial. And my aunt's been with her.'

'Good. You may need some support tomorrow. Now go home, try and get a good night's sleep. Lee, we talked about a character witness or two – any luck?'

'I'll let you know before court tomorrow. Something has come up and I need to take another statement.'

Chapter 27

That evening, Cassie asked herself again why Emma Gilbrook had made the allegation of rape. It was a question Sadler had asked her and she hadn't an answer. Why would any woman go through a trial, being questioned about their most intimate behaviour if it was not true? Would she herself have reported similar conduct as rape? She knew she wouldn't. She knew what a trial was really like. She was ruminating on what she might have done when her mobile rang.

'Cassie, I've just taken a statement from Linda Callender …'

'Who? Linda …'

'She's the ex-girlfriend. The one who went to Australia and then dumped him.'

'Did she call you?'

'She's here. She came to London when she heard about the trial. She wants to give evidence …'

'You sound doubtful?'

'She describes him as being keen on sex. She says they started having sex very early on in their relationship. She was underage … look I'll email it to you and you can make your own mind up.'

Outside court the next morning, Cassie and Lee met before Sadler turned up. 'I've read the statement and on balance I think I'd like to call her. What does she look like? Is she presentable?'

'Tanned. Good looking. A bit like Emma.'

At that moment Sadler approached them. 'Linda's back from Oz. She says she wants to help. Give evidence for me.'

'I took a statement from her last night. Miss Hardman is considering whether she would make a good witness for us,' Lee said.

'But …' Sadler said.

'It may look straightforward to you, but you were having underage sex with her and the way she describes your relationship – well,' Cassie said, ' I don't want the jury to think you're sex mad.'

Sadler frowned. 'I see. Does she say that?'

'You seem surprised?'

'We were at the same school and – we did make love quite a lot, but not every time we were together. She's come a long way to support me – to say I never forced her.'

'Lee, can you go back to her and perhaps ask her some more questions about their relationship. I am minded to call her.'

Cassie watched Sadler walk to the witness box followed by the security guard who stood behind him as if he was about to make a run for it. She thought it was ridiculous and designed to negate the fundamental principle that a defendant was innocent until proved guilty. Although Sadler was tall – she thought he was probably six feet – he was slim. Today he was dressed in a light grey suit and pale blue shirt, no tie. She had told him to wear whatever he felt most comfortable in. He was a very attractive man, his dark hair cut short, and had large dark eyes with long eyelashes. After taking the oath, he put his hands on the edge of the witness box. They were small compared to his height. As she got to her feet to conduct her examination in chief, Cassie looked at the jury. One of the younger women had leant forward, her attention directed towards the defendant. At times Sadler tapped his fingers on the edge of the witness box and as they reached the details of sexual intercourse, he stuttered. He was an attractive man but not a bully.

Once Cassie had finished her questions she sat down and waited for Hugh Palmer to begin his cross examination. She thought this stage of the trial was like throwing the witness to the wolves. As she had twisted the description given by Emma Gilbrook, so Hugh would insinuate Sadler was a brute, overpowering a younger girl to satisfy his sexual drive. She pulled her notebook towards her and then took a mint from the packet on the bench.

'Mr Sadler, Emma Gilbrook is ten years younger than you, she was clearly less experienced?'

'She told me she was twenty-four. I had no reason to doubt her.'

'She looked younger, did she not?'

'I didn't think so.'

'On the previous occasion the two of you met, she had paid for herself?'

'I think so. I'm not sure if I paid for coffee when we met in the park. I don't recollect. She had arrived before me and may have already had a drink. She did pay for her meal in the pizza place. As she says I paid a bit more because I had a beer.'

'Yet at the restaurant, you insisted on paying for dinner for the two of you?'

'I'd asked her out. It was, well, more of a date. I wanted to pay.'

'Wasn't it to make her more likely to agree to have sex with you? A form of grooming her?'

'Of course not. It was a date. My treat.'

'You left the restaurant together?'

'Of course.' Sadler was looking puzzled.

'Were you surprised when she suggested you went to her friend's flat?'

'Not really. She talked a lot about Anita and told me they were very good friends and she used the flat from time to time.'

'Did she tell you what she used the flat for?'

'I knew she lived at home with her mother. Having some privacy is difficult.'

'Privacy to have intimate relations.'

'I guess so.'

'Did you think Emma was inviting you to her friend's flat to have sex with you?'

'No. I didn't. She told me Anita may be there. She wanted us to meet.'

'Did she say why she wanted you to meet her friend?'

'I assume she wanted us to get to know each other. Confirm we were an item.'

'Anita Connor wasn't at the flat when you arrived?'

'She wasn't. Emma had a key and let us in.'

'Did you think Emma had invited you to the flat to have sexual intercourse with her at this stage?'

'I don't know what I was thinking. We'd have a bit more time together in private?'

'I'd suggest that by this time you were ready to have sex with her.'

'I didn't want to leave her. I wanted to spend more time with her.'

'When did you realise you were going to have sex with her?'

'It just happened … we were kissing and I caressed her. She was responding. It just went from there.'

'You took her into the bedroom?'

'We both got up and went to the bedroom together.'

'She was behind you, when you went into the bedroom?'

'I didn't drag her there. It's not a very big flat.'

'You held her hand and pulled her towards the bedroom.'

'No. I didn't.'

'Did you ask her if she wanted to go to the bedroom?'

'No, I didn't. She walked with me.'

'Once you were lying on the bed you were caressing her breasts?'

'She took her blouse off and her jeans.'

'Didn't you undo her jeans and pull them down?'

'We took her jeans off. They were very tight and had zips at the ankle. I don't think I could have got them off without help.'

'You went to get a condom?'

'They were in the inside pocket of my jacket. That was in the living room.'

'Why did you have condoms with you if you were not expecting to have sex?'

Paul Sadler looked at Hugh as if he couldn't understand the question. Hugh repeated it.

'I always carry a packet of condoms.'

'Are you always expecting to have sex?'

'It's just a sensible precaution. I can't remember when I put them in my pocket. I always carry them – in case.'

'In case you get the opportunity to rape a young woman?' Cassie saw one of the young men on the jury put his hand up to the breast pocket of his denim jacket. Was he checking he had a supply of condoms with him?

'No. I did not rape Emma.'

'Why do you think she is making this allegation?'

Sadler spread his arms out, the palms upturned. 'I don't know, I really don't know.'

'It was only your third meeting, your first proper date. Isn't that rather quick to start having sex?'

'I don't know what's usual.'

'Have you had sex on a first date before?'

'Once or twice. This wasn't a first date.'

Cassie looked at Hugh and not for the first time wondered what his sex life was like. She was quite fond of him but he was a little old fashioned. On one occasion when she had bumped into him as she was coming out of Temple Tube station he had bought an enormous bunch of flowers, thrust them into her arms and vanished before she could thank him. Hugh was relying on assumptions about sexual behaviour that were from another age. Had he, like too many lawyers, particularly the men, attended a single-sex school where they were taught nice girls didn't?

'Miss Gilbrook agrees, she helped you put the condom on. You knew she was trying to protect herself, didn't you?'

'I was nervous, that's why I couldn't get it on. She was quite willing to assist me. I took that to mean she was quite happy to have sex with me.'

'Did you ask her if she consented to having sex with you?'

'No, I didn't, we were … she was clearly enjoying the physical contact. Isn't that what happens, two people enjoying each other?'

Hugh didn't reply – witnesses weren't supposed to ask counsel questions – but Cassie could see he was disturbed by the question her client had posed. She turned her attention to the jury box and saw a few of the jurors nodding, hopefully agreeing. Cassie thought of her own relationships and how her body responded to physical contact. Had she always been in control? She thought not. Is that what had happened to Emma Gilbrook? Had there been conflict between what her head was saying and what her body wanted?

'You asked Miss Gilbrook if she was enjoying your attentions?'

'I wanted to …' Sadler paused and then stumbled over the next word '… satisfy her.'

'She didn't say she was enjoying it, did she?'

'She gave every appearance of doing so. Of wanting to have intercourse.'

'How did she do that?'

'She helped me with the condom. If she'd told me no or stop it I would have done so. She didn't.'

Cassie couldn't help but smile at how Hugh had made a mistake by asking one question too many. Hugh must have realised his error because his next question was about the interviews with the police.

'You were reluctant to answer the questions the police officers asked you?'

'At first I thought they were saying Emma was underage. I was confused by that.'

'As you were entitled to do, you stopped the interview and asked for a solicitor?'

'I did, and in the second interview I told them I did not rape Miss Gilbrook. I believed she was willing to have sex with me. The officer didn't believe me and he made it clear he didn't.'

Cassie leant forward – she was worried Sadler was going to refer to that part of the interview that had not been put before the jury. He didn't, and Hugh must also have been aware that he was straying onto evidence the judge had ruled inadmissible, because he said he had no more questions for the witness.

After Sadler had returned to the dock, Cassie asked Judge Tyte for a short adjournment.

He rolled his eyes towards the ceiling. 'I hope it's necessary, Miss Hardman.'

She assured him it was. She didn't want to say there was a possible witness in case she decided against calling Linda Callender. The judge told the court they could have ten minutes and the jury filed out of court. Cassie followed. Out in the marble-clad galleried hall, Cassie could see Lee standing with a tanned young woman with similar coloured hair to Emma Gilbrook, but it hung loosely round her face. Lee introduced them and then handed Cassie a document. 'It's a further statement from Linda. A bit more explanation about their relationship.'

'I really want to give evidence on Paul's behalf. I'm sure he wouldn't force himself on any girl,' Linda said.

'I do understand, but … Let me read this.' Cassie walked away along the concourse. Calling a witness was always a question of balance. Would Linda Callender's evidence help Sadler or would cross examination reveal facts that undermined her and because of that, the defendant?

Cassie finished reading the statement and then walked back to Lee and Linda Callender. 'Ok, let's go with it.'

'Linda Callender, please,' Cassie said. The black-gowned usher rushed out of the courtroom and seconds later appeared with the young woman following behind. The usher directed Linda into the witness box, handed her a bible and asked her to read the words from the card. When she had taken the oath she looked towards the dock and a smile lit up her face.

'Miss Callender, you know Paul Sadler?' Cassie said.

'Very well. We met at school. He was in the class above me.'

'Did you see each other out of school?'

'A lot. We were inseparable. Boyfriend and girlfriend. He came to my house often. His parents were divorced, his mother had remarried and he didn't get on with his stepdad. So he came to mine most days.'

'How did your relationship develop?'

'Do you mean when did we start having sex?' Linda looked at Cassie, who said she did.

'I think, after about six or so months. It was during the summer holidays. We were spending all day together. My parents were both out at work and we both wanted to do it.'

'How old were you?'

'I was fifteen and I think Paul was sixteen. He'd had a birthday about a week or so before. I'd joked about it being a birthday present.'

'You were underage. Did you know that?'

'I did, but all the girls in my class were having sex. Paul and I, we were good together and it seemed right.'

'How long did your relationship last?'

'Nearly five years. We both left school, Paul got a job at Heathrow. I wanted to be an air hostess, but it was difficult and I ended up working in various bars.'

'How did your friendship end?'

'I wanted to travel a bit before settling down. Paul had a job he enjoyed. He did want us to get married but I wasn't ready for that. My dad suggested I went to Australia and see how I felt then. While I was there I met my partner and I wanted to stay in Oz. Then I fell pregnant. I wrote to Paul explaining I'd met somebody else.'

'You've stayed in touch?'

'Sort of. Facebook, you know.'

'Where do you live now?'

'In Melbourne. I heard about this charge and flew over. I wanted to support Paul.'

'During that five years, were you having sex throughout that time?'

'Fairly often. We both enjoyed it.'

'Which of you initiated having sex?'

'Mostly Paul, but I did too.' Linda looked across the courtroom towards the jury box. 'He never once forced me to have sex with him. Not ever.'

There was no cross examination. Cassie knew Hugh didn't want to risk asking questions when he had no idea of what the answer might be.

Chapter 28

DCI Saltburn had decided to continue observation on the premises for the next few nights. They had secured the shop when they left and no one would have known the place had been searched. At night, the mews was unlit save for one lamp at the end closest to Ladbroke Grove. From the unmarked Vauxhall Corsa, Alex could see the lights from one of the houses illuminating a rectangle of the cobbled surface. Beyond, in the dark, was the print shop. They could not see the premises but the mews was a dead end so any vehicle arriving would have to pass by their parked vehicle.

Alex and Chris had been in position for over four hours. The smell of the pizza they had shared hung round her nostrils, and the floor of the car was covered in sweet wrappers. Chris Dundy reached for a can of Coke and pulled the tab away. 'Want some?' he said, holding it out towards her. Alex shook her head.

'I could do with a pee. We've been here for hours and nothing's moved on the plot since the guy at number four staggered back,' Alex said.

'How desperate?'

'What, the guy getting drunk?'

'No, for a pee.'

'We've not got that long to go before the others take over. I can wait.' It was alright for the blokes, they could find a dark corner in which they could relieve themselves; she'd have to keep her legs crossed.

She slipped down in her seat and pulled the bulky sweater she was wearing round her slim body. On her lap she held a log book; she turned the pages back and began to read the earlier entries. The comings and goings of the residents of the mews were recorded. The young mother, or was she an au pair with a child's buggy, an elderly man with his black Labrador, a couple of forty-something IC1 males carrying briefcases, probably architects, and a number of young men both IC1 and IC3 who had gone to the print shop and then left the mews. Were any of them Oscar Davenport?

Chris Dundy was sitting behind the wheel of the unmarked police car; from time to time he tried to stretch his bulk by arching his back. She closed the log, there wasn't any description that could have been Oscar Davenport.

She looked up as the lights of a vehicle shone through the back window of their car. Alex pushed the loose strands of her blonde hair into the band of her ponytail, picked up her Met Police baseball cap and slipped further down in her seat. Chris too lowered himself down to below the headrest and placed his hand on the ignition key. They remained motionless as a large white transit moved slowly along the cobbles. Once it had passed and they were in the dark again, they both sat up and watched the rear lights travel along the mews. Alex checked her watch, it was one thirty; she noted the time in the log book, then she began to record what she could see as Chris spoke softly into the microphone giving other officers waiting nearby the same information.

The van stopped and a tall overweight man got out of the driver's side. He ambled towards the rear and looked round before opening the doors. Another man got out from the passenger side; he remained in the shadows, his body indistinct. Faint shadows allowed Alex to follow him as he walked towards the print shop.

'Unknown male into premises,' Chris relayed. 'A second male, a big boy taking large package from rear and now into workshop. Instructions?'

A voice came over the radio, 'Stay in position. Unit two will take over.'

A marked police car swept past them and turned across the mews, blocking the van's exit, and behind that from another unmarked car four men ran towards it and disappeared.

'Back home, unit one.'

'We're not getting any of the action then,' said Chris as he switched on the ignition and reversed out of the mews. Alex briefly wondered if he thought they were being pulled away from the plot because the DCI was unwilling to have a woman in the front line. She pulled her hair loose and pushed the band into the pocket of her jeans. As Chris backed out of the mews, Alex saw the slim figure of a man standing close to the wall of one of the cottages. 'Slow down.'

'We're in the way.'

'Oscar Davenport. What's he doing out at this time of night?'

Back at the station, Alex wandered into the canteen to wait for the rest of the team to return with the prisoners. Chris joined her and they checked the log to make sure it was correct before both of them signed it. The remaining members of the squad arrived, swaggering, their faces all smiles. 'How much?' Chris asked.

'A couple of kilos of coke.'

The debrief was short. Within five minutes DCI Saltburn had organised the interviewing of the two suspects and made arrangements for the vehicle to be driven back to the station yard. He asked Chris Dundy to arrange for the examination of the van by the forensic team and to log the exhibits. Alex waited for her instructions.

'Right, don't forget the custody time limits. We need to crack on.'

The team of detectives stood up to leave but, as Alex made her way to the door, DCI Saltburn said, 'Alex can we have a word.'

She came back into the room and he motioned her to sit down. When the rest had left he leant against the table. 'Oscar Davenport. He's the guy from the chambers where Hales works? You say he was at his door when the van arrived.'

'Yes, sir.'

'Was that a coincidence? Had he heard us driving into the mews?'

'I thought he was wearing a coat. Of course he could have put it on to cover himself.'

'No one else came to their door that we saw.'

‘Not as far as I’m aware. We waited on the plot until the other vehicles had arrived. Then we backed out, and I didn’t see anyone else in the street.’

‘I’d like to interview him but there isn’t really enough to justify an arrest.’ He paused and walked over to the window. ‘If we could get his telephone and trace the calls he made and received last night … Have you any idea how we might do that?’

‘Not really. Barristers’ own phone numbers aren’t on the chambers website.’

‘But someone else in those chambers will have the number?’

‘I would have thought so. If you’re asking me to contact Cassie Hardman again …’

‘I am. She owes you, doesn’t she?’

‘But these are her friends and colleagues.’

‘All I want to do is see if Davenport made or received calls from either of the phones we seized last night. If he didn’t, then end of investigation. If he did then he’s probably involved in the supply of the contaminated drugs.’

‘Can’t we tell from those phones?’

‘We would have to trace them. This would make the whole process quicker.’

Alex closed her eyes for a moment. ‘You’re the boss.’

‘Good. Go home and get some sleep.’

Alex continued working on the files on known drug users. She wasn’t sure how it could help in the investigation of the contaminated drugs, but she had been instructed to look for connections to Cotburn Mews. So far she had found none. From time to time she thought about the man who was harassing Cassie. She had a vague recollection of having seen or heard the name Delaney before. She searched the computer records and found a Felix Delaney. An informant had said Felix sold small quantities of cannabis and possibly cocaine. No action had been taken as a result of that. The record had an address for him in Cambridge Gardens.

Outside the police station she walked north, her long stride quickly covering the ground. At the corner of Ladbroke Grove and Cambridge Gardens she heard cat calls from a group of men working on some scaffolding. She ignored them. Some things never changed. That couldn't be said of the houses in this part of London, which were always being renovated. A wolf whistle from one of the workmen distracted her and she half turned ready to put two fingers up to him, but then decided against it. She wouldn't give him the satisfaction of knowing he had annoyed her.

A few minutes later she was standing outside the gate to 20 Cambridge Gardens. The large, rather rambling house on the north side of the road had a basement and three storeys above. At one end there was a tower-like structure rising out of the uppermost level. The property was built of grey stone and the many windows were painted a startling white. The wide front door was decorated to look like the door of Number 10 Downing Street, but the similarity stopped with a row of bells indicating it was in multiple occupation. There were a number of cars parked in the driveway: a white Citroen, a black BMW and a red Mini. She made a note of the registration numbers.

There were six doorbells, each with a name by the side, but none said Delaney. Alex looked at them and struggled to decide which one to try. After a slight hesitation, she pressed the one at the bottom labelled Kelly. Several seconds later, a woman's voice on the intercom asked who was there. Alex said she was a police officer and she wanted to speak to Felix Delaney.

'I don't think he's around.'

'Perhaps you can help me. He's not in any trouble.'

'I'm not sure. Come in.' Alex heard the sound of the front door being released and she pushed it open. She walked into a wide hallway with a black-and-white tiled floor. It smelt of disinfectant. In front of her a white painted staircase curled upwards. She was taking a step towards the stairs when a door to her right opened and a woman in her forties, or so Alex thought, appeared. Alex took out her warrant card and held it towards the woman. 'Mrs Kelly?' she said.

'No, well, yes. Kelly Blackburn. What is it? What do you want?'

'I want to talk to Mr Delaney.'

'It might be better down here.' Kelly Blackburn stood aside and led Alex through the door and down the steps to the basement.

Despite being on a lower floor, the flat was very light. The living room was level with the garden which had been planted, at least close to the windows, with a profusion of roses. The room was carpeted in a pale cream and the sofas were cream and pink chintz. Alex nodded approval.

'How long have you lived here?'

'About four years now. Malcolm, that's the landlord, let me decorate the flat and I've got my own furniture.'

'And the roses?'

'I put those in as well. Improves the view. You mentioned Felix – what's he done?'

'I'm making some enquiries about drugs. He gave this address some weeks ago.'

Kelly pursed her lips. 'Felix gave this address. When was that?'

'A couple of weeks ago. If you don't want to tell me if he lives here it's up to you. I'm hoping he'll be able to help our enquiries.' Alex was betting that Kelly would provide the information she was looking for. She might be wrong.

Kelly rummaged around in her handbag, pulling out a packet of cigarette papers and a tin of tobacco. She took her time rolling a cigarette which she offered to Alex. Alex shook her head. Kelly lit the thin stick and took a deep breath. 'Sometimes he's here – the ground-floor flat with his brother and his dad.'

'They're called …?'

'Malcolm and Adrian.'

'The landlord is … Malcolm?'

'He owns the house. They have a really big flat on the ground floor. The bell for their flat is the one on the left in a kind of stone dish. It's the original one for the house.'

Alex nodded. 'Right. I'll try it again.'

'There's no point, they're all out.'

Malcolm – Malcom Delaney. The name of the man who was stalking Cassie. Alex wanted to know more about the Delaney family. 'Malcolm, he's a good landlord?'

Kelly grimaced and looked out of the window towards the rose bushes. 'I would say so. He wants the rent on time but he does any repairs quickly in return. That's what he does – he's a kind of handyman. He likes a quiet house so apart from the man in one of the top-floor flats, all the other tenants are women.'

'Likes women, does he?'

'The story I've heard is that one of his tenants ran off with his first wife, so no other men in the house. Although he isn't living with anyone now. But I really don't know him very well. He doesn't say much about himself.' She giggled. 'The girl who was here before me said he has another woman somewhere. I think that must have been some time ago.'

'It's a big house. How can he afford this place on a handyman's money?'

'He inherited it from his grandmother. She bought it when no one wanted to live round here. Now it's worth a bomb.'

'What about the sons?'

Kelly sat forward, smoothing the skirt she was wearing over light grey leggings. 'They're nice boys. Adrian, well, not boys really. Charming I'd say.' For a moment her eyes softened, and a smile flickered across her face, then she looked away and when her gaze came back to Alex there was hint of caution.

'Adrian, a bit of a ladies' man, would you say?'

'I've said I don't know them very well. Just when we meet, coming and going. Sharing a front door kind of thing. He's far too young for me.'

'Felix – any girlfriends?'

'If he has I've never seen them. He's hardly ever here. He's quite a talented musician, plays with a band. On the road a lot. Quite keen on sport as well. I really don't think I can help you.'

'Does the name Gilbrook mean anything to you?'

Kelly took a drag on her cigarette. 'Never heard it before.' As she spoke she stood up and walked towards the stairs leading to the hall above. Alex followed her. When Kelly reached the top step, she stopped to let Alex pass her out into the hallway. 'Sorry I can't be more help.'

Chapter 29

Cassie was wandering round her flat after court rose on the second day of the Montgomery trial. For once she couldn't be bothered to cook. Perhaps some pasta. She opened the tin in which she kept a packet of penne and then put it back. She got out her papers but couldn't concentrate and when her mobile rang she held her breath before answering. It was Marcus.

'Cassie, I've got a further statement to serve on you. It's …'

'What do you mean a further statement? Who from? What about?'

'Calm down, my dear. The witness came forward after reading about the case in the *Standard*. She saw the incident but didn't realise anyone had been injured. She rang the police yesterday, and the DS took a statement this morning. I want to send you a copy, if I can manage to scan it into the computer.'

Cassie gave him her email address and he told her he would send it straight away. She put the phone down and then telephoned James to tell him about this new witness. 'I'll forward you the statement as soon as I get it. From Marcus's tone I think it's probably a smoking gun.'

'Fine. I was doing an advice in another case. I hope Marcus has the IT skills to scan it in.'

'Don't be fooled by his protestations of ineptitude. I'm sure he can scan the document and email it to me. He likes acting as if he's computer illiterate. I'll ring when I've read the statement.'

They didn't have to wait long before the statement from the witness pinged into Cassie's inbox attached to an email from Marcus which read:

'*Quite a significant witness*.'

Cassie groaned, then she forwarded the email with its attachment to James and printed off a copy. As the printer clattered she began to read the statement onscreen.

The witness's description of the incident outside the sweet shop made Cassie swear. As she completed the final page she threw the three sheets of paper onto her desk and picked up the phone.

'Have you read it?' Cassie said.

'Not helpful.'

'That's understating it. It's a disaster for us. An independent witness who saw the whole episode and our client looks like a raving lunatic.'

'Doesn't paint a pretty picture.'

'It certainly doesn't. Any bright ideas about cross examination or do we just hope Edie Munroe comes across as unreliable?'

'We could ask about why she took so long to come forward? How did she miss the ambulance and police? Time delay caused a memory lapse. Do we need to get a copy of the report in the *Standard* and see what she may have picked up from the newspaper?'

'That's a great idea. I'll search for it online and can you do the same. Then make a list of the similarities between them. If we both do that we might have a way of throwing the witness. Better get on with it.'

Before she could start looking for the piece in the newspaper, the Skype pop-up box told her Ben was online. She opened the window and called him. He answered almost straight away.

'How's the trial going?' he said.

'Quite well, until a minute or two ago. We've been served with another eyewitness statement that demonstrates what a pillock our client is. What about you? How's the conference going?'

'It's ok. I've been to too many lectures and eaten too much. But there isn't anything else to do here.' He pulled a face. 'Any more problems with the stalker?'

'I'm still getting emails. He seems to dislike my cross examination. And the other night I thought there was somebody in the flat, but it was probably the girl downstairs. I called the police and the copper who came thought I was being paranoid.'

'Do you think it was her?'

'I was sure the noise was in the flat, but I was on the phone. I heard what I thought were footsteps going down, but no one left the building so perhaps it was her coming in.'

'I guess so. What …'

'Ben, I really have to do some work on this new witness. Looking at the newspaper reports and all that. Speak to you soon. Lots of love.'

'Sure, and keep the doors locked.'

Cassie smiled and blew him a kiss before clicking on the red icon. She was soon searching the *Standard*'s website and found the articles describing the three days of the trial, and then she looked for the report at the time the incident occurred. Before she had the chance to read it, her mobile rang.

'I gather the officer who came the other night thought you were a hysterical female,' Alex said.

'Did he?'

'Cassie, there's more to this than you're saying.'

'I've no idea who this Delaney is. What he wants. He started by referring to this case I was in – I told you, a rape case. Paul Sadler was the defendant. I can't see any connection. I've searched through the papers and there isn't anyone with that name.'

'You didn't mention it to the officer.'

'No, I didn't. I've so much going on and … the notes aren't threatening.'

'But disturbing … at least for the moment.'

'I keep hoping they'll stop, but perhaps when this case is over … The client is very difficult and I'm having to combat his prejudices all the time. I haven't the time to make a complaint. Alex, I have some work to do now. Can we leave it?'

'Sure, sure. It's your decision, but I think I know who he is or at least someone with the same name …'

'What? Who?'

'I've come across someone with the same name, but I can't see any connection with this case of yours either. You know, harassment can escalate very quickly. If you'll only make a complaint there would be a proper investigation into this man.'

'I can't. Not at the moment.'

'You're stubborn. Think about it. Make a complaint and it'll probably stop.'

'Not now. Really, I know you're trying to be helpful but …'

Cassie switched off her phone and turned back to her computer screen. The first mention of the incident the day after was very short. The report of Marcus's opening remarks was more detailed and outlined the facts of the case against Montgomery. Cassie listed the details of the event, separating out what she thought was the journalistic twist on the facts, and then highlighted the sections in the statement that bore a resemblance to the incident as described in the press. She was perplexed by the absence in Munroe's statement of any reference to the emergency services arriving and asked herself if the witness was describing the same incident. She did refer to the shopkeeper wielding a golf club, but she could have got that from the newspaper.

When she had finished reading and rereading the witness statement and the article, she felt ready to try and undermine this new witness or at least make the jury feel she might be unreliable. She printed her notes and the newspaper reports and was about to turn off her computer, but decided to check her inbox again.

There was only one new email. It was from Delaney. She opened it and then shuddered.

Chapter 30

Mrs Munroe was a tall, slim Afro-Caribbean woman of about fifty, dressed in a navy blue suit with an emerald green silky blouse. She looked around the courtroom and then walked to the witness box without any hesitation. She stood erect and held the bible in a firm grasp as she read the words of the oath from the card she had been given in a clear Scottish accent.

Robin Tasker asked her to give her full name.

‘Edie Kathleen Munroe,’ she said.

‘Yesterday you contacted the police and said you believed you could give evidence about this case.’

Mrs Munroe looked at Robin Tasker as if he was a simpleton, and then turned her attention to Judge Crabtree. ‘Yes, I’d seen the incident but thought nothing about it. I assumed the boys had been chased away from the shop by the older man. I thought he was probably the shopkeeper. I didn’t realise anyone had been hurt, much less died as a result of the incident. So when I read a report about the case in the *Evening Standard* I thought I ought to call the police.’

‘That was the edition of the paper published on Tuesday evening?’

‘Yes, of course.’

‘Tell us what you saw.’

‘I was walking along the road on the opposite side from the row of shops when I heard shouting and swearing. The voices were very loud, it was impossible to ignore it, so I looked across and saw a group of four boys standing on the pavement in front of the shop door.'

'Can you tell us what you heard? Please, the exact words as you remember them.'

'It's quite a while ago but I think someone was shouting wanker and paedo. It may have been perv. The implication being the older man was a paedophile.'

'Could you tell who was shouting?'

'The noise was coming from the boys but I couldn't say who was saying which words.'

'Was there anyone else apart from the boys? I should ask you first, did you know any of the youths?'

'No, I didn't know any of them, although I thought the youngest may have been a pupil at my school. I'm headmistress at Cotburn Primary.'

Cassie turned to observe the jury; Edie Munroe was an impressive witness even without knowledge of her occupation. The female juror who always wore a pink shirt was writing furiously in her notebook. Cassie and James had speculated on how many pink shirts the fifty-year-old had.

'Can you describe the boys?'

'No, not really. They had their backs to me, but they were all Afro-Caribbean or mixed race I believe.'

'In addition to the youths, was there anyone else near the door of the shop?'

'I didn't see anyone at first, the boys were standing in a circle and then as they began to move away, I saw an older white man waving a golf club at them. His words were very racist.'

'What was he saying?'

'I found it rather upsetting – he was calling them niggers. I did think about crossing the road and asking him to stop. I wish I had now.' She paused and looked around her, then said, 'He was very angry but, well, I did think the young men were being very abusive as well. I think that affected me. I didn't want to get involved in whatever they were arguing about.'

If only she had, thought Cassie, Albie Young might well be alive, Montgomery wouldn't be facing trial and she wouldn't be defending him. She was sure the jury felt something similar. Cassie heard the sound of someone sobbing in the public gallery; she looked up and saw her client's wife holding a handkerchief over her mouth. Mrs Montgomery looked directly at Cassie. Even at a distance Cassie could see her face was contorted with misery; Cassie tried to smile but then looked away to avoid the distressed but penetrating gaze.

'Which direction were the boys moving in when you last saw them?'

'The man was hitting out with the club, swirling it around, and they were trying to get away from him. Kind of spreading out in different directions in a sort of semicircle.' She shrugged her shoulders. 'I don't know how else to describe it. Moving out from the shopkeeper.'

'You didn't cross the road, so where did you go?'

'I kept walking along Ladbroke Grove in the direction of the Underground station. I could hear shouting for a little while, then it stopped and I assumed the lads had run off. I didn't look back.'

Robin Tasker thanked Mrs Munroe and asked her to wait as she would be asked some more questions.

'Do you need any more time, Miss Hardman?' said Judge Crabtree.

'No, I can begin cross examination,' Cassie said before turning towards the witness box. 'Mrs Munroe, you've told us you learnt of the death of Albie Young when you read the report of this case in the newspapers. Would it be right then to assume that the younger boy you saw was not a pupil at your school?'

'Yes, I would have known about the incident if he had been and last night I checked the pupil roll in order to be sure, but we had no one who could have been a relative of the dead boy.'

'I first received a copy of your statement last night, so would the newspaper report have been in the evening newspaper the night before?'

'Yes, I rang Scotland Yard originally and they took my name and address, then Miss Kotzeva rang me yesterday morning and we arranged for her to come to my school. I live in Lewisham, so that seemed the most convenient place to meet.'

'And no doubt the most expeditious. Did you see the report of the incident when the young man died in March?'

'Not that I am aware of. If I did I didn't make the connection with the incident I had witnessed.'

'What was it about the report in Monday's paper that made you believe it was the incident you saw?'

'I'm not sure. The location was described in detail, the sweet shop. I remembered it because it reminded me of similar shops when I was a child.'

'Did you see or hear the ambulance or police vehicles racing up Ladbroke Grove?'

'No, I didn't.'

'When you first noticed the group, how far away were they?' Cassie was being careful; the witness's description of the incident was different from the youths but also from her client's. If her version was believed by the jury then Montgomery had been chasing the young men, not defending himself.

'It's difficult to judge. They were about ten metres in front of me and across the road when I first heard the shouting, so I would guess about twenty metres.'

'They had their backs to you, so would it be right you could not see what, if anything, any of them was carrying?'

'No, I couldn't see.'

'The youngest of these boys, was he with the group or a little way apart?'

Mrs Munroe screwed her eyes up as if looking at a picture. 'I think he was by the window of the shop when I first noticed him.'

'Would this be right: looking at the group from where you were walking he would have been on the left of the other three?'

'Yes, that's right.'

'Did he move further to the left or towards the other boys?'

The expression on the witness's face changed as if she realised there was something inaccurate in her account. 'I thought they all moved away from the shop – you know, dispersed – but …' She paused. 'Actually, I think he must have run away first, because I can only remember three young men moving outward.'

'You're saying the younger boy had vanished?'

'He was there, then he wasn't. I don't know what happened to him.'

'The shopkeeper, when did you first see him?'

'He wasn't there when I first looked. I'm sure of that. I didn't stop to watch what was happening and there was traffic passing, so I suppose I missed him coming out. Also the youths were quite tall and blocked my view. But the next time I looked he was out on the pavement waving this golf club and shouting abuse.'

Cassie had considered suggesting to Mrs Munroe she was mistaken about the golf club and she had taken that description from the newspaper article but, having seen the witness, she decided against that line of questioning. Edie Munroe was not likely to have made that error and would not be persuaded she had, however clever the cross examination. Cassie had to go back to establishing Mrs Munroe had only seen part of the incident.

'How far had you walked by the time you saw the older man?'

'I was level with the shop by this time.'

'You've described the boys as being tall and around the door to the shop, blocking your view. Did the boys still have their backs to you?'

'Yes, they were in a kind of huddle and then – actually I think I saw the end of the club first. I wasn't sure who was swinging it around. Then they began to move away and I saw the shopkeeper, a man I assumed was the shopkeeper, and realised it was he who had the club.'

'Did they turn and run away?'

'Not really, I thought they were trying to keep out of the way of the club. Watching him swinging it around as they backed away.'

'You describe the boys as moving outwards, can you help us with how far away from the shop door they were when you last saw them?'

'Not far. A metre at the most.'

'Would this be an accurate description of your observations? You heard the shouting and looked over at the group of youths standing by the door to the sweet shop. At that stage nothing seemed untoward, is that right?'

'Yes, I thought a group of youths were being over-boisterous. Actually, that's being generous to them. Their language was, to put it mildly, very offensive.'

'You continued walking and then the next time you looked you saw the shopkeeper being abusive to the youths? Was it hearing the word “nigger” that attracted your attention?’

‘Yes, I think it probably was.’ Edie Munroe nodded, lips pressed together.

‘At that point you saw the youths backing away and assumed they were leaving the scene?’

‘I thought it was all over, whatever had caused the dispute between them and the shopkeeper. The shouting stopped suddenly and that confirmed my belief that the incident was at an end. Also I think one of the boys ran past me. I thought they had all gone in different directions.’

Cassie thanked the witness, scribbled a quick note on Mrs Munroe’s statement and then sat down. James leant over the bench and, keeping his voice low, said, ‘That was great. Doesn’t look so bad now.’

Chapter 31

Alex couldn't get away from thinking about Malcolm Delaney and, if he was the stalker, why he was harassing Cassie Hardman. She hadn't got the opportunity to ask for Oscar Davenport's phone number and was annoyed by Cassie's obstinacy, but she was worried about the risk Cassie might face from her stalker. She had an excuse for speaking to his son, Felix. From the files he was a frequent visitor to the nightclub under the Westway, so even though there was no link with the contaminated drugs, she thought she could justify talking to him. She headed back towards Cambridge Gardens.

Parked on the driveway were the white estate and a transit van decorated with a guitar-playing black male set against a background of blues and purples. She pushed the large white button set in the stone door jamb, and after a minute or so a man came to the door and peered at her. He was about fifty years old and probably about five foot ten. Younger and leaner he might have been thought handsome. Now his hair was beginning to go grey, his skin was pale and he had bags under his eyes. After a brief inspection of her, he asked who she was. She produced her warrant card from her pocket. The man shook his head, and said, 'What do you want, then?'

'I'd like to speak to Felix Delaney. You are?'

'I'm his father. He's not here.'

For a moment Alex paused and concentrated on the man standing in front of her. This was Malcolm Delaney. He looked such an unassuming man, not someone consumed by anger. She continued with the pretext for being there. 'Do you know where he is? We want to speak to him.'

'What about?'

'We're making some enquiries about drug use at Peaches.'

'He doesn't do drugs.'

'We just need to speak to him.'

He pursed his lips and looked up at the trees before making eye contact with her again. 'He's gone to the sports centre under the Westway.'

'When was that?'

'About ten minutes ago.'

Back behind the wheel of her car she turned towards the Westway Sports Centre. Much of the area was inaccessible in a vehicle, but she drove towards the car park under the football pitch and parked on a double yellow line. Her initial guess was that he would be on one of the practice pitches but there was no sign of him. She walked a little further past the tennis courts. The highway was above her and much of the grey concrete that supported the road was covered in garishly coloured graffiti, encouraged by the authorities to hide the depressing location. Alex tried to decide whether she thought this was art or not. They were nothing like Banksy's work. No wit, nothing political like the kissing policemen. Then she spotted Felix sauntering along about twenty metres in front of her. She called his name and to her surprise he looked round and then stopped. She caught up with him, told him who she was, produced her warrant card.

'What's this about?'

'Drug use at Peaches.'

Felix began walking west again. 'I've got a game of fives round the corner here. What do you want to know?' he said as he pointed the way round the climbing pyramids. Out of the corner of her eye Alex saw two ponies chasing each other in a small sand arena. She was distracted by their movements.

'It is a strange place for a riding school,' said Felix. 'Gypsies.'

'I know,' said Alex. She had been a frequent visitor to the site when she was still in uniform. 'Do you go to the club, Peaches, much?'

'Used to. Played there on occasions.'

'I noticed the van at …'

'You've been to my home?'

'I saw your dad, he said …'

'He's not keen on the police.'

'Look, why don't you come back to the station and talk to me there.'

'Are you arresting me?'

'I've no grounds. I'd just like a chat about a few things.'

Felix looked up at the sky and then at Alex. 'I'll come after my game.'

Alex nodded. 'Ok. See you later.'

She was surprised when two hours later she was told Felix Delaney was in the waiting room. She escorted him into an interview room where they sat down facing each other across a table scarred by cigarette burns.

'Have you been to Cotburn Mews lately?'

'Not sure where that is.'

'Runs off Ladbroke Grove. There's a square …'

'Right, I'm with you. Don't recall going there. Is there any reason I should have done?'

'We think someone is dealing in cocaine from some premises in there. Have you been there in, say, the last week?

'No. A week ago I've driven up north, played a gig, driven back – it's a bloody long way. So, no, not been there this week. If at all.'

Felix began to play an imaginary song on the table, and mouthing the words. He was a well-proportioned young man, with long fingers. She noticed the nail on his right thumb was long and she assumed one of the instruments he played was a guitar. His face was thin, the whites of his eyes bright against his tanned skin. He would not look at her. Was that because he knew something about the drug dealing?

'Do you know anyone who lives in Cotburn Mews, or works there?'

'I've just been thinking about it. There's a print workshop?'

'Used to be.'

'I got some stuff for the band printed there. A couple of posters, some fliers, that kind of thing. Haven't been there since then. Must be a couple of years ago.'

Alex told him about the drugs being contaminated. 'We've made a few arrests at Peaches for possession. We need to find the supplier.'

'I don't do snowy, never have. Mugs' game. Smoke a bit of weed. Can't help, sorry.'

'I need to fill in a couple of forms about speaking to you. You live in Cambridge Gardens?'

'With my dad and brother.'

'Still at home then …?'

'Can't afford to rent anywhere else. It's a big house and we live in the ground-floor flat. The rest is divided into small studios – that is apart from Kelly. She has a one-bedroomed flat.'

'You said your dad wasn't keen on the police. Any reason?'

'There's been some bother with my sister.'

'She lives with you?'

'No, with her mum. Different mothers.'

'She's called?'

'What's this about?'

'I've said, we're trying to prevent these drugs being sold.'

'What's that got to do with my sister? She's not an addict or anything.'

'So what's the bother with the police?'

'She was raped. She said the trial was like being assaulted again.'

'And he thinks the police were to blame?'

'I don't know what he thinks. He's pretty angry.'

'How angry? Just ranting and raving or …'

'Or what?'

‘Would he stalk someone he thought responsible for the verdict in the trial?’

‘I don’t know what you’re getting at. I don’t want to answer any more questions. I’m going.’

Felix stood up and walked towards the door. Alex didn’t try to stop him. He took hold of the door handle. ‘You’re barking up the wrong tree.’ Alex shook her head.

Chapter 32

The next witness in the Montgomery trial was Detective Sergeant Angela Kotzeva. The woman officer walked towards the witness box ignoring both the judge and the jury. She picked up the bible and, without looking at the card that the usher held out to her, she promised to tell the truth, the whole truth and nothing but the truth. She was wearing almost identical clothing to those she had been wearing when she interviewed Chris Young: a straight navy skirt and pale shirt, although this time it was green rather than yellow, and over the shirt a charcoal grey jacket. Her questioning of Chris Young had demonstrated how competent she was; she would be difficult to cross examine. At least this time Cassie didn't have to question the veracity of the officer's evidence.

After Kotzeva had taken the oath she gave her name and rank and then looked towards Robin Tasker, no doubt waiting for him to ask his first question but, as he lumbered to his feet, Judge Crabtree said, 'The two boys, Leon Campbell and Jonathan Wilding, are both juveniles, yet their evidence was not recorded. Is there any reason why not?'

'Yes, My Lord.' Sergeant Kotzeva turned away from Robin Tasker and towards the judge. 'The video was in use for another case with a very young child. The interviews with her were taking a long time. It was late evening and Leon and

Jonathan were getting very restless. I offered to get drinks and something to eat, but they wanted to tell us what had happened straight away. Leon's mother and a social worker were waiting as well. I became concerned that they would leave and we would have problems getting them to return. Also we had kept the two boys apart and if they left they would have more opportunity to talk to each other about the incident and be accused of putting their heads together.' She glanced towards Cassie. The officer had tried to eliminate any opportunity for the two boys colluding in their evidence. 'I spoke to a senior officer and as they were not the victims and … I took the view they were fairly robust, we decided the best course was to take written statements from them.'

'What view did the parents take?' Judge Crabtree said.

'Mrs Wilding was happy with the situation and Leon's social worker agreed to that course. They were all fed up with the delay. There was discussion about them going home and coming back, but we wanted to get their statements as soon as we could, for the reasons I've already mentioned.'

Cassie thought the officer had guessed she would be asked by somebody about the breach of protocol for interviewing juvenile witnesses and had prepared her response.

'Fine, Mr Tasker. Now we'll begin.'

Robin Tasker fumbled with his papers for a moment. 'On the third of March, were you called to the scene of an incident at a shop in Ladbroke Grove?'

'Yes. Montgomery's Sweet Emporium, it's called.'

'What did you find there?'

'It was three forty-five when I arrived in company with Detective Constable Craig Hadley. There was already an ambulance in attendance and they were putting a young man onto a stretcher. A boy of about nine was by the side of the ambulance with one of the paramedics. He was crying and clearly very upset. The medic told me the boy was the victim's younger brother and was called Chris. The lad on the stretcher was Albie. He hadn't been able to get any further names from the younger boy. He also told me …' She paused and looked towards Cassie as if asking for permission to continue. Cassie was well aware that the evidence of Albie Young's condition was hearsay and the words of the paramedic did not prove how badly injured he was, but she didn't want to insist on the ambulance man coming to court just to fill in the sequence of events; better to let the evidence go unchallenged from the officer.

Cassie leant across and whispered to Robin that she had no objection to Angela Kotzeva giving the evidence. The officer must have realised what had happened and continued. 'He also told me Albie was seriously injured and was unconscious.'

'Was there anyone else there?'

'Yes, Mr Montgomery was standing at the door of the shop. I went up to him and asked him if he was aware what had happened. He told me the youth with two others had been stealing from his shop and he had used a golf club to get them away from his premises. At that point I was concerned that an offence may have been committed and, in view of the possible serious consequences, I cautioned him and told him I was arresting him for assault occasioning grievous bodily harm.'

'You told him he didn't have to say anything but it may harm his defence if he did not mention anything when questioned something he may later rely on in court. Anything he did say could be given in evidence?'

'That's correct.'

'Did he say anything at all?'

'He started to say they had been a real nuisance and had done damage in the shop. I told him it would be better waiting until we were at the station and he had seen a solicitor.'

'Once at the station did you interview him in the presence of his solicitor, Mr Durrant, and DC Hadley?'

The officer read the transcript carefully. Montgomery's account of the incident in interview was the one he had maintained to Cassie in conference. There was one passage of the transcript that was problematic for his defence. Cassie had underlined it.

DS Kotzeva. Are you a racist, Mr Montgomery?

Montgomery. If you mean do I dislike all these immigrants, yes, but I don't care where they come from, they're foreigners, they should go back home.

DS Kotzeva. Is that why you hit Albie Young, because he's black?

Montgomey. No, they were stealing from me, threatening me. That's why I hit out.

DS Kotzeva. You could have closed the door on them, couldn't you?

Montgomery. I don't think so. I thought they were ready to rush me, to come back in. I really wanted them to go away.

'Members of the jury, I'd like to discuss a matter with counsel. Perhaps, go and have a coffee,' Judge Crabtree said.

When the jury had left the courtroom, the judge turned to DS Kotzeva. 'There's mention of turning a camera off. Is there a recording of the incident?'

'Yes, My Lord,' said the witness.

'Is the jury not to see the video? Mr Tasker.'

'I don't know why not … I'm not sure if Mr Pike wanted it played.'

Judge Crabtree frowned. 'We can't wait for Mr Pike to be here.'

Cassie got to her feet. 'We believe the prosecution thought it added little to the evidence. It's not the best of recordings. One of those intermittent cameras. It can be misleading.'

'I'm sure the jury are perfectly capable of sorting out what's happening. Unless there is very strong objection against it being played, the jury must see it. I'll rise while the video is located.'

'Ouch,' said James.

'I suppose it was inevitable,' Cassie said.

‘I’m going to see if I can speak to Marcus,’ Robin Tasker said as he left the court.

It didn’t take long to set up the video and to play the short clip to the jury. Cassie sucked one of her mints as the scene inside the sweet shop was played out, stuttering like a very old movie. The jury didn’t seem very surprised by its contents; although they all followed it closely, only two of them made notes.

Robin Tasker thanked DS Kotzeva and then said, ‘Was the video played back during the interview or was that the end of it?’

‘We didn’t have the recording at that stage. We ended the interview when I told him he would be charged with attempted murder.’

Cassie asked the officer just one question. ‘Mr Montgomery is a man of good character.’

‘He has no convictions recorded against him.’

Chapter 33

After court rose that evening, Cassie ushered Montgomery, James and Zac into a tiny conference room. There was only just enough space for them all to squeeze round the wooden-topped table.

'I thought the officer was very fair, didn't you?' James said.

'She was fine, and luckily for us there is nothing in the interview that we need to deal with, no lies to explain away. It's the clear evidence of prejudice we have to contend with.' She then turned to her client. 'Mr Montgomery, as you know, the Crown have closed their case and tomorrow it's your turn to give evidence. You don't have to, but if you don't the judge can comment on that and tell the jury they can take it into account and draw such inferences as they think appropriate – and that they may hold it against you. He'll say something to that effect to you. My advice to you is that you should tell the jury what you say happened. I believe jurors take the view that if they were charged with an offence they would want to tell the court what happened and not hide behind a shield of silence. Do you understand?'

Montgomery took a deep breath and nodded at her. There was little in his expression to show what he felt about the prospect of going into the witness box.

'Right. Tonight I want you to read through the copy of the statement you made to Mr Durrant and make sure you can remember what you said to him – it's the basis of the case I've been putting to these lads. When you give your evidence, just answer the questions I ask you and keep your replies short. If I think the jury should hear more I'll ask you further questions. Do you understand that? The difficult time will be when Mr Pike cross examines you. He'll pick up on every inconsistency in your evidence and he'll try to provoke you into making racist comments. I do not want to hear them from you. No swearing, no name calling. Do you grasp what I'm saying?'

Mr Montgomery looked stunned as if she had hit him, but he said he did understand. Cassie waved at him to lead the way out.

'See you tomorrow,' she called after him as he walked towards the lifts.

'That was a bit tough wasn't it?' said Zac.

'He needs to think about what he says. The case against him could turn on what they make of him. He's got a run on self-defence but they have to believe that Loveday had a knife and that Montgomery had no opportunity to retreat. I think we've established the lad did have a knife or, at least, they can't exclude it. But on the issue of whether he went a step too far out of the shop they may decide that on the question of his motives.'

'So, if they think he hit out because they were black then they'll decide he could have closed the door on them?' Zac said.

'Exactly. Let's hope he takes on board what I've said to him.'

Once in the robing room, she turned on her mobile phone then took off her wig and gown.

There was a message from chambers asking her to go in after she had finished in court, but nothing from her stalker.

Cassie turned left out of the doors of the court and walked slowly south along Old Bailey, the street that gave its name to the Central Criminal Court. At the junction with Ludgate Hill, as she drew level with the black painted telephone kiosk by the Leon café, a voice called her from behind. At first she didn't recognise it and she felt her stomach turn and the muscles in the side of her neck stiffen, but then she realised it was James and she relaxed. 'James, I was … I thought it was somebody else.'

'Don't worry, I'm not your phantom stalker. Are you going back to chambers?' he said.

'Yes. And you?'

'Yes, I'm rather hoping some money will have turned up.'

'Not you as well. I suppose it's the tax bills arriving. Always a problem. I don't know about you but I always seem to spend my fees twice – when I'm doing the trial and then when I actually get the money.'

James laughed. They continued walking in a companionable silence. Cassie's thoughts returned to Delaney; he seemed to have invaded her life. She was determined not to think about him and the Sadler case so she concentrated on observing the street scene. She noticed the sign above the Punch public house, a gold profile of the character holding his truncheon aloft. A few doors along she saw the three gold balls of a pawnbroker's, next to a sign proclaiming they were pawnbrokers of distinction. She wondered how long there had been a need for them so close to the Temple and what the phrase meant. She asked James whether he thought some of their colleagues used pawnbrokers. 'I've never heard anyone say they did,' said James, 'although I can see some might if their fees haven't been paid for a while.'

'It says pawnbrokers of distinction. Do they only deal with people of distinction or only lend money against objects of distinction? Whichever, it would rule me out.'

James laughed. 'At least you've not lost your sense of humour.'

Retreating into her own thoughts she looked into an optician's window and smiled at the large poster displayed there. She wondered how long it would be before she needed glasses; her eyes were often sore from so much time spent under artificial lighting.

As they drew level with the faded sign of the three squirrels outside Goslings Bank, she heard James's voice as if it was coming through water, asking her something about accounts. She shook her head as if to shake out fluid from her ear. 'Sorry, I was miles away. You were saying?'

'I hear there is some sort of disagreement between Eleanor and Richard. Do you know anything about it?'

'You've been talking to Stephen – he always knows all the gossip. But, no I don't. Eleanor does think we should do more to curb chambers' expenses, but she can't get Richard to even think about it.'

'She's right, isn't she? Fees seem very low and the delay in getting the money adds to the problems. I've heard some talk of rent not being paid.'

'I'm not surprised. Sometimes there are delays in payment and people have mortgages and tax bills to pay. We could do with some tightening up of fees collection. Eleanor really wants to change the whole clerking arrangements. Richard and a few others like the way it is. I'm not getting embroiled in the dispute between them. The real problem is Jack. Richard will protect him from Eleanor. She thinks Jack hasn't done enough to get her work. We've been here before and what usually happens is she's instructed in some big case and she hasn't the time or energy to continue fighting. At least for a while. Anyway, enough of that,' she said as she pushed open the door into the clerks' room.

There was an unnatural silence as they entered and an unusually large number of members of chambers were standing by the pigeonholes with their backs to the rest of the office. As she walked across to her own, she caught the sound of Jack arguing with somebody. She pulled out the bundle of papers and letters that had accumulated, at the same time straining to hear what was being said. It was difficult, but Jack sounded angry. She caught a few words but thought he was telling whoever was on the other end of the phone that there was nothing he could do. He looked up towards where she was standing and threw the phone down on his desk.

His face had reddened and his eyes were a flinty grey. She inspected the contents of her pigeonhole; there were a couple of additional instructions for a mortgage fraud, some circulars from law publishers, an invitation to the South East Circuit dinner and a couple of letters. She turned the envelopes over in her hand; one had the address of her bank on the back but the other was unmarked. As she began to walk out onto the stairs, she opened the mysterious envelope. Before she could look at its contents Jack called out to her, asking her how the trial was going.

'Not too bad, it's early days. It's what happens when Marcus Pike starts on the defendant. It won't be a pretty sight, I'm ...' She pulled from the envelope a postcard showing a painting of *The Rape of the Sabine Women.* She turned the card over and on it was the typed message: 'It happens all the time. Delaney'. She stuffed it back into the envelope and forced her mouth into a grin. 'Not a pretty sight, I'm afraid.'

'Are you alright?' Jack said, getting out of his chair and walking over to her. He took hold of her shoulders and held her. She tried to avoid his gaze as scrutinised her face.

'I'm fine, really. Rather tired of holding the dogs of prejudice at bay.'

'There's some new instructions for you. You'll get the download soon. It's a good case at Southwark – probably last six months. You're leading with Mike Harris as junior.'

'When's it due to start?'

'The date hasn't been fixed yet, but at least six months away. Plenty of time to prepare.'

'I'll need some time out of court to work on that,' Cassie said.

'I'll see, but you can't turn down good work when it comes in.'

'I need a life of some kind, Jack. Anyway, what's this meeting about tomorrow?'

'I'm sworn to secrecy, Miss Hardman, sworn to secrecy.'

She knew that meant he had no more idea what the meeting was about than she did. She shook her head at him.

'When will Montgomery end?'

'Jury should go out Tuesday. Don't fix anything, I'd like a day or two off. I think I might go home for a long weekend.'

Jack sighed as he checked the onscreen diaries. She thought he was going to attempt to persuade her to start another case or do a list of sentences on the following Friday. She waited and made sure he marked her diary with the word 'Away'. Great, she thought, she knew she needed a break and the Lake District was beautiful in summer. Amanda and her nephews would be on holiday and it would be good to spend some time walking with them in the countryside.

'Could Mr Callan do a plea tomorrow morning? It's not in your court, but next door,' Hamish called out to her as she moved away from Jack's desk.

'I'd rather not. My client's starting to give evidence tomorrow and I need a really good note of what he says.'

'Ok, I'll ask Mr Burnett.'

'Ask me what?' Stephen Burnett said as he walked into the clerks' room.

'There's a plea in mitigation at the Old Bailey tomorrow: ten o'clock, Court 6. It's a drug importation. Instructions will be here sometime after six.'

'I was hoping to get home early. The other half has been in a bit of a huff. But I need the money. How about a drink, Cassie?'

A glass or two of wine might steady her nerves and chatting with Stephen would be a distraction from both her case and the stalker.

Daley's wine bar was on the corner of Fleet Street and Essex Street and was a favourite haunt of lawyers. It was often packed but tonight they were early enough to find seats. The bar was large and Cassie spotted a couple of unoccupied chairs by a table in a corner where she hoped they would not be interrupted. This was a good opportunity to ask Stephen what he knew about the chambers meeting the next day.

'Not much,' he said, 'but I think Richard is really looking for a vote of confidence in the way he runs the set. Eleanor thinks we aren't on top of financial things, and, well, I've heard something about downsizing the premises.'

Cassie was taken aback. She felt they were stuffed in like sardines as it was. 'No way, it's like a cattle truck in there, we're hot-desking as it is.'

‘Yes, but how much work do you do in chambers? We all work from home now. We only come in to collect papers and it’s somewhere to house the clerks. Some of that can be done at home as well. Zoe only comes in twice a week.’

‘I know, I quite miss her and her brightly coloured jumpers. When I was a pupil we used to take bets on what colour it would be that day.’

‘What about the Hales problem?’ Stephen said.

‘I’ve passed on the Cotburn Mews address … they can’t take that any further, Alex says.’

Before Cassie could say anything more, she saw Hamish coming towards them. ‘Thought I’d find you here, sir,’ he said, handing Stephen a thin brief. ‘I was coming this way and thought I’d bring it for you. Save you going back to chambers.’

‘Thanks. Do you want a drink?’

‘Not here, sir,’ Hamish said, looking round at the groups of barristers in their detachable collars collecting round the bar and tables. ‘I’m meeting some of my colleagues in the Cheshire Cheese. See you.’

Chapter 34

Cassie spent the evening writing out her speech in the Sadler case. She was meticulous in her preparation; two lives hung on it. She knew that, but her objective was the acquittal of the defendant – he was her client, not the young woman. Sadler was facing seven years in prison, his life totally destroyed. Even the fact of the allegation left him vulnerable. He'd already been suspended from work and for the rest of his life he would have it hanging over him. She caught her own emotions and trapped them in the recesses of her mind; they were not for now.

She liked to have a narrative to her speeches: a beginning, a middle and an end. What was there about this case to which members of the jury would relate? What would make them say they understood what had happened that night? Cassie believed the very ordinariness of the events were the key to a not guilty verdict. Boy meets girl, they like each other, there's a mutual attraction and after meeting a few times they make love. The hurdle she had to leap was why Emma Gilbrook had cried rape. She was sure Hugh would make that point with great force. Cassie thought she could argue the answer lay with her mother. Rose Gilbrook's outburst about her daughter's virginity had been a significant moment in the trial.

She began tapping the keys of her computer.

‘There is only one issue in this case and that is: did Emma Gilbrook consent to having sexual intercourse with Paul Sadler or did he have a reasonably held belief that she did? She says she didn’t want to have sex with him and that she simply submitted to him because she didn’t know what else to do. Was that really what happened? The defendant, it has been suggested, used the Rush Hour Crush notice to entice this young woman to meet him. Again, there was nothing unusual about that. Many relationships begin online these days. Emma Gilbrook responded to the message; she didn’t have to do that. Unlike online dating Paul Sadler had no other information about her. If she had ignored it he couldn’t have pestered her or put any pressure on her. She contacted him because she remembered him and she thought he was an attractive man. What was it she said, he was smartly dressed, handsome?

Emma Gilbrook had met the defendant on three separate occasions and she says she enjoyed his company. Presumably that’s why she agreed to see him after the first meeting in Holland Park and again after seeing him a week later in the pizza parlour. If she hadn’t liked him she wouldn’t have met him on the night in question. The Crown suggest that by asking her to an expensive restaurant, he was grooming her. If that’s right, an awful lot of dates are grooming. Isn’t it just ordinary for a man to ask a woman out and to pay for her meal?

Throughout the first two meetings there was nothing to make her afraid of him. She wouldn't have met him if there had been. He had walked her to her bus stop, held her hand, kissed her on the cheek as they parted. All very normal, just what you would expect from any young couple feeling their way in a new relationship. There was a little more physical contact on their third date. In a romantic gesture they held hands across the table in the restaurant.

Like a lot of young people today neither of them lives in their own home. It's difficult to have any privacy to explore a relationship. Emma Gilbrook, however, had access to her friend Anita Connor's flat. She was the one who suggested they should go there. One of the questions you will have to consider is whether she is telling the truth when she says she thought her friend would be there. Anita Connor, reluctantly you might think, told you she had said she would be out and didn't know what time she would be back. Knowing the flat would be empty, why did Emma Gilbrook take the defendant there? At the very least it must have been to spend time alone with this man who she found attractive. To pursue their romance.'

She stopped typing. What was she going to say about Rose Gilbrook? She didn't want to criticise the mother too forcefully. A mother who tried to control her twenty-year-old daughter's life. A mother who believed her daughter had not had sexual intercourse before. Had Emma made the allegation to save herself from explaining to her mother where she had been the night before? From being questioned too closely about who she had spent the evening with and what had happened.

Was it to deflect attention from behaviour of which she knew her mother disapproved? It was Rose who had phoned the police, not Emma. Rose who had screamed at Sadler on the phone accusing him of mistreating her daughter.

She continued with her speech.

'One piece of evidence you may want to think about is Rose Gilbrook's response to Paul Sadler's call the next day. There is no real disagreement that Rose Gilbrook was so angry she wouldn't listen to anything Sadler said. She told you he wanted to persuade her daughter to withdraw her allegation, yet he could not have known she had made a complaint. He didn't mention the night before. He was asking Rose Gilbrook to pass on a message about his inability to contact Emma as he had said he would because of his shifts. Of course, it is understandable she was angry, but not to jump to the conclusion she did.

What too of her statement that her daughter was a virgin? As we know from the doctor's evidence, that was not the case. Most of us don't discuss our sex lives with our parents, but even so, to assume a twenty-year-old has not had sexual intercourse in today's world seems unusual. Has Emma encouraged that belief? Did Emma want to maintain a mask of innocence? Was that what Emma Gilbrook was afraid of, her mother's anger?'

From defending in many similar case, Cassie believed that jurors looked at their own sexual experiences and compared the events they had heard described in court to their own. Some of the men, she believed, would identify with Sadler and think they had been fortunate not to have a similar allegation made against them. Others, perhaps, had daughters and would want to be as protective towards Emma as they would their own child. There was little she could say to them, but to the women, she could rely on a shared understanding of life. When she addressed them about the issue of consent, she would say there were many situations where we don't want to do something but we agree to it. She often used the example of going to work or doing jury service. Then she would add that the same applied to sexual intercourse where consent is given for many reasons: love, not worth the argument, the easiest way. Inevitably most of the female jurors would nod in agreement.

What was she going to say about Paul Sadler? The prosecution had spoken about the age difference. She continued writing.

'He is twenty-nine. Some years older than Emma, but she was used to having older friends, indeed seemed to prefer them. He had a long-lasting relationship with Linda Callender. Throughout that time, some seven years, they were sexually active, and she says at no time did he force her to have sex. Encouraged, yes, but she was not pressurised into having intercourse when she did not want to. She describes him as loving and affectionate, not the man for her, but she was clear she did not believe he was a rapist.

Paul Sadler's account of the events that evening don't differ very much from those described by Emma Gilbrook. He says at all times throughout that evening he believed she was consenting to sexual activity. Apart from one occasion when she said no, and he stopped, she never told him she did not want to go any further. She says she simply submitted to what he wanted. Is that an accurate description of what was taking place?'

Cassie stopped and read over the paragraphs she had just written. She didn't want to say the young woman had lied, although that was always the implication. Wasn't there room for confusion by the complainant, at one moment not wanting to have intercourse but seconds later physical desire overcoming the reluctance. She didn't think it was possible to say that in her summing up. She had to rely on the way Emma had responded to Sadler's advance. She began typing again.

'She had a number of opportunities to stop Sadler from having intercourse with her. She took off her blouse, folded it and placed it on a chair. She helped him remove those tightly fitting jeans. When he went to get the condom from his jacket pocket in the sitting room, she stayed on the bed. When he struggled to get the condom on, she helped him. And then having had intercourse with him he left to go to the bathroom and she remained on the bed waiting for him to come back. The second time they had intercourse she was on top of him. I have no doubt the learned judge will tell you that people react very differently to the threat of rape, some fight all the way and others simply submit. He will also tell you that some give consent reluctantly. Perhaps confused themselves about what they want in that relationship at that moment. You have to be sure Emma Gilbrook did not give her consent and that Paul Sadler did not believe she was consenting. I submit that Emma Gilbrook was attracted to Paul Sadler, and by her actions that night she indicated she was consenting to having sexual intercourse with him. How could he have believed anything different?

Members of the jury, one final comment. The prosecution bring this case and they must prove it. It is not for Paul Sadler to prove anything. Before you can convict you must be sure Emma Gilbrook did not consent to sexual intercourse with Paul Sadler. If you think she did consent or you think she may have consented then you must find Paul Sadler not guilty of the offence of rape. If you think Paul Sadler believed she was consenting and that belief was not unreasonable, or you think that he may have held such a reasonable belief, then again you must acquit.'

She would then thank the jury for their attention and sit down, hoping she had done enough to persuade them Sadler was innocent.

Before he began his summing up, Judge Tyte addressed Cassie and Hugh. 'I have prepared a summary of the directions I intend to give in this case.' He passed a sheaf of papers to the clerk sitting in front of him. She waved them at the court usher who dashed forward, grabbed the bundle and then handed them to the two barristers.

‘You should have two pages. Do you want time to consider them?’

Hugh Palmer didn’t look at his copy before saying, ‘Yes, My Lord.’ Cassie confirmed she too would like the opportunity to consider the directions.

‘Of course. Fifteen minutes then.’ Judge Tyte trotted off the bench.

Cassie wandered out into the concourse and sat down on one of the leather-cushioned marble benches. Lee came and sat beside her as she read the document.

‘The case you are to try is an allegation of rape. I have already told you to put out of your mind any stereotypes or assumptions you might have. In particular you should bear in mind that there is no one classic response to the trauma of a serious sexual assault.

It is for the prosecution to prove that Emma did not consent to Paul Sadler having sexual intercourse with her and you must decide this issue by looking at all the evidence. When you do so it is important to recognise that the mere fact that Emma took the defendant to her friend’s flat and willingly engaged in kissing him does not mean that she must have wanted to go on to have sexual intercourse and must have consented to it. A person who engages in sexual activity is entitled to choose how far that activity goes and is also entitled to say “No” if the other person tries to go further.

It is not suggested that, before or at the time Sadler had sexual intercourse with Emma, he either threatened her with force or that he used any force upon her, and it is clear Emma did not put up any struggle. It is also common ground that she did not suffer any injury. The defence say that this is because Emma fully consented to what took place. Emma on the other hand gave evidence that when Sadler led her to the bedroom she became frightened and did not know what to do. You will have to resolve this issue by looking at all the evidence, but it is important to recognise that the mere fact that Sadler neither used nor threatened to use any force on Emma and that she did nothing to prevent him from having sexual intercourse with her does not mean she consented to what took place. As I have already said, experience has shown that different people may respond to unwanted sexual activity in different ways. Some may protest and physically resist throughout the event, whilst others may, whether through fear or personality, whilst they did not consent, be unable to do so. It is important to draw a distinction between consent and submission. A person consents to something if, being capable of making a choice and being free to do so, she agrees to it. Consent in some situations may be given enthusiastically, whereas in others it is given with reluctance, but nevertheless it is still consent. But when a person is so overcome by fear that she lacks any capacity either to give consent or to resist, that person does not consent but submits to what takes place. It is for you to say, having considered all the evidence, what the situation was in this case, bearing in mind that it is for the prosecution to prove that Emma did not consent to Sadler having sexual intercourse with her.

If you are satisfied so that you are sure Emma did not consent then you should go on to consider whether Sadler believed she was consenting. If you come to the conclusion that Sadler, as he says he did, believed she was consenting then you should ask yourselves if such belief was reasonable. There is no obligation for him to have taken any specific steps to ascertain consent. Look at the evidence and use your experience of life to decide if that belief was reasonable or may have been reasonable. It is for the prosecution to make you sure he did not reasonably believe she was consenting.'

'Nothing we can complain about there, is there?' Lee said.

'Not really. It's such a thin line between reluctant consent and submission. How can any man be acquitted?' Cassie said.

'But they are. Often.'

'I think jurors rely on their own experiences. If they decide this is a normal courtship routine and it reminds them of their own sexual relationships and how they had begun. Sometimes the media make it seem so black and white when it's really a murky shade of grey, particularly in this type of case.'

She read the directions again. This time she thought about her own background and her failed marriage.

Hugh Palmer had no objections to the directions either, so Judge Tyte had the jury brought into court and summed up the case to them. As he told them what consent meant, Cassie noticed a number of the jury frowning, their brows furrowed. Judge Tyte must have seen that as well because he told them they would have a copy of his legal directions to take to the jury room with them. Cassie didn't think it was the words that confused them; it was wondering how to apply that test to the evidence they had heard.

Once Judge Tyte had finished, Cassie asked for bail for Paul Sadler. 'Within the precincts of the court,' the judge said. Cassie pulled her papers together, leaving them stacked neatly. Out in the concourse, Paul Sadler sat down on one of the marble benches, covered his face with his hands and bent over. Cassie sat beside him. She couldn't tell if he was crying or not. She put her hand on his shoulder and, after a minute or so, he lifted his head.

'What happens now?' he asked.

'We wait.'

'How long?'

'I don't know. I don't think the judge will give them the majority direction before this afternoon.'

A shadow crossed Sadler's face. 'A majority?'

'After the jury have been considering their verdict for over two hours, the judge can tell them that if at least ten of them are agreed on a verdict that's enough. I think this judge will give them longer than that if they don't return a verdict quickly.'

Sadler shook his head and lowered it down towards his knees again. He breathing was irregular and from time to time he shuddered. Cassie remained sitting next to him. She didn't want to leave him alone in such a distressed state. She turned to look along the gallery towards the stairs and the lifts. To her relief she saw Lee walking towards them. Lee could take over chaperoning Sadler while she made some phone calls.

About an hour later she returned to Court 12. Lee was outside the court, sitting on the bench she had vacated, but there was no sign of Sadler. She was about to ask Lee where he was when she heard footsteps behind her. She hadn't seen him as she had made her way along the concourse. He walked, head down, to the end of the gallery, turned and retraced his steps to the other end, turned and headed back in the direction he had just come from.

'He's been doing that for the last half hour,' Lee said.

'I can't imagine what it's like. Your whole life in the hands of twelve men and women who don't really know who you are and what you're like.' Cassie paused. 'Do you have a brother?'

Lee shook her head. 'Do you?'

'No. I have a sister and she has two young sons. I sometimes think how easy it is for a young man to misread a situation and find himself accused of rape. Your life destroyed for a mistake.'

'Men have the power.'

'Do they? Does he?' Cassie nodded towards Sadler still pacing the floor. 'He's quite vulnerable too. From what his ex said, he's had a difficult time. His mother effectively abandoning him. Leaving him with an aunt. Linda Callender thought he was very dependent on her, wanting a permanent relationship too soon.'

'Wanting sex too soon.'

'You were positive he was innocent.'

'I still think that. The beginning of a relationship – it's a difficult time. We've all been there. You want the sex. You're not sure if you should say yes and he'll think you're a slut and never see you again, or you say no and he thinks you're too cold or you don't like him, and you never see him again. In the meantime you're responding to him physically and before you know where you are you're having sex with him and it's too late to stop it.'

'Not just the beginning of a relationship either.'

Cassie's thoughts were interrupted by the usher. 'The jury have asked for sandwiches. Judge Tyte won't take a verdict before two.'

Cassie and Lee interrupted Sadler's pacing and told him nothing would happen until after the luncheon adjournment. Sadler shook his head. 'I couldn't eat anything.'

'Come and have a cup of tea, at least,' Lee said, taking him by the arm and leading him towards the staircase.

Cassie returned to the outside of Court 12 at two. Lee was sitting reading a newspaper and Sadler was slumped next to her. Cassie sat down next to her solicitor. A few minutes later the usher walked towards them. 'Judge Tyte is having the jury back into court.'

'Is there a verdict?' Cassie said.

'I think he wants to give them a majority direction.'

Cassie called Paul Sadler over to the courtroom door. 'The judge has asked for the jury to be brought into court so I think he intends to give them the direction about reaching a majority verdict. You'll have to go back into the dock.'

When Cassie and Hugh were in their seats, Judge Tyte said, 'Mr Palmer, Miss Hardman, I propose giving the jury the majority direction. Do you have anything to say?'

The both said they did not.

Cassie always watched the jury carefully as the direction was given. She wanted to see their reactions; it might provide an indication as to what was going on in the jury room and how close they were to agreeing on a verdict. Sometimes it was obvious that getting ten to agree was just as difficult as getting a unanimous verdict. The oldest of the seven women looked directly at Sadler and shook her head; the woman with the dark curly hair looked puzzled, and the young male with the single earring had lost the grin he'd worn throughout the trial. Only a man in his forties looked down his nose at Cassie. She turned to Lee. 'Looks like it might be a hung jury.'

Outside the courtroom, Sadler was shaking as he asked what the majority direction meant. Cassie explained. 'It's not a simple majority. At least ten must agree.'

‘What happens if they can’t agree?’ said Sadler.

‘The case will be heard again.’

He turned away from her, walked towards the plate-glass window and leant his forehead against it. She heard him weeping. Lee went over, put a hand on his shoulder and led him back to one of the benches in the hall. He sat down, his head in his hands.

About half an hour later, they were called back into court. Cassie watched closely as the jury filed into the jury box. The juror Cassie had named ‘the golden girl’ looked at the dock. Did that mean they would acquit? She considered that a good sign. The clerk stood and asked the foreman to stand. A large man in his fifties had taken the seat at the front of the jury box closest to the judge. He pulled himself to his feet and said they had.

‘Mr Foreman, do you find the defendant guilty of rape or not guilty?’

Cassie held her breath and closed her eyes. It seemed a long time before the foreman said, ‘Not guilty, My Lord.’

There was a cry from the public gallery and the security staff were bundling someone out of the door. It looked like a young man, but Cassie didn’t get a good look at him. She did see DI Crawford stomping out of the courtroom.

Chapter 35

'I'll call the defendant, My Lord. Mr Montgomery, please.' Cassie watched him walk from the dock to the witness box and noticed for the first time that he had a rolling gait as if he were still at sea. He was dressed in a white shirt, a navy jacket and grey trousers, but he had abandoned his tie. Despite his Adam's apple bobbing up and down, he read the words of the oath in a firm voice and an aggressively neutral accent.

Under Cassie's gentle questioning he told the court about the shop and how he'd inherited it. She asked him about the problems he'd had with the young men from the school. He appeared to have taken her advice and stuck to describing the events without being abusive towards his tormentors.

'Let's turn to March third. What time did the boys come into the shop?'

'It must have been soon after three thirty, when school finished.'

'You've told us about youngsters from the school coming into the shop and stealing from you. Had you seen the lads who came into the shop that day before?'

'Oh, yes. I recognised all three, although they may not have all been together before.'

'When they came in the shop, what were you doing?'

'I was standing behind the counter on the telephone, I think, to one of my suppliers.'

‘What did the boys do while you were on the phone?’

‘They started to take down magazines from the top shelf.’

‘What type of magazines?’

‘I think they would be described as … pornographic. Mildly pornographic.’ For the first time Cassie thought he looked a bit sheepish; a bit of humility wouldn’t go adrift with the jury. She glanced towards them and noticed a grin on one of the younger men’s face, before asking her next question.

‘What was your response to them taking the magazines?’

Montgomery had rotated a little in the witness box and was looking at her instead of the jury. She did what Marcus had done and turned away from him so that she was facing the judge and could see both the defendant and the jury with only a slight turn of her head.

‘I told them to put them back. I didn’t say, but I won’t sell them to schoolkids.’

Now Cassie was able to observe the jury, she could get some idea of their reaction to Montgomery’s comments. Some of the women on the jury nodded, she hoped in approval.

‘Did they do what you asked?’

‘No. They started to tear the plastic wrappers off the magazines.’

‘What did you do about that?’

‘I put the phone down and shouted at them. I swore at them.’

'What did you say?' Cassie said. Montgomery hesitated and looked first at her and then at the judge, who said, 'We've all heard the words before so please tell us exactly what you said.'

'I think I called them black bastards and told them to bugger off.'

'Did they leave the shop then?'

'They threw the magazines on the floor. They went to pick up bars of chocolate from the shelves in the middle of the shop.'

'Did they pay for the chocolate?'

'They were in front of the counter, but they didn't offer to pay. They asked for sweets, sweets and cigarettes.'

'Where do you keep the sweets and cigarettes?'

'The fags, cigarettes, are on shelves behind the counter and the sweets are in large jars along the front.'

'If we look at photo three in the bundle does that show the counter?' There was a pause while the jurors shuffled through their papers, found the bundle and opened it. Cassie looked along the two rows and thought they were rather enjoying listening to the defendant. None of them had the blank look they sometimes wore when a case seemed impossible to defend.

'Did you sell them any sweets or cigarettes?'

'I told them as far as the fags, sorry, cigarettes, they were underage and they couldn't have any.'

'Did they accept that you were not going to sell them cigarettes?'

'They said their mother had sent them.'

'Did that make any difference?'

'I have sold cigarettes to underage kids when they have assured me they were buying them on behalf of adults. I know I shouldn't, but, well, some of them do get sent on errands by their parents. This time I said no, I wasn't going to let them have any.'

'What was their reaction to your refusal?'

'They became very abusive. Called me a silly old wanker, stupid. Told me to fuck off. I was shouting at them to get out. I swore at them.'

'Can you remember what you said?'

'Not really, but if they say I called them fucking niggers and black bastards I probably did.'

Cassie heard the slight click of disapproval from James, but she hoped the jury would think her client was being truthful rather than confirming how prejudiced he was. She moved on to her next question.

'Had they moved away from the counter?'

'No, they were right up against it, pushing at it, leaning over. Swearing at me, calling me a wanker and a cunt. Then one of them said I was a paedophile, paedo or pervert. Something like that. I picked up that golf club,' he gestured in the direction of the exhibits table, 'and waved it at them. They moved back and went towards the door but one of them picked up some chocolate, bars of chocolate. I yelled at him to put it back.'

'Did he do that?'

‘They just kept going out of the shop. I went round the counter and followed them towards the door.’

‘Why did you follow them?’

‘I wanted to get the chocolate back and I wanted to make sure they left.’

‘Did you still have the golf club?’

‘I did. They’re big lads. I couldn’t push them out.’

‘Did they leave the shop?’

‘They went outside on the pavement and then stopped and turned towards me. It was then I saw the knife. The one in the middle was holding a knife out towards me. Campbell I think it was.’

‘What did you think was going to happen?’

‘I thought he was going to stab me with it so I swung the golf club and then … it was so fast. I think I caught him and there was a scream. I could still see the knife so I hit out again and as the club came down it hit the one running between me and the lad … the one with the knife. He went down, then this much younger boy came. He bent over. The youngster jumped up and ran at me shouting I’d killed his brother. I ran inside and called an ambulance and the police.’

‘Did you intend to hit Albie Young?’

‘No, I wanted to get the knife out of the other lad’s hand. I didn’t want to hurt anyone.’

Cassie turned round to James seeking assurance there was nothing else to cover with the defendant. He nodded. She thanked Mr Montgomery and told him he would be asked some more questions.

Marcus was already on his feet but Judge Crabtree intervened and said he thought a break would be appropriate. Montgomery was led back to the dock.

'Can you tell him we can't speak to him while he's giving evidence,' Cassie said to Zac.

'I thought he gave his evidence quite well,' said James.

'What did you think the jury made of him?'

'They seemed to understand where he was coming from.'

'A break now may help. The jurors will be considering his evidence and deciding whether they believe him or not. That's why Marcus was anxious to start cross examination. They may have decided he's being truthful so Marcus must make them change their minds. That's harder than while they're still uncertain. But if, under pressure, he starts ranting he'll quickly lose the jury's sympathy and I think Marcus will provoke him into losing it.'

Marcus Pike was clearly relishing the thought of cross examining Montgomery. Cassie could see the glint in his eyes. His lips puckered as if he was holding in the words and the tension as he flicked the pages of his notebook. She watched as he spoke in hushed tones to Robin Tasker. Montgomery was standing in the witness box, his hands gripping the sides. He looked towards her and she smiled at him. She wondered if she had been too strident in her advice about answering Marcus's questions, but she knew how skilfully Marcus would try to provoke him into showing his anger and his dislike of these young men.

'You're still under oath, Mr Montgomery,' Judge Crabtree said.

'Yes, yes, I understand,'

'Right, Mr Pike.'

Marcus stood and looked across the room at the jury, his eyes washing over them as he sought their attention. When they were watching him he turned to the man in the witness box. 'It must be very difficult trying to run a small shop these days, without having young people stealing from you and damaging your stock?'

'It is. The profit margin on these items is so small. I can't afford to lose it, any of it.'

'Are most of your customers children from the school?'

'It depends on the time of day. In the morning I get people on their way to work. They don't want to walk the extra distance to the supermarket. They'll buy cigarettes and sometimes a magazine. Not newspapers really, not now the *Metro* is free.'

'Yes, the free daily. But I guess the supermarkets don't stock the top-shelf magazines, so you make some sales with those?'

'That's right.'

'But later in the day it's the children from St Colombs?'

'Lunchtimes some of them come in and browse round the comics. Buy a Coke – I think they've banned them at school. The younger ones like buying sweets as I can weigh out a couple of ounces for them. Or they buy a bar of chocolate for their dinner.'

'Just like children always did?'

Cassie kept her eyes down on her notebooks and scribbled her own record of the exchange, combining the questions and answers to create a narrative on which she could rely. It was a skill she had acquired over the years and she was very good at getting the essence of the exchanges down on paper. She didn't want to look at either the jury or her client, certainly not her client. Marcus was being sympathetic, lulling Montgomery into letting down his guard. She knew her client would respond to that and would begin to feel comfortable and it was then that Marcus would spring his traps.

'Would it be right to say that you were on edge the moment these boys came into the shop?'

'I thought I recognised them and I assumed they would probably steal or cause some damage. I was watching them closely.'

'You weren't going to throw them out?'

'Not if they behaved themselves.'

'You were prepared to sell them whatever they wanted?'

'Up to a point. I've already said I don't sell top-shelf magazines to anyone under eighteen.'

'Cigarettes – you would sell them cigarettes?'

'I might have sold a single packet on the understanding it was for a parent.'

'Even though they were underage?'

'I've said I did from time to time.'

'So you did, so you did.' Marcus paused and Cassie looked towards him wondering what Marcus was trying to establish.

'You were on the phone when they first came into the shop, but you didn't ring off immediately?'

'I can't remember what the call was about, but I was probably speaking to the people who deliver the magazines. I wanted to get whatever it was sorted out.'

'That was more important than the possible threat from the boys?'

'I was keeping an eye on them. Watching them. Trying to see what they were up to.'

'You were expecting problems from them because they were black?'

Montgomery said nothing, his eyes fixed on Marcus who swivelled round to look at the jury and then turned back to him.

'Isn't that right?'

'That's what you say.'

'What do you say?'

'It's what's happened before.'

'It was while you were on the phone the lads began to misbehave?'

'Yes, they took some magazines from the top shelf. That was when I finished the call and told them to put them back.'

'Did you shout at them?'

'Probably.'

'Shout that they were black bastards?'

'I don't know if I said that straight away but at some time I did. I've had nothing but trouble from these, these black kids, youths. I hoped they would leave the shop, but they threw the books on the floor so I went round to pick them up.'

Cassie turned and said to James in a rather loud whisper, 'Have you got that? Can you underline that passage?' She then looked at the jury; at least some of them had been distracted by her comment.

'The boys had got fed up waiting for you to finish your call and then they asked to be served?'

'Not before they'd damaged some of my stock.'

'They wanted to buy some sweets?'

'Yes, and fags.'

'Cigarettes. You said you'd sold them cigarettes before but on this occasion, you declined to do so. Can you explain why?'

'They'd damaged the books, tearing off the wrappers and throwing them on the ground. They were underage and I knew that they were fibbing when they said they'd been sent by their mum.'

'What made you decide they were telling lies?'

'The time. They'd come straight from school, it seemed unlikely they'd been home, or seen their parents.'

Montgomery was tapping the edge of the jury box, just as Marcus planned, Cassie thought.

'Not because of their colour?'

'Whatever the colour I wouldn't have believed they wanted the cigarettes for their mum or dad.'

'If they had been white, would you have decided they were lying?'

Montgomery paused. 'I think so. It's not happened so I don't know.'

'Are you saying you have not had any problems with the white pupils?'

'Not as often and usually only if they come in with black kids.'

'Let's go back to this incident. At what point did you tell them to leave?'

'When they began to call me names, after I refused to sell them cigarettes.'

'That was when you called them black bastards and niggers?'

'They didn't seem very upset by me swearing at them. They were calling me names. I'd had enough.'

'So you picked up the golf club?'

'They're big lads. Bigger than me. I wanted them out of my shop. They weren't for going, so I thought I'd give them a reason to leave.' Montgomery began to rock backwards and forwards and his hands gripped tightly on the edge of the witness box.

'And they did leave?'

'They got to the door.'

'Outside on the street?'

'They were standing round the door.'

'Were they still swearing at you?'

'No, I don't think they were. But I saw the knife.'

'Were you swearing at them?'

'There was a knife.'

'You were inside the shop. The boys were outside?'

Montgomery stared at Marcus Pike before answering, 'I've said so.'

'One of them with a knife? Are you sure of that?'

'Yes, yes. I'm not a liar.'

'Why not step back into the shop and close the door?'

'Because, because I didn't. I didn't want to give way. I didn't know what they'd do.'

'You didn't want to give way. You wanted to show them who was boss?'

'I thought they might try and rush the door before I could close it.'

'You didn't want to let the niggers, as you would say, have it their way, did you?'

'I just saw the knife.'

'You thought they were black bastards and you were going to deal with them.'

'I don't like them. They are a nuisance, don't work, steal, take drugs, beat people up. I wasn't going to be another one of their victims.' Montgomery was breathing heavily and his eyes looked as if they were popping out of his head.

'So you hit out at them?'

Now Montgomery was red in the face, the knuckles of his clenched hands white. He half raised his fist and leaned forward, as if he was about to punch somebody.

Montgomery closed his eyes and pulled himself up. 'I hit out to get the knife out of the lad's hand. I did not want to be stabbed by him. There were three of the black bastards. I wanted to make sure they didn't get to me.'

'You could have closed the door and telephoned for the police?'

'By the time the police arrived, they'd have scarpered.'

'That was what you wanted, wasn't it? They would go away?'

'I wanted them to leave. I wasn't going to turn my back on them.'

'Why not back away from them and then close the door?'

'I didn't think of that. I don't know.'

'You were angry, weren't you? Very angry?'

Montgomery said nothing.

Marcus continued, 'You saw what you thought was a knife, but instead of stepping back and closing the door, you struck out at them? You were swinging that golf club around, hitting out. You didn't care who you hit. Wanted to teach them a lesson. Wasn't that what happened?'

Montgomery leaned forward and glared at Marcus. 'I thought I was going to get hurt. That's what people like them do. Use a knife on anyone who gets in their way. That's why I swung the golf club. It was me or them.'

Marcus had changed tack with Montgomery. For some reason, Cassie wasn't sure why, he thought the jury would believe Loveday had a knife, so he was concentrating on the reasons for the defendant striking out and whether he could have escaped being hurt by retreating into the shop.

She decided not to re-examine Montgomery; he had stood up well to Marcus's questioning. The case would turn on whether the jury thought her client had acted in self-defence.

Chapter 36

Judge Crabtree adjourned after Montgomery had given evidence. Cassie went back to the Temple to wait for the chambers meeting to begin. While she waited, she sorted out her post and tried to tidy her desk. A telephone call from Alex annoyed her; she wasn't an informer. She returned a few unwashed mugs to the kitchen, shredded a number of papers and put some receipts in a file for her accountant, but her mind wandered to the reason for Richard calling all the tenants together. Their Head of Chambers was not known for his interest in the views of the more junior members; he had always considered the set of rooms they rented, the clerks and the rest of the barristers, his own personal fiefdom. Nor was he particularly concerned about the efficiency of the clerking team. Had he finally realised, over the last few weeks, the murmurings about the collection of fees had risen to a crescendo? Did he know or care that the squeeze on Legal Aid had resulted in a sharp decline in incomes, particularly for the more junior members? Then there was disquiet about the distribution of work. Cassie knew she was lucky; Jack seemed able to secure some good cases for her. Some of the other female tenants didn't do so well. Some were keen to expand their work into different and more lucrative areas than crime; barristers doing Legal Aid work weren't called 'the worthies' for nothing. But Cassie loved the courtroom, the preparation for cross examination, composing and delivering speeches to the jury. Acting as she saw it for the individual against the might of the state. She wanted to continue doing that kind of work. She appreciated Jack's efforts on her behalf. She knew he hoped she would apply for and become Queen's Counsel. She was ambitious and she did want to take Silk. There were downsides to being elevated to one of Her Majesty's counsel; being sent to different courts all over the country sometimes for weeks or months on end was one. She knew it interfered with marriages and family life, but unless she and Ben …

Stephen stuck his head round the door. 'I think Jack's a bit pissed off about this meeting. He's wandering around downstairs like he's lost his wallet. Eleanor suggested he went home and he plonked down at his desk and told her that as she was grumbling about fees, he had decided to check on whether there was something wrong with the accounts process.'

'On a Friday night?'

'Quite, he's usually in the Cheshire by now, crowing over how much work he's brought into chambers. Anyway, this meeting is about to start. Coming?'

Cassie picked up her handbag and followed Stephen to the library.

Richard Jago was pouring out the Champagne when Cassie and Stephen wandered into the already crowded room. Stephen leant towards Cassie and whispered, 'Amazing what the offer of champers will dig out of the woodwork.'

Cassie grimaced, pushing her way to the other side where she had spotted a vacant chair. She leant back against the library shelves and looked round. Stephen was right – nearly every tenant was there, including Oscar Davenport. Cassie was troubled by what she had seen in the Devereux Arms the week before. She was sure Roger had given Oscar something else besides a brief. She turned her attention to the Head of Chambers.

'Right, I think we can begin. Has everyone got a drink? Now, I've heard some of you are troubled by the delay in fees being paid,' Richard said. There was a murmur as a number of tenants signified their agreement. 'I've spoken to Jack and he tells me he believes the problem lies with the Legal Aid.'

'It isn't just Legal Aided work. I've got a couple of private cases,' said Eleanor.

'That's down to the solicitors and we all know what they're like. Hang on to the money as long as they can,' Richard said.

Someone said, 'The same goes for the government.' At that a chortle rippled round the room.

Eleanor looked round and scowled before shaking her head. 'If we don't get paid it impacts on the payment of rents and Jack's percentage. Then there's VAT and tax bills to pay as well.'

'I haven't heard Jack grumbling about not getting paid.' Richard remained largely unruffled.

Eleanor snapped back, 'That's because he gets so much he doesn't notice if he hasn't had a few hundred.'

Richard smoothed the leg of his Savile Row dark grey suit, but he showed no other sign of concern, as Eleanor continued to argue. Suddenly a large number of the tenants were speaking at the same time, some of the them supporting Eleanor about the fees. One or two said chambers should be discussing the development of their practices.

'What are you suggesting. Do you want to replace Jack as our clerk and if so, who is to be clerk in his place?' Richard said.

The room went silent and then Eleanor said, 'We can't afford to go on paying such a large percentage to him.'

'He contributes to the expenses, particularly the other clerks,' Richard said.

'A fees clerk who doesn't chase our fees. Or are they sitting in chambers' account?'

Richard was unruffled. 'Do we want to replace Jack? I know he will not accept a reduction in his percentage.' He was right to be confident; although a number of Cassie's colleagues agreed with Eleanor, no one wanted to change the clerking arrangements or cause a rift in the set. 'Right now we've settled that. Drugs. As some of you may know, it appears that a wrap of, I think, cocaine, was brought into chambers some weeks ago. We don't know who did that, indeed it may not have been any tenant or member of staff, but I do not want to hear of this happening again. Anyone caught with any drugs in chambers will be forced to relinquish his or her tenancy. Now, unless there is anything else …' There was a momentary silence and then everyone began talking except for Oscar who left immediately. Richard picked up a bottle of wine and began filling the glasses of those closest to him.

As the meeting broke up both James and Stephen asked Cassie if she wanted to join them for a drink in the Devereux Arms.

‘Not tonight, I’ve things to do.’ When she saw the disbelief in their faces, she added, ‘Seriously, I wouldn’t be very good company.’

As she left the entrance to 3 Burke Court and was about to turn right towards Fleet Street, she saw the figure of a man standing by the covered archway alongside Brick Court. His collar was up, partially hiding his face. The lighting was dim in Middle Temple Lane, but something about his posture made her think he was waiting for someone. She paused and continued to peer into the dark trying to discern the face, but he moved back further into the shadows towards Middle Temple Hall, as if he had seen her observing him. It crossed her mind that the unknown male had been waiting for her and that he must be Malcolm Delaney, but the figure made no move towards her. She wanted to run, but instead turned back north and quickened her pace to the gate at the top of the lane, listening for footsteps in case she was followed. The large wooden gates, open during the day, were closed so she moved to the side, under the jetted upper floor of the gents’ outfitters and out of sight of anyone standing in the main thoroughfare, opened the pedestrian gate and stepped out of the eighteenth century and into the lights and noise of twenty-first century London.

Within minutes of getting home, Cassie's mobile pinged the arrival of an email. She pulled the phone from her bag and looked at the message.

'*Have a good weekend before I come looking for you!! Delaney*'

Chapter 37

Alex didn't wake up until 10 a.m. She felt groggy after three nights with very little sleep. She wouldn't have come to then but for her mobile ringing. She reached out for the phone on her bedside table and squinted at the screen. The call was from her father.

'I thought you might like to come and have lunch with me some time. Now the flat is furnished.'

'I'd love to, but I'm really tied up at the moment.'

'Are you alright?'

'We've been on surveillance for three days and I haven't had much sleep.'

'What about the weekend? Saturday.'

'That sounds fine. You'll send me the address? Text.'

'Of course. See you then about noon.'

Before she could say anything else the line went dead. There was no point in trying to contact Cassie at this hour, she would be in court.

She waited until five before ringing Cassie. 'I'm very sorry about this. The guvnor has asked me to …'

'To what?'

'Do you have Oscar Davenport's telephone numbers? Home and mobile.'

'Why? What do you need them for?'

'Do you have them?'

'Alex, I'm not giving out the contact details of other members of chambers.'

'I know it seems disloyal, but it would help our investigations into the source of the drugs Hales had.'

'Are you suggesting he got them from Oscar, or ...'

'Look, you said you'd been told the drugs came from an address in Cotburn Mews. That is right. And Davenport lives there.'

'What are you saying? I don't imagine for one moment Oscar would be involved in the supply of drugs, or indeed use them.'

'Last night a van containing over two kilos of coke drove into the mews. The driver and his mate have been arrested. Now it's probably just a coincidence but as we were moving away from the scene Davenport came to the door of his cottage.'

'I'm sure it was a coincidence.'

'We need to eliminate him from our enquiries ...'

'You want to check his phone numbers against those on the suspects' mobiles?'

'Exactly. We can get them from the usual channels but that will take some time and we may have to arrest your friend.'

Cassie said nothing.

'Cassie, Cassie are you there?'

'I'll think about it. I'll have to find the list of numbers in chambers. I don't have it with me. And I have a meeting this evening. You'll have to wait.'

There was silence. Cassie had terminated the call.

Alex rang the station and asked to speak to DCI Saltburn. She told him she had failed to get the information he wanted. 'But I have another idea,' she said.

Back home she dressed in her black leathers and rode her Ducati to the Temple. It was a fine summer's evening and the roads weren't too busy going east. She zoomed along the Bayswater Road, round Marble Arch and down Park Lane. She had to slow up at Hyde Park Corner but she was enjoying riding her bike, something she hadn't been able to do for some time. Her last free day she'd gone to have lunch with her mother and didn't dare turn up in her leathers. Constitution Hill was quiet and then, just for fun, she went twice around the statue of Victoria before navigating Birdcage Walk, into Parliament Square and on to the Embankment. As she was parking her bike in Arundel Street, she searched her memory for the pubs and wine bars Cassie had spoken about. She didn't pay at the meter; if she was booked she'd get the DCI to fix it. She took off her helmet and let her blonde hair fall loose.

The first pub she came to was the Cheshire Cheese. The bar was small and she didn't recognise any of the drinkers, so she walked up Milford Lane towards Fleet Street. A little way east along the Strand and facing the Church of St Clement Danes was Daley's Wine Bar. It was very busy and it took Alex a little time to check the person she was looking for wasn't there. A man dressed in the dark suited uniform of a lawyer tried to speak to her, but she sidestepped him and left.

She didn't know where to go from there. Further down Essex Street she could see the sign of The Edgar Wallace. She walked towards it, peeked inside but again there was no one she recognised. The Edgar Wallace was on the corner of Essex Street and an alleyway, Little Essex Street. At the entrance to the pedestrian walkway she could see another public house. She walked towards it. The sign swinging above the door identified it as the Devereux Arms. She stepped inside, looked around and standing at the bar clutching a pint glass was someone she recognised, Stephen Burnett. He looked towards her and smiled. Then he pushed through the crowd towards her. 'Alex Seymour, isn't it?'

She nodded. He asked her if he could get her a drink. 'Soda and lime, please.' She looked at her leathers.

'Sure.'

Once they both had a glass in their hands he motioned her towards a table that had just become vacant. 'You ride a bike?'

'A Ducati 848.'

'Nice.'

'Do you?'

'No. Not my thing. Prefer something less exposed to the elements. Anyway, what brings you here? Seeing counsel in a case?'

'No, actually I was hoping to meet Oscar.' She hadn't meant to say that; it implied she had arranged to meet him. She hadn't anticipated

Stephen Burnett being there when, and if, she saw Davenport. She had hoped to make their meeting accidental.

'Oscar. I didn't know you knew him.'

'I met him when I was here a couple of weeks ago. I spoke to Cassie about …'

'Roger and the great drug mystery.' Stephen sat back and tipped his chair onto its back legs. Alex suddenly felt uncomfortable. He was scrutinising her, trying to assess her and what she did or didn't know. Suddenly he let the chair down with a crack. 'Well, here he is.' Alex turned and across the room she saw Oscar Davenport.

Stephen Burnett called out, 'Oscar.'

Davenport acknowledged them, got himself a drink and came over to their table.

'You know Detective Constable Alex Seymour, I gather, a friend of Cassie's.'

'We met on the stairs a couple of weeks ago,' Oscar said. Alex felt flustered as he studied her.

Stephen looked from one to the other. 'Ok, well, I'll be on my way then.' He finished his beer in one and left them.

Oscar pointed to the chair Stephen had vacated. 'Can I sit here?' He put his glass of wine down and sat facing her. 'Now, why are you here? Not meeting Cassie, I assume.'

'I remembered seeing you two weeks ago and then yesterday …'

'Yesterday?'

'We've been keeping observation in Cotburn Mews. You live there. You were at the door of your house.'

'I wondered why someone was parked up in the street. So why come here?'

Alex smiled. Oscar leant forward, put his hand on her leg and stroked her inner thigh. She didn't try to stop him.

'Neutral ground,' she said.

'You spoke to Cassie about the wrap our junior clerk was caught with?'

'Do you know anything about it?'

'Why should I?'

'We arrested two men last night delivering two kilos of coke to the print shop. It was one thirty in the morning. You came out into the street.'

'And you think I'm involved. There's no way I'd get mixed up in anything like that.'

'I hope not.' Alex took hold of his hand and ran a finger round his wrist. 'I hope not.'

'Why don't we go somewhere a little more private? Your place or mine?'

'I live just off Kensington Park Road. Why don't you meet me there? Then I can get out of these.' Alex pointed to her leathers.

Oscar said he had to go back to chambers to collect some papers and then he would get a taxi. She gave him her address.

'Just in case there are any problems, give me your mobile number.' She took out her phone and entered the number he gave her. Once she was back at her bike she called DI Saltburn.

It was a warm evening and the motorcycle outfit had made her hot. She hadn't intended to go back to her flat, but when he had touched her she had felt a shiver run through her body. Oscar Davenport was an attractive man, but he was a suspect in the supply of contaminated drugs. She decided to keep the assignation and once she got home she had a quick shower pulled on a pair of jeans and a white T-shirt, and sprayed her neck and wrists with her favourite perfume, Jo Malone's Basil and Lime. She was unsure of what she wanted from him. She poured herself a large glass of whisky.

Oscar turned up a short while later. He was carrying a large holdall. 'I've not come to stay.' He dropped it onto the floor in the hallway. 'Robes.'

Alex ushered him into the living room and asked if he wanted a drink. He indicated her glass and said he'd have the same. As she poured the whisky, he wandered round the room.

'What made you join the Met?'

'I wanted to do something different. Thought it might be exciting.'

'But it isn't?

'Sometimes. Definitely when Cassie Hardman is involved.'

'Ah yes, our Cassie.' He put on a faint Lancashire accent.

'You don't like her?'

'I don't really know her. We don't mix in the same circles.'

'At work?'

‘I’ve never co-defended with her. She has a reputation for being a fighter. Jack, our clerk, likes her and he’s pushing her to take Silk.’

‘Will she?’

‘She probably should but it’s a bit of a lottery. Anyway, I don’t want to talk about her. Tell me about you. What about before you became a police officer?’

‘There’s not much to say, private school in Ascot. I’m not academic, so university wasn’t for me. I spent a year or so travelling. India, Thailand and then Australia. I didn’t want an office job. I’d learnt to ride a bike in Oz. Loved it. Joining the Job seemed obvious. And you?’

‘Boarding school, Oxford, the Bar. Following in Father’s footsteps. Not enough of a rebel.’

‘Not what you wanted to do?’

‘I can’t think of anything else. Not everyone loves being a barrister like Cassie.’

‘You didn’t want to talk about her.’

‘No, I don’t. I can think of better things to do.’

He sat down on the sofa and stretched out a hand. She let him pull her closer.

‘Mind my drink,’ she said.

He took the glass from her, placed on the side table next to his own and then he drew her towards him.

The next morning when Alex woke up, Oscar Davenport was stretched out naked next to her. She admired his slim muscular body as she recalled how turned on she had been last night. She slid out of bed, pulled on her dressing gown and went into the kitchen. Her mobile was on the work surface. She checked her email and messages. There was one from Mel Haskins asking her to call and a text from Cassie saying she had received another email from her stalker. She had to persuade Cassie to report the harassment. She filled the kettle and leaned back. She was pouring water into a teapot when Oscar came into the room with a towel wrapped round his waist.

'That can wait,' he said, slipping his hand round her breast and letting the towel fall to the floor.

After they had made love again, Alex got up, went to her wardrobe and selected a pair of black trousers and a grey silk shirt.

'I'm having lunch with my father. He's just moved into a flat near Nine Elms.'

'And your mother?'

'She's living in Richmond, Ham actually. They're separating.'

'Bad news?'

'It's been on the cards for a while, ever since …'

'Since?'

'My brother was killed in a skiing accident five years ago.'

'The man in the photograph on your dressing table.'

'We were close. We all miss him.'

Oscar dressed while they were talking. Alex took out a lipstick, looked into the mirror and began to paint her lips. Oscar came to stand behind her and placed his hands on her shoulders. 'We must do this again.'

Her father's flat was on the tenth floor of a high-rise block. She stood on the rooftop terrace, a glass of Champagne in her hand, and watched a barge carrying the contents of city rubbish bins edging its way downriver towards the Houses of Parliament.

'Like it?' her father said.

'Great. The panorama is amazing. Big Ben, St Pauls, the Eye and the Shard. Still, I prefer …' Her mobile buzzed at her. She checked the screen and tapped to accept the call. 'Mel, sorry I didn't call back.'

'That's ok. I thought you'd like to know Davenport made a couple of calls to one of the guys we arrested last night.'

She closed her eyes. 'Thanks, thanks for letting me know.'

'We arrested him this morning, as he got home. Spent the night somewhere and by the smile on his face he got his leg over. The governor thought you might want to be in on the interview.'

'It's difficult.' She turned away from her father. 'I can't talk now. Family problems …'

'Anything the matter?' her father said.

She put her hand over the phone. 'Work colleague. Won't be long.' Then to Haskins, 'Let me know what he says. He won't cough, will he? He knows the law.'

Mel laughed. 'Bit of evidence to explain.'

Alex's father took the glass from her hand and repeated, 'Anything the matter?'

She shook her head. 'I'll speak to you later,' she said as she ended the call. And then to her father, 'No, Dad, I'm fine. Just something's come up at work. But let's have that lunch. Did I see some lobster in the fridge?'

Her father put his arm around her shoulder and led her back downstairs into the living room.

After lunch Alex made her way back to her own flat and made some tea. She sat holding the mug in her hands, wondering what she was going to do. If the DCI found out she'd spent the night in bed with a man they were investigating as a possible drug dealer she would be out of the force. What had Oscar said to her boss? Would he have told him about them having sex? She was sure he would not admit being involved in the supply of the contaminated drugs. After several minutes she plucked up the courage to ring Chris Dundy.

'Where've you been?' he said.

'At lunch with my father. I gather Davenport's been arrested.'

'Arrested and released.'

'Interviewed?'

'Sort of. The boss was told to lay off. So he asked Davenport why he was out in the street when the drugs were delivered to the print shop. He said he lives there and was up late working on a case when he heard the noise and went to have a look.'

'And the telephone calls?'

‘He buys from time to time. Everyone on the street knows they supply good stuff.’

‘We can’t prove anything else.’

‘I don’t think we’re going to try. The guvnor is furious, but …’

Alex let herself breathe more slowly. She hoped Oscar wouldn’t contact her again, but already she knew it was what she wanted.

Chapter 38

Cassie had difficulty sleeping, the Sadler trial haunting her. She got up early and walked to Portobello Market, not the southern end where the stallholders would be setting up their pitches. The antique stalls and shops were for the tourists and wouldn't be really humming until later. Instead she made her way to the section of the street where fruit and vegetables were stacked up for sale. She made a few purchases – strawberries, olives and bread. As she wandered along the street a voice called her name and she looked round. Standing by his stall was a man she knew as Sammy and he was holding out a bunch of rosemary. 'For remembrance,' he said.

She felt herself blush; he had been kind to her in the past and she frequently bought vegetables and herbs from him, but today she was so wrapped up in her own thoughts she had forgotten to seek him out. Sammy was still wearing a dirty green Barbour with a brown corduroy collar over his bulky figure.

'Sammy, how are you?'

'Bit better now it's warmer.' He held up his hands, the fingers twisted with arthritis. Cassie looked at his weather-stained face, his grey hair and the eyes which had a roguish twinkle. 'But you're looking a bit down in the mouth. Witness problems again?'

'You could say that, but …' She shook her head. 'Nothing I can do. I'm not hunting for an alibi witness this time.' While she was speaking a man with a small child came to the stall and Sammy turned his attention to his customer, pushing the rosemary towards her.

'Thanks, I need to get on.' She walked away quickly; she didn't want to explain to Sammy what was going on.

A couple of hours later she was back in her flat with nothing to do for the rest of the day.

She pulled her blue notebook from the library shelf by her desk and leafed through the pages, looking for the notes she had taken of Emma Gilbrook's evidence. The page began with Emma's name underlined and then the numeral '*20*', her age. She had written a description: '*Innocent, pale, no make-up, scraped-back ponytail.*'

The difference from the woman Sadler had photographed in the restaurant was extreme. She could have been fifteen. Without eyeliner or lipstick she had looked irreproachable. Asking her questions about her behaviour with Sadler had seemed almost like sacrilege, but she had to do that. She was relieved that the screens protecting Emma Gilbrook from her client had prevented him from seeing her. Cassie knew he would have been livid at what he would have seen as a deliberate deception. At least she had been able to get copies of the photograph for the jurors. They showed a different Emma Gilbrook; one whose eyes sparkled with laughter, whose make-up enhanced her natural beauty, and whose hair was loose and curled across her forehead.

She began to read the summary. She was sure she had not asked any questions that were not necessary. She hadn't needed to cross examine about Emma's previous sexual history. She tried to remember the questions she had asked. Her notes were very sparse; it was hard writing when one was standing and asking questions.

First Meeting – talk music – work – clothes. Light-hearted.

Second Meeting – work again –that week's incidents. Physical contact – held hand crossing road. Kiss on cheek said goodbye. + kissed on lips few times.

Looking forward to dinner, enjoyed company, made me laugh.

Not nervous – didn't want to have sex.

Then Cassie had noted a change in Emma's demeanour. *Stiffened.* She remembered that she had asked Emma if she found the defendant attractive and she had said, 'Most women would.' There had been a ripple of laughter in the courtroom, quickly squashed by a frown from the judge.

There was a name written down which Cassie couldn't read, but it was the name of one of the jurors. The juror, a pretty woman with a kind of golden glow to her round cheeks, had smiled at the defendant prompting Cassie to make the note. It was a reminder to make eye contact with her and try to establish some rapport.

The next thing she had recorded was *No change in behaviour – good time. Lovely meal.*

Cassie knew the restaurant Emma and Sadler had gone to. It was usually crowded and noisy – not the sort of place one would choose if the aim of the date was seduction.

Suggested friend's flat – wanted continue – not for sex.

Thought Anita there – not surprised when not. Had key.

If there have coffee – if not I'd make coffee.

Cassie remembered Emma had said something about knowing where the coffee was and that had caused another outburst of laughter. Emma became upset, blinking, tears beginning to roll down her cheek.

The notes continued. *May have said Anita would be out.*

Not sure why went into bedroom — hold of hand. Pulling a little. Could have refused. Didn't say anything. Afraid? Not sure.

That section was heavily underscored. To Cassie it had been a turning point in the case. If she wasn't afraid of Sadler, why had she let him lead her into the bedroom? Why not say she didn't want to go with him or say something to show what she thought.

Kissed him. Thought no further. Didn't say no.

Didn't get up when went for condom. Don't know why not.

Helped with condom. Knew going to happen – protection.

That had been a difficult moment. If Cassie remembered correctly Emma had not answered her question at first. Had she blushed? Bitten her lip? It didn't matter … the jury would draw their own conclusions.

Had sex again. Could have got up. Didn't.

Didn't know what to do. Held my arms and rolled me over on top. No bruising.

Afterwards got dressed.

Anita came. Introduced them. Chatted for a few minutes. May have been fifteen. Paul said at work first thing.

Didn't say anything to Anita. Embarrassed – at her flat when she not there.

Went home – bed. Overslept. Mum cross – angry. Not the first time – missed work.

Mum rang police when told her.

Cassie could picture Emma Gilbrook as the young woman standing in the witness box, her eyes wide like an animal caught in headlights. She didn't enjoy cross examining her. It brought back memories of her ex-husband Tony. Not that the incident had been the reason for her leaving him, but it had been the precipitating factor. She had not reported it to the police, not least because although she was certain she did not want to have sex with him, she wasn't sure whether she had consented or not. If she wasn't sure, then how could a jury be. He would have said he believed she had consented and she had come to the conclusion he would be believed. So often their arguments, and there had been a lot of them, had ended with Tony, holding her in his arms, nuzzling her neck, kissing her and telling her to stop arguing. She would struggle with him, hitting his chest with her hands and saying no, but always she had given in to him, it was easier.

Further, if he had been convicted he would have been sentenced to six or seven years in prison and she didn't want that. She didn't hate him that much.

She was lost in her memories when the phone rang. 'What did you think about the meeting last night?' Stephen said when she answered.

'I thought it got a bit acrimonious at times, but nobody wants a split in chambers, and as soon as the money comes in again, it will settle down.' She paused. 'Although I do think we should be looking at our expenses more carefully.'

'I know you get on with Jack, but some members of chambers don't get the same service as you do. He sees you getting Silk so he's supportive, gets you good work.'

'Stephen, I know that, but I don't think I'm in a position to do anything. What happens really is down to Richard and Eleanor. My guess is they'll sort something out in the next few weeks. Eleanor is very good at getting her own way and Richard will have sensed the mood in chambers is for some changes.'

'And the warning about the drugs.'

'He couldn't say much more, could he?'

'Nobody seemed surprised.'

'I guess not. I suppose too many use recreational drugs for it to shock. Apart from me.'

'Getting old, Cassie. Out of touch.'

'Maybe.'

After lunch, a salad of spinach leaves, blue cheese and toasted walnuts tossed in a vinaigrette of balsamic vinegar and olive oil, she wanted to leave work behind her. Looking out, she could see the sky was the bright metallic blue of a hot afternoon. She thought about the domestic chores and decided she wasn't going to do any of them, not even cook. She would go out to Kensington Gardens, take a book and spend the rest of the day doing nothing. She was determined not to think about the Sadler case anymore. He had pleaded not guilty, she had represented him as any other barrister would, she had cross examined the witnesses with skill and consideration, perhaps more sensitively than many; the verdict was the responsibility of the jury, not her.

She returned home in the late afternoon and turned on her computer with the intention of downloading a film for the evening. As she searched through for something she wanted to watch, a pop-up notified her Ben was online and a few moments later she heard the ring of the Skype programme. She accepted the call and the screen came to life with Ben smiling at her.

'How's things?' he said.

'Fine.'

'I've been trying to contact you for a few days.'

'I know, but I've been very busy working. The Montgomery trial is really hard. He's so difficult. I'm having to spend too much time controlling my temper, but it's nearly over. And then the time difference gives such a short window to make calls to the States.'

Ben's face showed he thought she was making excuses, but she wasn't going to apologise.

'We've got speeches and summing up left before the jury goes out. And, well, if he goes down then I've done my best.'

'Will he?'

'He shouldn't, but you never know. He's such an unlikeable character. I frightened the life out of him before he gave evidence and he got through it without making any major boobs.'

'Are you still having problems with the guy harassing you?'

She bit her lip. 'I got an email last night.' She didn't tell him the sender had threatened to come looking for her.

Ben took a deep breath. 'Look, Cassie, I know it's a bore, but I think you need to change all your passwords. I think this guy's hacked your computer. Some of the people here are real techies and they were talking about something called ratting. It stands for remote access technology. It's the same thing you get with a help line for software. I've done that, said I couldn't get something to work, and they ask to take control of your computer. Quite a number of trustworthy companies in IT do it, but similar programmes are available on the dark web for free.'

'And that gives access to my computer?'

'Whoever wants to control your computer sends an email which is obviously spam. You delete it and that sets off a worm that lets the hacker take control of the computer remotely. You've not noticed any changes in the way it's working, have you?'

'No. I don't think so.' She frowned and her voice trembled.

'No emails deleted? They were there and then they've gone.'

She shook her head. 'No, no. Nothing like that.'

'It sounds like he's using your email account to find out what you're doing and your interests. You're very easy to find online – chambers' website, legal directories. I had a quick look and found quite a few sites that could have given a stalker enough to hack into your email account …'

'Do you really think so? It's supposed to be secure so that I can get the documents from solicitors.'

'That's maybe what's limiting what he can do. I guess that software is harder to get into and he can't do that.'

'He knows I like Lowry paintings. And when I went to the shop the defendant owns …'

'That's what they do. It's an intrusion into your life. It's the same as trolling. Needs similar technical skills and a similar pathology. My guess is you've looked at some paintings on the computer, or had an email about the artist?'

Cassie looked away from the screen and felt her face pucker up. 'Amanda's been to see the exhibition at the Lowry Centre. Oh, and I did look at one of the auction houses. Can I stop it?'

'I'm not sure. Change the password on all your accounts and see if that stops him. You may have to disconnect your computer from the internet and get an IT expert to see what's going on. But try the password route first.'

'Right. I'll do that. It's going to take ages.'

'Try not to worry too much. There's not much you can do over the weekend.'

'I guess not.' She tried to smile. 'Anyway, how are you? Missing me?'

Ben paused and she could see he was looking for the right words, the downside of video calls.

'Like you, in the gaps between work.'

She let her breath out and they chatted for a few minutes before she said she needed to start on changing her passwords. Before she went into the settings window, she looked at her emails. There was another one from Delaney. Just one word.

'*Bitch.*'

Notting Hill Gate Tube Station

She was standing on the right of the escalator: a young woman, probably about twenty years old. She didn't notice the crazy frieze along the walls, a strip cartoon of journeys to outer space, strange figures with antennae on their head, and the message 'Beware of spaceships'. Her eyes were looking inward at something no one else could see. The updraft from the platforms caught her floral print dress, white and yellow daisies on a blue background, and the hem drifted upwards; she didn't try to hold it down and it settled back in place around her knees.

Once off the first escalator she walked past the tourists on their leisurely way to London's heart and joined the throng of workers heading for the City and the West End. The large white handbag she carried hit the shoulder of a woman who was pointing out a poster for the production of *Thriller* at the Lyric Theatre. She didn't apologise, even though the other woman swung round and rubbed her shoulder.

The east-bound platform of the Central Line was all hustle and bustle: males in suits, shirt necks unbuttoned, women wearing colourful cotton dresses. They moved around like flocks of birds as they looked for a little extra space and hoping to find a place where the doors of a not-over-full carriage might stop. On the walls of the tunnel there were large cinema-screen-sized posters. One carried the logo of a well-known bank, another had a photograph of vegetables. Further along was a picture of a can of beer and then the red and white of a mobile phone operator. The waiting commuters were more interested in their own mobiles or copies of the *Metro* than the advertisements. The woman made her way along the platform towards the western end of the tunnel from where the train would emerge. The time on the information panel was 08:33:04.

A man in the striped trousers of a lawyer or restaurant manager got in her way and she pushed past without saying anything. She was nearly crushed against the wall by a very tall young man, blond, probably Scandinavian, carrying a large rucksack who stepped back into her path. He apologised but she didn't acknowledge him. A woman with a child dressed in a school uniform of brown gingham rushed past the woman in the floral dress and the white handbag caught the child in the face. The little girl began to cry. 'Look where you're going,' the mother said. There was no reply and the mother didn't pursue her complaint; the woman's eyes were unresponsive as if she had not seen them.

When she reached the end of the platform the woman stopped and looked back towards the indicator panel which displayed the length of time before the next train arrived. There were three trains on the panel; the first one was due in one minute and was for Epping, the second a minute later was for Stratford. The third was due in six minutes. The time was now shown as 08:34:49.

As the front of the first train arrived at the end of the tunnel and began to brake, the woman moved forwards but the six-inch heel of her bright blue right shoe caught on one of the studded tiles. As she stumbled an overweight man in a navy suit caught her elbow and pulled her back from the track. 'Don't want you going in front of a train, do we?' he said. She stared at him and shook her head. The man let go of her arm and moved away, his lips pursed. The train stopped and when the doors opened a group of tourists chattering in French got off and pushed past the woman. She dropped back towards the tunnel wall, letting the doors close and the train leave the station. The time on the information display was 08:35:13.

The platform began to fill again and a young woman carrying a multi-coloured striped holdall was on the left-hand side of the woman. Slightly behind her and to her right was a young male who admired the slim figure in the daisy print dress. The train for Stratford appeared at the entrance to the platform and the woman stepped forward off the platform into its path. She rose in the air like a high jumper about to flop over a bar. The blue dress cascaded around her and vanished under the train. Her handbag somersaulted along the track, spilling some of its contents onto the platform. The sound of the brakes squealing in anguish as the driver brought it to a halt began to impact on the waiting passengers. There was a smell of burning as the wheels ground along the track. The train stopped. There was silence. Then someone screamed. The time on the digital display was 08:36:40.

The screaming rose and fell before turning into a muffled sob as station staff dashed along the platform. The crowds of commuters pressed themselves even tighter together and moved towards the passageway out of the tunnel. The doors of the train opened and those inside huddled together as they stepped onto the platform. Some looked back as they made their way out of the station, but most kept their eyes averted. The woman with the multi-coloured holdall saw a black-and-gold coloured wallet on the ground. She picked it up and opened it. Inside was a credit card with the name Emma Gilbrook embossed on it.

Chapter 40

It was Monday morning and the final days of the Montgomery trial were in front of Cassie – just speeches and summing up – then the jury would retire to consider their verdict. If he was convicted she'd let James do the plea in mitigation.

She set off for Notting Hill Gate Tube station. The sunny weather encouraged her to walk at a leisurely pace rather than scurrying. She checked her watch; she had plenty of time. She strolled along Pembridge Road past pastel-painted terraced cottages, and then, as she got closer to Notting Hill Gate, a couple of retro clothes shops and one selling vintage records. One of the second-hand shops sold handbags cast off by their wealthy owners, which carried such prestigious names they were far too expensive, despite their battered appearance, for her to consider buying. She peered into the window in the hope something might be within her budget. There was nothing. In front of her was the Gate Picture House; it was the cinema she and Ben went to if they fancied seeing a film. He was returning from his trip to the States and she knew the time was fast approaching when she would have to make a decision about their future.

As she got nearer to the junction she noticed a number of police cars and ambulances stationary in the road around the entrances of the Tube station. She sighed and quickened her pace; she just knew the Underground was closed. She swore under her breath, annoyed that she had loitered along the way. She checked her watch; it was already nine fifteen. She would have to try and get a taxi, although she would be lucky if she did. She wasn't the only commuter looking for an alternative way to get to work, and most of them were trying to hail a cab. Taxi after taxi sped by but none with their yellow lights on. She began to walk towards Queensway, hoping she was wrong and she'd be able to find a cab. A tall man about her age caught up with her and as he drew level asked her in a polished accent if she was going in the direction of the City. When she replied she was, he suggested they stopped and waited for a moment or two to see if they could get a cab. 'We can watch both directions,' he said. They waited on the pavement for about five minutes. Cassie was checking her watch all the time and as the seconds grew into minutes she was feeling more and more resentful that somebody had thrown themselves on the line and prevented her from getting to the Bailey on time. No sooner had the notion crossed her mind than she berated herself for such a cruel thought; no doubt whoever it was had been so distressed that they had felt life was not worth living. By this time Cassie and her companion were facing the entrance to Kensington Palace Gardens. She checked her watch again; it was nine thirty already. She said, 'I think I'm going to walk through to Kensington and get the Tube to Blackfriars.'

'That's not much help to me, I need Liverpool Street. I'll keep walking this way and see if I can pick up a train further along the line,' he said. He strode away from her, turned and put up a hand in salute. Cassie crossed the road and stepped out along the tree-lined road, past the security booth that guarded the entrance to the most expensive real estate in the country. Further down she passed the sentries at the gates to Kensington Palace. She cut through Vicarage Gate, where she had to skip past a large man with an equally large dog on his way to Kensington Gardens. She was almost running by the time she turned left into Kensington Church Street towards the former department store which was now a trendy organic food shop. At the T-junction she crossed the road and hurried west along Kensington High Street towards the Tube station. Here she was lucky, and she had no sooner reached the platform than a Circle Line train arrived.

Cassie wasn't the only one who was late; so were two of the jury, who had been stuck on the Tube. Judge Crabtree thanked them all for the effort they had made to get there and then asked Marcus to make his closing speech.

Marcus Pike was a talented jury advocate. His speeches were succinct and he could be very theatrical. She'd told James about his speech to the jury in the Barker case, where he'd held aloft the deceased girl's red high heels throughout his speech, and said she wondered if he would wave the golf club around during the course of his address. 'Does he play golf?' said James. Cassie snorted.

Marcus stood up, moved the lectern standing on the bench in front of him and faced the jury. He picked up his papers, the bundle of photographs and the plan of the shop, and placed them side by side on top of it. The golf club was laid in front of the lectern along the bench where the jury could clearly see it. His eyes scanned each of them. He waited until they were all looking at him.

'Members of the jury, although in due course My Lord will give you directions on the law and you must follow the directions he gives, nevertheless I will say a little about it as I place the prosecution case before you. There are a lot of misconceptions about what the law permits and doesn't permit. The press seem to take the view that if you protect your person or your property the law will turn against you, and you will be tried and convicted of an offence and the perpetrator of the violence against you will be exonerated. That is not the case.'

Cassie heard the disapproval in his voice. She had heard his views on the way newspapers reported cases before, and their lack of knowledge of the law. Although she agreed with much of what he said she knew most of the court reporters had very little choice in what was eventually printed. Very few of the editorial staff had sat through a trial, although she had been in a case where she later learnt one of the members of the jury had been the editor of a Sunday broadsheet. The journalist had written an article in praise of the jury system, so she had been prepared to forgive his misunderstanding of the legal principles involved in the trial.

‘What the law demands,’ Marcus said, ‘is that any action you take is appropriate and proportionate. What does that mean? It means, for example, that you don’t need the same amount of force against a child as you would against a full-grown man. It means if you have the opportunity to retreat, to escape the violence, you should do so. You are expected to act reasonably but you are not expected to judge to a nicety the exact amount of force you use in order to protect yourself or your property. Is that clear?’

Cassie looked at the jury and saw a number of them shaking their heads. Of course it was a difficult test to apply but usually the facts of a case made it obvious. She had successfully defended a young man who had used a knife against another youth who was using only his fists and feet in the attack, but the difference in height and weight had been substantial and explained the use of a knife. Each case was different and each depended on the exact circumstances. Was Marcus laying the ground for arguing that her client was a full-grown man and the victim was a mere child? She wasn’t sure the jury would buy that, but it was a valid argument for the prosecution to make.

‘What then are the circumstances that you need to take account of in this case? I don’t suppose you will have any doubt that the three youths behaved very badly when they went into the defendant’s shop. They committed a number of offences, criminal damage, yes, theft, certainly. Their language left a lot to be desired, although so did that of the defendant. What there was not was any assault, nor were there any threats of violence, nothing happened to put Mr Montgomery in fear. Yet he picked up a golf club and threatened them with it, chased them out of the shop brandishing the iron.' Marcus picked up the golf club and raised it above his head, then brought it back to eye level and inspected the shaft. 'A number nine iron, I think.' He halted, his eyes scanning the jury. 'Was that reasonable, was that proportionate for the theft of a chocolate bar?' His voice rose towards the end of the sentence as he emphasised the word 'bar'.

Cassie had to put her head down to hide her face; she couldn't help being amused at the way Marcus was approaching this case, suggesting considerable force had been used to prevent the theft of such a trivial item as a bar of chocolate. A quick glance at the jury revealed that one or two of them were openly grinning. She made a note to make sure she placed emphasis on the totality of the three lads' behaviour.

'I'm sure my learned friend here will say they were refusing to leave the shop, what else could he have done? We say he could have called the police. They may have threatened him, saying they would accuse him of being a paedophile, but that was untrue and he knew it. Indeed it is probable they would have run away if he had picked up the telephone. We will never know. The phone was in the shop and must have been close to where he was standing – he had just finished a call. He could prove they had stolen from him – he had the CCTV recording of the events of that afternoon.

'Not surprisingly, when Mr Montgomery ran at them with the golf club all three boys left the shop and he stormed out after them. What then happened? Did Leon Campbell produce a knife and threaten the defendant with it? You must decide if he did. But the prosecution say that once they had left the premises, the defendant no longer had any need to continue wielding the golf club, swinging it around as he did. We say the reasonable person would have retreated inside his property and closed the door on the young men. This defendant didn't do that. Mrs Munroe, the headmistress of a local school, thought the boys were trying to get out of the way and the shopkeeper, this defendant, was very angry. He says he didn't want to risk turning his back on them, particularly as one of them had a knife. Is that right or is he, as we say, simply trying to account for his loss of temper fuelled by his dislike of these young men, for dislike them he did. Think about the names he called them, terms that have been discredited, and rightly so, for a long time now.

'We say you can be sure he acted in anger and his attack on these three youths was unlawful. He intended to cause them really serious harm and he did so. Harm that resulted in the death of Albie Young. And that means he is guilty of murder, the verdict we ask you to return.'

'Miss Hardman, we'll break for half an hour,' said Judge Crabtree.

Cassie stood and nodded at him but he was already halfway towards the door. Up in the Bar Mess she turned on her mobile. Since she had changed her passwords she had heard nothing from her stalker; she hoped he was no longer interested in harassing her. On the screen of her phone she saw the familiar heading 'Paul Sadler'. She was dismayed, but she opened the message. There was one word.

'*Murderer.*'

At first her voice was shaky but after the familiar opening sentence of her speech she forgot the threats and was soon speaking with her usual fluency. She had decided to meet the allegation of racism head on. 'Over the last few decades we have come to accept that racism is wrong, we cannot judge a man or woman by the colour of their skin. Mr Montgomery has some very strong views about that, he has never tried to hide his dislike of those who are not white and British. Like many, he resents the increased immigration into the UK.'

She paused. This was very dangerous ground and she wanted a moment or two to look carefully at the members of the jury and to make some assessment of how uncomfortable they were finding her remarks. Would they meet her gaze or turn away in disgust? She scanned the two rows; at least they weren't looking away from her.

'But there is no evidence that he has ever been involved in any racist organisations or has threatened or assaulted anyone because of their ethnicity. He has run the shop in Barlby Road for a number of years, yet there is no evidence of him discriminating against any group of people who have come to the shop as customers.

'Not only has he been the proprietor of the shop, but his father was before him. The business has been run by his family for over fifty years. Mr Montgomery has seen many changes, but the little store is on a knife edge and he knows that. He cannot afford customers who steal or damage his goods. We know, and there is no dispute about this, that groups of pupils from St Colomb, including Jas Wilding, Loveday Campbell and Albie Young, came into the shop and did just that – they stole sweets and chocolate, damaged magazines and generally made a nuisance of themselves. It is with all that in mind that I ask you to look at the events of the third of March.'

She reminded them of the evidence the boys had given and the differences between them, before she turned to the final minutes of the incident.

'The young men left the shop but at the door they turned and faced him. You will have to decide what happened next. Mr Montgomery told you that one of them, Loveday, pulled out a knife. Loveday has denied it, but we know from Chris Young that he often did carry a knife and Jas Wilding thought he had waved a knife at the defendant. Why did he do that? They were outside the shop and they could have kept running or walking away. They were in a position to retreat.

'You have to ask yourselves if what Mr Montgomery did was reasonable. Standing at that doorway with three young men who may be, in law, children, but they were all over six feet tall, facing him, one with a knife in his hand, was it unreasonable to try to disarm the youth? Keeping

Loveday at a distance, you may think, was a sensible precaution.

'Did he use too much force? Was using a golf club to get Loveday to drop the knife disproportionate? It's suggested by my learned friend that once the youths were outside the shop Mr Montgomery had no need to continue to follow them out onto the pavement. He should have stepped back and closed the door on them. His actions, the prosecution say, were in pursuit of the young men because he was angry and he is a racist. You have seen the DVD showing the position he was in when he struck the fatal blow with the golf club and you must ask yourselves if he had gone a step too far. In any act of self-defence you do not have to weigh to a nicety the exact degree of force you use. We submit Mr Montgomery did nothing more than seemed reasonable to him.

'We say that what happened was a tragic accident. In trying to disarm Loveday the golf club hit Albie Young as he ran towards his brother. Mr Montgomery was acting in self-defence and therefore you should return a verdict of not guilty.'

As she sank into her seat she looked up at the public gallery but the only person there was the defendant's wife. It was over; soon she would be able to forget about Montgomery even if she couldn't forget Delaney.

Cassie and James returned to chambers after the court rose for the day. The clerks' room was unusually quiet for the time of day. Cassie thought it was probably the fallout from the chambers meeting, which had shown a number of tenants were dissatisfied with the clerking arrangements. These hours between four and seven were the busiest for the staff, who were responsible for allocating work to those available the next day, answering the telephones, checking court lists on their computers and making calls to solicitors and other sets of chambers. By the time they left later that evening every case listed for the next day would have a barrister to attend court on behalf of the client whether prosecuting or defending. Some of them would only have received the brief late in the afternoon and would spend the evening preparing the case for the next morning. Today they were in a sombre mood.

Roger Hales was dashing from room to room, picking up briefs from barristers' desks so that they could be handed to whoever was free to do the work. He acknowledged her presence but was reluctant to look her in the face. Other members of chambers wandered in. There was none of the usual banter. They checked their pigeonholes for correspondence, any new instructions they had received and hopefully a list of the payments made to chambers on their behalf and which would soon be in their own bank accounts. Spencer Watson drifted into the room; it was the first time Cassie had seen him since she'd teased him about not disturbing the papers on Eleanor's desk. She watched him pull the papers he was carrying to his chest and his features froze as if he was trying to avoid eye contact with her.

'Spencer,' Cassie said, 'how are you?'

He bent down to the pigeonholes reserved for pupils and pulled out a collection of papers, including a thin brief tied with pink ribbon. He looked at the front page and then raised his head and said, 'It's for me.'

'Is that your first case?' Cassie said.

'Yes, it is.' He looked as if he was about to give a whoop of delight, his mouth opening wide before a huge smile broke across his face.

'I'll be at home later if you want to run things over with me. You have my number on the chambers list.'

'Thank you. I'm sure I'll be alright,' he said as he almost skipped out of the room.

'He's over the moon. What's it for, Hamish?' James said.

'Applying for an adjournment at West London. The defendant's ill and there's a sick note. Even you couldn't go wrong, sir.'

Hamish's joke lightened atmosphere. James laughed and said, 'Just you watch it.'

Some time later Cassie was walking along Chepstow Villas towards her home; she wasn't paying much attention to her surroundings, pleased the Montgomery case was coming to a conclusion until a voice said, 'Cassie,' and she looked up into the face of Alex Seymour.

'I have something to tell you. I think it would be better inside,' said Alex.

Chapter 41

'What's happened? You've not arrested Oscar, have you?

'It's something more serious, and … you … I think you may be in danger.'

'Why? Who? Delaney?'

'Yes, Delaney. This morning his daughter committed suicide.'

'What's that … was she …'

'Emma Gilbrook.'

Cassie closed her eyes and sank down onto the Chesterfield. 'Oh no, no.' She leant forward, clenched her fists and beat her knees with them. She felt Alex's hand on her arm but only for a moment before it was withdrawn, and when Cassie looked up Alex was standing by the desk looking at her. Cassie could feel the tears pricking at her eyes. She swallowed hard, determined not to cry.

'I've been at the mortuary and he was quite threatening. I don't know if he'll actually do anything, but he blames you for her death.'

It had not been a pleasant time at the Coroner's Office in Horseferry Road. At first the officer on duty had been reluctant to tell them whether Malcolm Delaney was at the mortuary, but after Alex explained who she was and that she was investigating a case of harassment, he relented and told them two men, Felix and Malcolm Delaney, were in the mortuary at that moment to assist in the identification of the dead woman. He asked them to wait until there was further information. They must have waited for about half an hour. Chris had wanted to know what the reference to a stalker was about; she had refused to fill him in on the details.

When Felix and Malcolm Delaney were ushered into the waiting room they looked pale and the older man was swallowing hard. They flopped onto seats without a word. Neither of them paid any attention to Alex and Chris. The officers waited, not wanting to intrude on their obvious misery. A couple of minutes later a woman came in with two mugs of tea and handed one to each man.

Malcolm's hand was shaking as he took a sip of the tea. Felix had put his mug down on the floor and leant over, holding his head in his hands. Then Malcolm's demeanour changed. "it's your fault. Police didn't do their job.' He gulped as he struggled for breath. 'You lot letting a rapist loose. My daughter. Raping my daughter.' He put up his hands as if trying to push someone or something away. 'The police and those posh talking lawyers. That woman she was the worst.' Felix put his hand on his father's arm. That seemed to calm him down and he became quite still, staring at Alex. It was his final words before he left the office that rang in her ears.

'And that woman lawyer, she'll pay for this. She hurt my girl and I'll hurt her.'

After Alex had explained what Delaney had said, Cassie felt numb, as if she had been drained of blood, and she could hardly breathe. 'Because of the rape trial?'

‘I guess so. She didn’t leave a note or anything. No explanation about why she threw herself under the train, but her stepbrother Felix says she was distraught after the verdict. They knew she was depressed but they didn’t think she would go this far.’

‘I tried to be considerate. It’s almost impossible to defend in these cases without at least implying the witness is lying, but I didn’t call her a liar to her face.’

‘You do what you have to do, but …’

‘I know it’s traumatic, the offence, giving evidence, and at the end of the trial I can walk away. You can’t’

Alex nodded. ‘Cassie, is there someone who could stay with you tonight? It’s only a precaution – just in case. I would offer but I’ve got to go back to the station. The squad I’m with have a lot of work and I need to get back there.’

Cassie wished Ben was back, but he was somewhere in mid-Atlantic. The only person Cassie could think of was James. She was reluctant to ring him, but she did so. He was eager, too eager, to agree to come over and said he would be with her in half an hour.

As soon as the arrangements had been finalised, Alex said she was going. ‘But don’t open the door to anyone you don’t know.’

James took considerably more than half an hour to get to her flat, and she was very agitated by the time he bounded up the stairs. She was relieved to see him. She wanted to give him a hug but stopped herself. She didn’t want to encourage him.

He had a large plastic bag from which he pulled a dark blue sleeping bag, a toothbrush, shaver, clean white shirt and a bottle of Chablis.

'I think you like this wine. What about ordering a takeaway?'

'I'm not sure if I want to eat anything, but the wine would be nice.'

'Well, I want something and I can't leave you so let's get a couple of pizzas. You don't have to eat anything.'

James ordered the food and opened the bottle of wine.

'Want to talk about it?' he said.

'I was defending this guy Sadler on a charge of rape. I looked at my notes over the weekend. I cross examined the girl about putting on a condom and their position during intercourse. I didn't need to call her a liar. I don't think I was that hard on her. It was one of those cases that turned on the facts.' She paused for a moment but something urged her on. 'You know the sort. The jury acquitted after a majority direction but I don't think they had much doubt it wasn't rape. She's killed herself, and apparently her father has threatened me. He's the man who's been sending the emails. And I do feel responsible. I do, I do. It's terrible. I never expected this. It's almost enough to make me give up defending.' She pulled out a tissue from the pocket of her black jacket.

'You were doing your job, representing someone who pleaded not guilty. That's what we do, isn't it? Someone has to do it and if Sadler had been convicted, he'd have to serve a lengthy prison sentence.'

'That's what's so terrible. No one wins.' She breathed hard. This was what she did, the job she'd trained for, worked hard for, had against the odds secured a place in chambers and established a successful practice. Whatever happened she couldn't give it up.

The food arrived and Cassie decided she was hungry enough to eat. They sat at her pale oak dining table talking about the Montgomery case and what the jury might be thinking and, having exhausted that, James asked her about the disagreements in chambers.

'I really don't know what anyone can do about this row. I don't like it any more than you do, but I guess I'm on the right side of Jack. He's very supportive, gets me some good work, introduces me to the right solicitors. Nobody wants chambers to split – it happened before I was taken on. My pupil mistress told me … caused a lot of heartache.' Cassie pushed a hand through her hair. 'It's a pity she's not here any longer.'

'Jack thinks you'll take Silk. Will you?'

'I'd like too, but …'

'You're not afraid of failing, are you? Not Cassie Hardman. Or is it the relationship with Ben?'

Cassie threw her head back. 'No, of course not. He'd be thrilled.'

'Would he?' said James. 'Makes married life difficult, travelling around the country.'

He took her hand and stroked the fingertips. For a moment she wanted him to hold her in his arms; she needed, wanted, the security of physical contact. She moved towards him, but then stepped back. He was a junior tenant in her chambers, she had to maintain their working relationship. 'I think I'll try and get some sleep. Do you need anything?'

'No, I don't think so.' He let her hand slip out of his.

She slept fitfully. Was she responsible for Emma Gilbrook's death? Could she have treated Emma more kindly in the witness box? She went over and over the Sadler case, trying to reassure herself that Emma Gilbrook's death was not her fault and she had only been doing her job. She remembered her frustration when she had found the Tube station was closed. She pushed her face into her pillow and began to sob.

Alex got back to her flat from telling Cassie the news about her stalker to find Oscar waiting in his Porsche outside the entrance. She stopped and watched as he uncurled himself from the car. Her pulse began racing. He took her hand and tucked her arm through his and walked her towards the block.

'I'm not sure …'

'Not here. Once we're inside.'

She let him take her keys and unlock the door. Once inside he pulled her to him and kissed her. She didn't respond and he stepped back. 'Now, what's this? I mustn't sleep with a drug dealer. I've given my explanation and it's all over.'

'I don't know …'

He took her in his arms again. 'This is too good to pass up.' This time she didn't resist.

Later, as they lay naked in her bed, she said, 'I've had a bad weekend …'

'Thinking about me?'

'I'd have lost my job if …'

'A gentleman doesn't kiss and tell.'

Alex sat up and rolled over so she could see his face. 'Tell me the truth, did you have anything to do with those drugs?'

'Alex, Alex. Just leave it. It's better you don't know. You're a beautiful woman and at this moment I want to forget you're a police officer and just enjoy your body.'

Chapter 42

Cassie and James took a taxi to the Bailey the next morning and, as they got out by the front entrance, they bumped into Stephen Burnett, who greeted them with a look of surprise that faded into an incorrect assumption. Cassie grimaced at him. As she opened the door into the court building she heard Stephen say 'What's wrong with her?' to James. She didn't hear any reply but as she turned to let the two men in, Stephen was shrugging his shoulders.

As they went through the security barriers, Cassie couldn't help scrutinising the face of every unknown male she saw. She was sure Delaney knew how to get past the security systems and into the courthouse. He could be anywhere.

She felt safe in the robing room, but as she went downstairs she continued to look for possible strangers. Outside Court 10 she found Zac in the middle of a scrum of reporters. 'What's going on?' she said.

Amongst the journalists was Ruth Pymlott. 'Miss Hardman, that rape trial you did a couple of weeks ago, the girl has committed suicide.'

Cassie couldn't bring herself to say anything. She put her head down and pushed through the crowd and into the courtroom without a word and sat down in her usual place. She looked up at the public gallery, shook her head and then balanced her notebook on her files. She ignored Marcus as he took his seat.

Judge Crabtree sat promptly at ten thirty. He clearly planned to sum up and get the jury out that morning. Cassie watched them closely. She was on her own today; James had been sent to another court. Zac had moved to sit right behind her. Once the judge was seated he looked at Cassie and raised his eyebrows, then tapped on the pale wooden top of the bench until the court clerk got up and turned to face him. He whispered something to her, which caused her to write on a scrap of paper which she motioned to the usher to hand to Cassie. The note asked her if she was ready for the trial to continue. When she looked up she became aware Judge Crabtree was watching her. She nodded at him to indicate she was fine and, with that, the judge commenced his summing up.

Although she had made it clear there was no problem, it wasn't true. She and James had drunk a little too much wine, Cassie trying to suppress her fears in an alcoholic haze. She hadn't succeeded. At home, each and every noise had left her stiff with fear until she had identified its source. Her downstairs neighbour had come in late and bustled around, the hinges of the front door sighed, and, when a heavy lorry went past, the window frames rattled with the wind. From time to time she had got up and peered out of the windows onto the Chepstow Road, looking for anything strange, anyone hanging around for no apparent reason. But the road had been quiet and she had only seen the odd late-night party goer on their way home. She had tiptoed into the kitchen to get a glass of water but she hadn't been quiet enough. James wriggled out of his sleeping bag and stood up.

'Can't you sleep?'

'I keep thinking he might come here. He's been before.'

'I'm here. I won't let anything happen.' He had taken her by the hand and led her into her bedroom. She had got back into bed and he had lain down beside her. 'It's all right. Let me just hold you.' Cassie hadn't protested, she was too weary.

Now, although she was sure Delaney couldn't get into the courtroom and the number of staff was reassuring, still from time to time she looked up at the public gallery. Judge Crabtree's voice was melodious and she soon found herself settling into the rhythm of her work, listening to the judge's summing up to ensure there were no mistakes.

She noted he'd told them of their respective roles in the trial and then he said, 'I have drafted a few questions that I think will help you come to your decision.' He handed a sheaf of paper to the clerk in front of him and she passed them on to the usher. Cassie looked at the copy she had been given and she checked that the questions were appropriate. Once the jury had been given their copies Judge Crabtree continued. 'The law of self-defence is really common sense. If a man is under attack he is entitled to defend himself so long as he uses no more than is reasonable force. In this case, when Montgomery struck Albert Young, did he believe he was about to be attacked by one or more of these boys? If on the evidence you are sure that the defendant was the aggressor and did not believe he was under attack but acted out of anger fuelled by racism then you will return a verdict of guilty. If however you consider it was or may be the case that Montgomery believed he was under attack or about to be attacked you must go on to consider if what he did was reasonable. If you consider that what he did in the heat of the moment, when fine judgements are difficult, was no more than he reasonably believed was necessary, that would be strong evidence that what he did was reasonable. It is for you to decide whether the force used was reasonable and you must do that on the circumstances as you find the defendant believed them to be. If you are sure that even allowing for the difficulties he faced in the heat of the moment he used more than reasonable force, he is guilty.

'Well, that's the law. As you can see, I've listed those questions on the sheet of paper for you to have while you consider your verdicts. We'll take a break now and I'll remind you of the evidence you've heard.'

Outside the court, Marcus told them he was leaving to go back to the trial he had started in another court in the building. Cassie grinned at him. 'Another murder then?'

'No. It's a multi-handed fraud.' He put his hand to his mouth as if to stifle a yawn.

'Have fun,' she said. She was a little envious of Marcus, able to leave this trial and go on to something different, while she had to remain and wait for the jury to consider and deliver a verdict. It was one of the advantages of prosecuting; the client was the prosecuting authority and they were not as involved in the outcome of the case. She wondered how long the break would be and then decided she had time for a coffee in the Bar Mess.

The large room upstairs was furnished as a self-service café with a servery at one end and long tables in rows. Where the room narrowed because of the stairs, there was a green leather sofa and a few easy chairs that looked like the leftovers from a gentlemen's club. The coffee table was covered with this morning's newspapers and copies of *Country Life*. There were no women's magazines, nothing that gave any indication the users may be interested in anything other than country pursuits and large houses. Cassie sat down in one of the chairs and picked up a copy of the *Daily Argos*. She flipped through the pages, reading a paragraph here and there until a photograph caught her attention. She folded the paper and examined the picture carefully. The picture was black and white, and, although, the young woman was wearing make-up, the eyes heavily rimmed with kohl and the eyelashes encrusted with mascara, the face was that of Emma Gilbrook. Cassie began to read the article, which although it didn't name her was highly critical of the trial process and the cross examination. The implication was that the verdict was wrong and Paul Sadler had only been acquitted because of the wiles of his barrister. She suspected she had not been named only because some libel lawyer had thought a personal attack on her would be actionable. If Delaney read this, would his anger be fuelled by the insinuation she had been brutal with her cross examination? And as the tannoy called her back to Court 10, she wondered how Sadler would feel as his acquittal was called into question.

The jury box was empty when she hurried through the door. Robin Tasker was standing in front of the clerk's bench chatting to a small redhead who was sitting behind it, her curls poking out from under her wig. She didn't notice Cassie at first, but as soon as she did, she said, 'The judge wants to see you in chambers.' With that she got up and led the two of them up past the judge's chair and out into the expensively carpeted corridor where the judges had their rooms.

The usher knocked on the inner door and, when a voice invited them in, opened it and stood aside to let Cassie and Robin enter the room. Judge Crabtree stood up as they walked in and pointed to the chairs in front of his desk. Photographs of the judge in slacks and a white shirt holding various model yachts were still hanging on the walls. When she and Robin were seated, Judge Crabtree sat down at his desk, which was covered with copies of different newspapers opened at similar items to the one Cassie had seen in the *Daily Argos*.

'Cassie, I understand this case,' he pointed to one of the papers, 'was one in which you were defending?'

'Yes, My Lord. Paul Sadler was acquitted and it was a perfectly reasonable verdict on the evidence. '

'It's very sad for her family. Terrible thing to happen. Sadler will find this difficult too. He's been acquitted, yet the press is behaving as if he was guilty ... I don't think if our jury read this it will affect this trial, will it? Having you all over the press at this stage. ' He waved his hand over the collection of papers.

'No. I'm sure not. Actually I don't think they say who defence counsel was. They do make it clear it was a woman.'

'Yes, I thought one of them did say something about a Miss Hardman. Described you as an ambitious lawyer.' He nodded and smiled at her, and then said, 'Robin, do you think there are any repercussions for the trial?'

Robin Tasker shook his head. 'I can't think of any.'

'Good. We'll reconvene the court and I'll continue with my summing up.'

Cassie was furious as she considered Judge Crabtree's remarks; all he was concerned about was whether the trial would be prejudiced in any way.

Back at her place in court, she found an envelope on the bench in front of her. She turned it over in her hand; there was nothing written on it. It was not sealed. She opened the flap and pulled from it a photograph with the name of a West London photographer's studio stamped on the back. She turned it over and the eyes of Emma Gilbrook gazed into hers. Cassie stifled a sob. She couldn't cry here.

Chapter 43

As Judge Crabtree made his closing remarks, James slipped into the courtroom to stand under the public gallery. Cassie waited for the judge to finish and then asked for Montgomery to be granted bail within the precincts of the court. Judge Crabtree must have decided Montgomery wasn't about to bolt under the stress of waiting for the verdict and, to her surprise, acceded to her request. It was ironic, she thought, that while her client's future was decided by the jury he had to spend the time waiting with a man whose race challenged all his prejudices. She spoke briefly to Montgomery and then left him with Zac, admonishing them both to stay together in the canteen and on no account to leave the building. Montgomery asked her how long she thought the jury would take to consider their verdict.

'I've no idea. We have to wait for as long as they take. Go and get yourself a coffee or something.' She relented a little and added, 'I know it's difficult but there's nothing we can do now, just hope they return the right verdict.'

She walked with them to the lifts. 'I have some telephone calls to make. I'll see you later. James, you might like to stay with Mr Montgomery for a while. Oh, and see if you can arrange for Mrs Montgomery to come into canteen, rather than stay in the public gallery.' James said he would although he didn't look too pleased, but he was her junior and he would do as she asked.

Up in the Bar Mess, she sat down on one of the green leather chairs and looked at the selection of newspapers on the coffee table in front of her. Nearly all of them had an article about the suicide of Emma Gilbrook. Cassie looked at the report in *The Guardian*. It didn't seem any more balanced than any of the others but there was a quote from Emma's brother, Felix Delaney. 'My sister was very upset by the verdict in the recent trial of Paul Sadler. She always maintained she had been telling the truth and that he had raped her. She felt the trial was like a second rape, being cross examined about her previous sexual experiences and called a liar. She believed that if the jury had heard all the evidence they would have convicted the defendant, but some relevant parts were excluded by the judge after an application by the defence lawyer.'

She thought about the brother's comments and the evidence she had persuaded the judge to eliminate from the prosecution case. His assertion that she had cross examined his sister about her previous sexual experience was not true. The issue had been raised because of her mother's claim she was a virgin. In addition, the evidence he was referring to was the messages on the Rush Hour Crush web page in the preceding three months. Cassie didn't think they would have helped the prosecution case at all. Had the messages been adduced before the jury she would have called the young women who had responded to the posts. Their accounts of meeting with Sadler would have confirmed he was not placing the requests to find women to sexually assault. All it would have done was prolong the trial. The only problem was that when the police first questioned him about it he had denied the messages were his, because he thought it made him look a fool. Cassie had objected to the evidence because it seemed to her irrelevant in the totality of the case. Certainly the prosecution's suggestion he had lied because he had posted the emails in order to find other victims to rape or sexually assault could be undermined. He claimed it was a way of meeting attractive women without using a dating agency and without paying any fees for introductions.

Cassie picked up another newspaper and saw the same quote repeated there. She was checking the rest of the pile when her mobile rang. She checked the screen and saw it was Lee Shaw.

'Hi, Lee, I'm waiting for a jury at the Bailey, so I might have to run. How are you?'

'I'm fine, but Paul Sadler isn't. He's very upset and angry about the way the press are assuming he's guilty despite the verdict. And that the publicity will get him the sack.'

'I'm not surprised. He's been acquitted by a jury and is being tried all over again in the newspapers.'

'What do you suggest? He's talking about a defamation action.'

'I don't know. I'm not a libel lawyer – and aren't there problems with funding a libel case? As I recollect Sadler was on Legal Aid for the rape trial. I suppose we could draft a statement for him with some explanation about the facts of the case, but sometimes it's best to let these things go and ignore it. It's never long before something else takes over the front pages and this will be forgotten.'

She had just finished speaking when the tannoy summoned all parties in the case of Montgomery to Court 10. 'We've been called back into court. I'll speak to you later.'

'It's a verdict,' James said as she settled into the seat in front of him. She turned towards him and saw Montgomery in the dock; his face was grey and he seemed to have aged in the time the jury had been out. Marcus had returned and, although his face was impassive, he was tapping the edge of the oak bench in front of him.

Once Judge Crabtree was back on the bench, the usher led the jury into the court and motioned them to take their seats. 'Anywhere will do, members of the jury, except the foreman should take the seat nearest to me in the front row.' There was a shuffle as the jurors rearranged themselves. The woman who always wore a pink shirt took the foreman's seat. She looked directly at Montgomery and Cassie closed her eyes, hoping that was a sign that the verdict was favourable.

The clerk stood and, holding the indictment in front of her, asked the jury foreman to stand. The woman rose to her feet holding a sheet of paper in her right hand and with her left she pulled at the collar of her shirt.

'Members of the jury, have you reached a verdict on which you are all agreed?' the clerk said.

'Yes, we have.'

'Do you find David Winston Montgomery guilty or not guilty of the murder of Albert Young?'

Cassie picked up a pen, flicked the pages of the notebook in front of her, and leant forward. Her eyes flickered along the two rows of jurors. They weren't looking at Montgomery. She dreaded the thought of a guilty verdict, drafting grounds of appeal and then standing before a bench of High Court judges and being interrogated by them as she tried to argue Montgomery's case.

The forewoman looked down at the paper in her hand and said, 'Not guilty.'

'On count two, do you find the defendant David Winston Montgomery guilty or not guilty of the unlawful killing of Albert Young?'

There was brief pause and then, 'Not guilty, My Lord.'

Cassie heard James breathe out and her heart resumed its regular beat. She asked for Montgomery to be discharged and as Judge Crabtree granted her request she allowed herself to turn and look at her client. He was standing with his eyes closed and his hands clutching the bar of the dock. She watched him as he looked up at the public gallery and she followed his gaze to where his wife was sitting and smiling down at him.

Cassie heard the judge thank the jury and then say he was adjourning. He left the bench and the jury began to file out of the courtroom. One of the jurors, an older black woman, stopped on the way out to speak to Albie Young's mother who must have slipped into the courtroom without Cassie noticing her. She didn't want to think about how the dead boy's mother or family were feeling. She began to bundle her papers together and as she did so Marcus walked the length of the bench. 'Well done. Not the easiest of clients.'

'Thanks. I must admit there were times when I thought we would be lucky to get away without a conviction for manslaughter.'

'I understand the case all this fuss in the papers is about was a trial you defended in.'

'Yes, that's right.'

'Don't let it get to you. It's bad, the girl committed suicide, but that isn't your responsibility. The newspapers love it, but they're worse than lawyers when they think they have a good story. Just think of hacking into people's telephones. At least when we question witnesses we're controlled by a judge. I'm sure it will blow over.'

'I hope this does,' said Cassie, 'I hope it does.' *Not only the newspapers*, she thought.

Chapter 44

There was scrum of journalists, photographers and TV cameramen outside the Old Bailey when Alex arrived. She pushed her way through them and into the foyer of the Central Criminal Court. She asked the security guard what had got the press so excited and he told her there was a paedophile ring being tried, and also some of them had been asking about the barrister who had got a rapist acquitted.

Alex grimaced. Not only was Cassie Hardman at risk from Emma Gilbrook's father but the press were harassing her as well. She walked upstairs to the outside of the courtroom where the bail application was listed. Stephen Burnett was waiting in the wide hallway and walked towards her.

'Are you here for the bail application in Court 6?' he said.

She told him she was.

'Cassie's really upset about the girl's death. Is she really at risk from the father?'

'Malcolm certainly made threats yesterday when we were at the mortuary. I suppose you know he's been harassing her for some time.'

'She's a tough cookie and hasn't said much.' He frowned and then tapped the brief he was holding. 'Are you still opposing bail?'

'It's a large quantity of coke. You'll have to speak to prosecuting counsel for the full reasons for remanding them in custody.'

'I was hoping you'd help me a bit – advance warning.' He shrugged his shoulders. 'DC Seymour, Alex, isn't it. Fancy a drink, coffee or lunch afterwards?'

Alex shook her head. 'I was warned about you.'

Stephen laughed and went on his way to the cells.

The bail application didn't take long. The two men arrested delivering the cocaine to Cotburn Mews were remanded in custody for trial. They both indicated they would plead not guilty, alleging they did not know the packages contained illegal drugs. From the expression on the judge's face she didn't think they had much chance of an acquittal. Nor did Alex, but defendants liked to put off the day of reckoning. It allowed them time to arrange their affairs.

Outside the courtroom, Stephen Burnett approached. 'These guys are small fry really. Couriers. Are you anywhere near catching the sharks?'

'No way. They never get out of the water.'

'Can I repeat the offer of a drink some time?'

'Better not.'

Stephen laughed. 'Oscar?'

As he walked away, Alex turned on her mobile phone; there was a text from Felix Delaney.

'*Very worried. Dad not been back home since left Coroner's.*'

Alex hoped Cassie was still safe in one of the courtrooms on the floors above her. She pushed her way through the revolving doors and out into the swarm of reporters and their cameramen. They were pushing each other, jostling to get the best position for their lenses to catch anyone emerging from the front door. She tried to move to her right, towards Newgate Street, but there was such a throng that she had to force her way through. With some difficulty she managed to escape onto the periphery of the tightly packed crowd. She paused for a moment and looked back south along the street. To her right and partly hidden by a television camera on the other side of the crush of journalists she saw Malcolm Delaney. Alex thrust herself back into the morass of pressmen to try and reach Delaney before he saw her. She found herself stepping first one way and then the other, around the photographers and journalists, avoiding cameras and backpacks. Someone stepped on her toes and she felt an elbow in her back. But for every step forward she was pushed back further from Delaney.

The pack suddenly moved towards the courthouse doors and she heard a plethora of voices all speaking at once. She couldn't see what was happening but guessed someone from the paedophile trial had emerged onto the street. On her left she saw the helmets of two City of London police officers; it looked like they were trying to control the herd of reporters. Alex pushed harder with her elbows at the men immediately to her right. 'Watch it,' one of them said.

'Let me through,' she said. 'Police, I want to get through.'

At the word police a small gap appeared in front of her and she was able to get to within an arm's reach of Malcolm Delaney. She shouted his name and he looked straight at her. She reached out and took hold of the sleeve of his jacket. She called his name again. He didn't acknowledge her, pulled free from her grasp and forced his way in the opposite direction to the edge of the crowd and once he was unimpeded he began to run south along the street. Alex tried to follow him as he ran. Then she saw the figure of Cassie Hardman some fifty metres or so in front of Delaney. The gap between the two was narrowing. Then Cassie stopped and turned towards Delaney, no longer moving away. 'Cassie,' Alex screamed. She knew she couldn't reach Delaney before he got to Cassie so she cried out, 'Cassie, run, Cassie,' hoping she would hear. 'Let me through, police, police!' One of the uniformed officers must have heard her because a path opened up and she began to run towards Cassie.

Chapter 45

Outside the main door of the courthouse was a crowd of journalists and photographers. As Cassie and James wriggled through the mêlée to walk south along Old Bailey towards Ludgate Hill, someone from the pack of reporters pushed in between the two of them. The long lens of a camera poked into her face. She looked away but not before the light from the flashgun burst across her eyes almost blinding her. She heard the sound of a commotion behind her but with her eyes half closed against the flare, she couldn't see the scuffle that had broken out near the entrance to the public gallery.

'You're Cassie Hardman, aren't you? What about this girl killing herself because you got her rapist off?' a voice said into her ear. She turned to look at the man who was accusing her.

'Who are you? I have no comment,' Cassie said. A microphone was pushed towards her, its fur cover almost touching her nose.

'Do you like humiliating young women?'

'Will you please leave me alone?'

'So you enjoy calling a young girl a liar, do you?'

Cassie put her head down and quickened her step but they kept pace with her. The cameraman continued to take photographs of her face, while the other man kept repeating his accusations. James tried to push between the men and Cassie first from one side then the other but he was in danger of tripping over each time he made the effort and in the end he gave up and walked alongside Cassie and the two reporters. The line of four wavered along the pavement. A taxi travelling north had to stop as the cameraman forced James onto the road. James asked the driver to take them to the Temple, opened the passenger door and got in, shouting for Cassie to follow him. The cameraman stepped back and stood between her and the open door, and then he reached behind and slammed it shut. James got out at the other side and ran around towards Cassie and put an elbow into the side of the sound recordist.

The noise of the commotion behind them had risen and it was the sound of shouting that finally made the two pressmen turn back and train the camera on the crowd around the entrance to the court. Once their attention was focused back along the street, Cassie broke into a jog away from the courthouse and the noise. She didn't get far before she realised James wasn't with her and then she stopped and looked back. He was standing watching the crowd about three metres from her. Some distance away, close to the entrance to the Bailey she could see a group of people pushing and pulling at each other. There was shouting but she couldn't make out any of the words. Most of them were men and she noticed the helmet of a City of London police officer fly into the air. Some security staff came to the door and looked out onto the street. The fighting continued and she took a step back towards the crush. Then she saw a man break free from the crowd and come running in her direction. At first she thought it was one of the two newspaper men trying to catch up with her but then she realised this man wasn't carrying either a camera or a microphone. She didn't recognise him and assumed he was struggling to get away from whatever fight was going on. She was turning to continue walking towards Ludgate Hill, when she heard a woman's voice call her name, and again she looked back along the street towards the doors of the Old Bailey but couldn't see anyone she knew. The fighting appeared to have stopped and the group was now following the man approaching her. James was coming towards her. She turned her attention back to the man who was getting closer and closer. She heard a familiar voice shouting her name in the distance – telling her to run, warning her she was in danger. The man was staring at her and was, she realised, intent on reaching her. When he was about four metres away it came to her. 'Delaney,' she whispered.

For a moment fear rooted her to the spot. He had something in his hands that glinted in the sunlight. She wanted to run away. *Don't turn your back on him. That's a knife. Don't let him get too close.* The distance between them was narrowing. She lifted the bag containing her robes. It was heavy but she swung it from side to side in front of her. Delaney ran to her right. He was within touching distance. Cassie threw the bag as hard as she could towards Delaney's chest. The holdall hit him. He stumbled with the impact. James grabbed hold of her, pulled her towards him and put himself between her and Delaney. Almost immediately

Delaney was back on his feet and rushing towards them. He swerved round James, grabbed Cassie's jacket and pulled her away. He was shaking her and screaming, 'Bitch, bitch. You killed her.'

Cassie shoved at him. 'Let go! Let go!' He lessened his grip, but as she backed away he grabbed her arm. He caught hold of the sleeve of her jacket and it tore. 'You're a killer,' he shouted, over and over. She turned to face him; he lunged out at her but she moved to one side. He turned again and now the holdall, still on the ground, was between them. Delaney reached for her arm again but she sidestepped him and for a moment they were engaged in some macabre dance. Cassie took a couple of steps back and Delaney tried to follow her, the knife held in one hand. Her eyes were glued to the knife as he pushed it towards her. It was inches away when he was pulled backwards and fell. Cassie looked up and saw Alex holding on to his right arm. Alex pulled him to his feet and said, 'I'm arresting you under Section 2 of the Protection from Harassment Act 1997.' She cautioned him but Delaney only grunted.

'Are you alright?' she said to Cassie.

'I think so …'

Cassie put one hand to her mouth as if to prevent a scream as she watched him led away by two uniformed police officers. James was holding her round the shoulders. She pointed to the tin containing her wig, which had fallen out of her bag and rolled a few feet into the gutter. James went to pick it up. Without his support she felt unsteady and thought she was about to faint, but Alex grabbed her arm and held her as she swayed. 'Take a deep breath. I don't think you'll want to see a photograph of yourself on the ground in the newspapers tomorrow,' Alex said.

James came back carrying her bag as well as his own, and said, 'Shall I get a taxi?'

'I think you should,' said Alex. 'I need to go with my prisoner.' She pointed in the direction of Snow Hill. 'I'll need to get a statement from you, but tomorrow will do.'

'No, I want to get away. I'll be alright. Yes, sorry, a statement. Tomorrow is fine,' Cassie said as she took a few tentative steps in the direction of Ludgate Circus.

Cassie struggled to walk along Fleet Street towards the Temple. She kept her eyes focused ahead of her and didn't speak. James kept pace with her, carrying her robe bag and his own. He asked twice if she was alright but she didn't reply and he gave up. She could still feel her heart thumping and the noise of the traffic seemed to explode in her head, but she felt a little stronger with each step she took. Then she saw the sign of El Vino's. 'I think I could do with a drink.'

'In here?' said James.

'Mm. A large glass of Chateauneuf, the best they have.' They walked to the back of the bar where there was an ill-assorted collection of small tables and chairs. James dropped the two bags by the side of one of the tables as she sank into a chair facing the street. She handed him a twenty-pound note. 'Two large glasses.' While she waited she glanced around; she didn't want anyone she knew to see her. A group of men were leaning against the bar, and sitting at another table were a man and a woman. From their dress, Cassie assumed they were lawyers; the journalists who had loitered there when Fleet Street was the centre of the newspaper industry had long ago been exiled to Canary Wharf. She was relieved she didn't know any of them; she didn't want to tell the story of the attack just yet. One of the barman, wiping glasses, was scrutinising her and she ran her hands through her hair. She hoped it wasn't obvious she was distressed and, she realised, angry. She had won her first leading brief and instead of celebrating her victory she was nursing her worst fears.

James returned with the two glasses and put them on the table in front of her. She picked up one and examined the dark, almost purplish liquid, then she swirled it round in the glass and sniffed it. 'One of the most complex wines produced in the world. Did you know that?' she said.

'No, I didn't.'

Cassie tried to raise the glass to her mouth but her hand was shaking so much she spilt a few drops onto her white shirt. She looked at it and, for a moment, even though she knew she had not been hurt, thought they were bloodstains. She squeezed her eyes shut in an attempt to stop herself from crying, but she failed. Her lips began to quiver and then silently the teardrops ran down her face.

James took a handkerchief out of his pocket and handed it to her.

'He looked such an insignificant little man. She was so beautiful. I can't imagine him being her father,' Cassie said.

She took a deep breath, dabbed at her eyes with the handkerchief and then picked up the glass and gulped a mouthful of the wine. She searched through her memory, wanting to concentrate on anything other than the events of the last few minutes. She didn't want to talk about the Montgomery case or discuss the verdict; instead she told James about her pupil mistress.

'You know my pupil mistress … the day of the High Court case … the one the owner of this wine bar took to exclude women from coming in without a man … they wanted to continue to refuse to serve women on their own and wouldn't allow them to stand at the counter … she was one of the first women into this bar …'

'They may have lost the case but it doesn't look as if much has changed.'

'No. It doesn't.'

Cassie heard herself laugh; she was safe and had won a great victory in court. She raised her glass. 'I suppose we should congratulate ourselves on the not guilty verdict. But …'

'This takes the shine off it.'

They finished their wine and then walked slowly the rest of the way to 3 Burke Court. James pushed open the doors to the clerks' room and let Cassie enter first. The chatter ceased and Jack sprang up from his chair and rushed towards her. He held her by the top of her arms and said, 'Are you alright?'

‘I’m not hurt … no bruises, nothing. But I was very frightened.’

‘She was fantastic,’ James said. ‘Hurled her robe bag at him and winded him. That friend of hers was there with a couple of other coppers and they intervened.’

‘He’s been arrested, has he? That’s good,’ said Jack. ‘Ben called, he’ll be at your flat when you get home. Anyway, you got a great result in the Montgomery trial. Of course the attack is all over the Temple and I guess it’ll be in the newspapers tomorrow. Great publicity, can’t do the work any harm.’

‘Jack, really,’ Cassie said.

A telephone rang and Hamish picked up the receiver. Cassie heard him say, ‘Kingston Crown Court tomorrow. Let me see.’ He put his hand over the mouthpiece. ‘Can you do a bail app in a fraud case tomorrow? It’s a sure not guilty and he wants to introduce counsel straight away. Are you up to it?’

Jack held his hand out for the telephone. ‘Miss Hardman needs a few days off after the events of this afternoon. You’ll hear about it on the news. Mr Callan, her junior, will do the bail application. I assume there’s a Legal Aid certificate for two counsel.’

Epilogue

For the first time in weeks, Cassie spent an untroubled night, safe in her own home and with Ben. They made plans to drive north to Lancaster but first Cassie had to make a statement about the emails and messages Delaney had sent her, as well as the assault. She went to the police station in Notting Hill where she was met by Alex Seymour.

After she had made her complaint, Cassie said, 'Thanks for the warning about him. When I saw him coming after me I guessed who it was. That's what saved me from getting hurt. You've saved my life again. Hopefully you won't get into any trouble this time?'

'No, no trouble. The boss approves even if I took a bit of time away from the drug investigation. He's asked me to join his team – Serious Crime Squad.'

'I gather Oscar was interviewed. Did you really think he was involved in drug dealing?'

'I hope not. I really hope he isn't. You're off for a few days?'

'We're going to my parents' in Lancashire. A few days with my mum's cooking, Dad fussing over me. I've a sister as well and her husband … is there something wrong?'

Alex smiled, opened the door and ushered Cassie out. 'No, not really.'

Alex went home that night and thought of Cassie heading north to her family. She poured herself a large glass of whisky. After a few sips of her drink, she went into the bathroom and ran a bath, adding some sweet-smelling oil. She retrieved her glass from the table beside the sofa and went into her bedroom, got undressed and pulled on a thick towelling robe. She sat at her dressing table and picked up the photograph of her brother and then put it down again. As she was heading back to the bathroom she heard the revving of a motorbike, the ring of her mobile. She looked at the screen and saw the caller was Oscar.

If you enjoyed reading this book the author would appreciate it if you could leave a short review on Amazon or Goodreads.

If you would like to contact me you can email me at contact@scribblingadvocate.com

Printed in Great Britain
by Amazon

61176215R00218